SHADE CITY

A DANTE BUTCHER NOVEL

DOMINO FINN

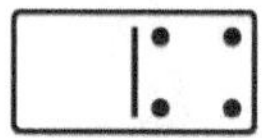

Copyright © 2014 by Domino Finn. All rights reserved.

Published by Blood & Treasure, Los Angeles
Second Edition

This is a work of fiction. Any resemblance to reality is coincidental.

No part of this work may be reproduced or distributed without prior written consent by the publisher. This book represents the hard work of the author; please read responsibly.

Front Cover by James T. Egan of Bookfly Design LLC.

Print ISBN: 978-0-692-24295-7

DominoFinn.com

Ghosts are Real

And they're everywhere. Lost souls unprepared to move on, they desperately cling to our world with every fiber of their haunted beings.

You can't see them. Shades hide in plain sight, possessing our bodies. Our hearts and minds. They drink and smoke and revel in the pleasures of the flesh, with no regard for the broken victims they leave behind.

What you need is a misfit. Someone with open eyes who can see the shades. The fakers. A fighter too stubborn to know when he's in over his head, and one with a trick or two to send them back to where they came from.

What you need is Dante Butcher, a work-hard, play-hard, fight-hard hero.

Welcome to the dark world of *The Dead Side*, where on the nightlife circuit, anything goes.

Shade City by Domino Finn follows an irreverent urban fantasy misfit who gives readers an outsider's inside-perspective of a shadowy Los Angeles.

★★★★★ "Keeps getting **more intense** the further you read."

★★★★★ "It's rare to find something actually **worth adding** to the mythos of supernatural fiction."

★★★★★ "**Edgy, aloof, and cool,** no one hones the same edge that Domino's characters have."

SHADE CITY

Sometimes, when a person is killed, the spirit suffers more than it can bear. It clings to a piece of this world and endeavors never to let go.

Chapter 1 - Saturday

I've been called a hipster before. I smoke cloves. I carry around a century-old pocket watch. Don't get me started on my exceptional taste in indie music. To be fair, I *was* currently having a drink in a bar under a widescreen TV playing *Point Break* (Pure Adrenaline Edition).

In black and white.

Hey, *Casablanca* it ain't, but Keanu Reeves and Patrick Swayze made a damn entertaining flick.

A hipster, though? Gimme a break. I don't sport a Victorian-era beard once popular with British magistrates. I can't stomach Pabst Blue Ribbon. I don't wear ironic clothing. Skinny jeans need not apply.

I'm a pretty straightforward dude when it comes down to it. Longish hair creeps over my eyes. My short goatee is the only facial hair to speak of (except when I get lazy about shaving). I do wear tight T-shirts because I'm thin and work out, but that's not a crime, it's style.

Hey, I'm young and living in Los Angeles. A guy's gotta make due, right?

I squeezed through the crowd in the small, backroom bar. The faint lighting and cramped seating exuded the feel of a house party. That was good on lazy nights. I could do the rounds without breaking a sweat. As I scanned the crowd, my gaze passed over the collection of Mexican crosses nailed to the wall. Some painted with bright colors, others sporting their natural weathered wood. Each with its own story, just like every person I brushed against.

I'm not a local, of course. Nobody here is. I've been around four years, but the first twenty of my life were spent in Miami. You might see that and think I wanted to be an actor, but it was nothing like that. I just wanted to get away from my fucked up childhood—the doctors, the drugs, the depression. I've had issues, you see, as long as I can remember. Moving west was like the old frontier settlers escaping the puritanical cities that stifled them. No more family for me. I was all alone now. And I loved it.

I'm a game programmer, if you can believe it. You know those old-school puzzle games you play on your phone, the ones that don't require much thought or coordination? Yup, you can blame me for contributing. But I work from home on my laptop and it's a steady paycheck so I'm riding this train as far as it takes me. Besides, I have to fund my partying somehow.

Maybe I don't take my career seriously enough, but I'm all about living in the present. I'm kinda rock and roll like that. There's a lot of fun to be had in this town. Honestly, there's a lot of trouble to get in as well. Especially when you know the things I know.

They call it the City of Angels. Well... angels, demons... I don't really know the difference. But I do know bad things are out there. I've seen them. Or felt them, anyway.

So why was I wasting my time at a small bar in the Valley? There was nothing wrong here. Nothing to see. I waved to the bartender on my way out.

Tonight, we're going clubbing in Hollywood.

Chapter 2

Full-on nightclubs are majestic articulations of wonder. I'm not talking about bars or lounges or other places where friends can gather and drink and bullshit—I mean dark halls and blinding dance floors, music that prohibits conversation, and crowds that make it difficult to maneuver.

Electronica was the weekend anthem at Avalon, a converted theater that was as much a staple of Hollywood as the manic club scene allowed. The venue was all about mass business. It didn't have the most refined interior or subtle offerings, but what it did have it had in spades.

Five bars lined the cavernous interior. A side alley housed smokers and the terrace upstairs had an open-air ceiling with a view of the Capitol Records building. The mezzanine seats were mostly intact and provided ample opportunity to engage in passionate rendezvous. The entire layout, of course, wrapped around the main stage. The accompanying area was clear of chairs to afford the kinds of crowds that should never be contained in one place. State-of-the-art lights spun wildly above, sequenced with the blaring of countless speakers. It was an old theater, beat up by the throngs of partiers, stripped of its beautiful propriety and made magnificent anew.

I hovered on the edge of the dance floor, palming my pocket watch. It was a Hamilton 940, a shiny brass number. An antique. A partner in crime.

"You're officially eighteen today," I said to the watch.

The timepiece ticked along and music filled my ears. Frowning, I slipped it back into my jeans and continued my lookout.

The mass of people was an ocean, sometimes drifting together like a slow current, other times crashing against each other in waves. Clubs are all about limiting activity in a way as to focus it, restricting the senses and squeezing them into uncomfortable positions where the only recourse for enjoyment is to let go and become completely free.

Free. It's a funny word that means a lot of serious things. I saw a lot of free people here. But any time you had an amalgamation of this much fun and exhilaration and sex, you'll always attract some fakers. And I saw every single one of them for exactly what they were.

The ocean swelled, the life within as diverse as any real body of water. Lowlifes, trust fund kids; businessmen, drug dealers (were those the same thing?); party girls, working girls; white, Chinese, Mexican, and more; pretty, cute, and ugly. It took all kinds.

A group of well-dressed guys loosened ties that still clung to their necks. They didn't get out much and used a special occasion as an excuse to fly the coop.

Couples grinded on the dance floor, trading partners until they found an acceptable pairing (if only for the moment). They wouldn't have been here if they had someone to go home to.

A group of friends egged each other on, pressing to make the most of their ill-advised antics. This was their release. After a long week of menial labor, they came here to discover new ways to stay sane.

Others, like the old man at the bar, ignored the raucous activity except when it begrudged him a bump or a shove. He just came here to indulge his addictions. He wanted to feel normal so he surrounded himself with crazy.

Back on the dance floor, four girls in a circle wore high heels and tight skirts. They thrived on the social atmosphere. They wanted to feel wanted. Needed to be needed.

And of course, there was the tall girl next to me who watched them. Like me, she wasn't dancing, but for entirely different reasons. It was obvious she was dragged here and hated every minute of it. The only thing she hated even more was being labeled uncool by her friends. So she came along, swallowed the contents of her cups, and was sometimes even persuaded to dance.

You'd think it was hard to fake it more than she was, but you'd be wrong.

I could relate, but not because I was shy or balked by the

lights. I may be a transplant but I belonged. New to the city, but not blinded by its brilliance. Mine is an outsider's inside perspective of Los Angeles.

I'm a studious drinker. I crave the adrenaline. Feed off the camaraderie. This scene was a rare opportunity to cut loose. And as for those participating in the charade of fun, well, I wasn't dragged here and certainly didn't seek anyone's approval, but I was the biggest faker of them all.

This was work for me. Simple as that. But who ever said that work couldn't be a little fun?

The DJ was capable, spinning a good Daft Punk remix that had the horde swimming on the sticky cement. I wanted to be out there. These moments made the hunt pleasurable, if not distracting. Even though I was clubbing, the discipline to remain fully alert was my priority.

As I saw the girl break away from her compatriots in the field and make for a spot at the bar, I killed my third drink.

I was *mostly* alert, anyway.

I traced each step of her candy heels along the moldy carpet. Her red blouse hung loosely over a black skirt that was tighter fitting than it should have been, but her legs were more appealing for the effect. Her supple thighs mesmerized me as they danced ahead, slightly sweaty but awash in a bath of perfume that was ever sweeter as I closed in.

I forced myself past some kids who downed shots to build up liquid courage. The girl flicked her long brown hair to the side, waiting for the attention of the bartender. I didn't need courage or patience. I brushed my chest against her arm as I put my side to the bar, ready to reload.

She didn't even grace me with a glance.

A blonde woman mixed cocktails, a little older than the crowd but with big enough tits that most men would settle for the cleavage. She did her best to ignore her customers, but the girl with the brown hair was doggedly determined to change her mind.

I smiled and signaled the guy working farther down. He was occupied as well—that was one of the signs of a good bartender—but he immediately saw me and nodded. That kind of notice wasn't afforded to just anyone. As I pulled my leather money clip from my pocket, I took that as a sign I was a good customer.

The brown-haired girl next to me pouted and put a hand on her shapely hip, giving me a jab with her elbow in the process.

"This stuck up bitch won't even look at me," she complained to no one in particular.

"Of course," I cut in. "She works off tips."

The girl turned to me. Her nose looked bigger up close and I could see the pale hairs above her fat lips. But she had big, seductive eyes.

"I was going to tip her."

"Don't get me wrong," I said. "I'm not questioning your ability to give her a dollar. And she might be stuck up—I can't say. But I think her target audience would say she was doing a bang-up job."

She watched as the blonde bartender bent over to grab a beer from the cooler. Her miniskirt rode up and her pink underwear flashed the onlookers. Then she spun around and placed the bottle in front of a pack of guys, leaning forward and looking down, innocently unaware that all eyes were on her chest. The old lady was a pro.

The brown-haired girl pretended to be dissatisfied with my explanation, but her eyes held an envious tinge. "I wish I had boobs like that."

"Me too," I agreed.

She widened her mouth in surprise, but the corners of her eyes wrinkled playfully. Her hand swatted my chest in admonishment. Her fingers lingered an extra moment. Her nails were short and painted a bright red to match her outfit, and she wore an engagement ring with an expensive diamond.

"Maybe if I had boobs like that, I wouldn't give you the time of day either."

I nodded at the probable truth. "Well, since you don't and you are, you might as well give me your name so I can buy you a drink."

With perfect timing, the male bartender put another Captain and coke down in front of me.

"Thanks, man," I said, stirring the glass with the cocktail straw. "And one for her."

"Two actually," she said, almost apologetically. "Long Islands."

I raised an eyebrow at her but nodded for the bartender. This was a trade, after all. Most men think it a necessary part of their repertoire to buy women they're hitting on drinks. I say they're suckers. You want to find women that want you, not want something *from* you. Drink after drink after drink; they might get lucky, but they're not doing themselves any favors. Me? I wasn't often seen buying women drinks for the purposes of pleasure. Let's call this an exception.

"Pam," she said. "That's my name. But I'm not one of those girls who'll grind on you for a drink. I can pay." Pam reached inside her purse.

"No," I insisted, "it was my offer. I have a hookup here. I'll get it." I put my hand on hers to stop her from retrieving her wallet. She didn't shy away from the contact. "My name's Dante Butcher. And I'm not in the mood to dance."

Chapter 3

The bartender returned with the other two drinks. "Twenty-seven," he said.

Nice. He'd given me mine for free. I handed him two twenties and told him to keep it.

"So let me guess," said Pam, flitting her lashes at me suggestively. "You're one of those smooth-talking guys who's used to sweeping girls off their feet?"

I raised an eyebrow. "Are we talking about sex already?"

Her smile tapered a little. "Maybe I've got you wrong then. Maybe you're just a dick."

I smiled plainly. "Now you've got a bead on me. I am."

"You are what?"

"A dick. There's no maybe about it."

She pursed her lips as she decided how to respond to that admission. Always beat them to the punch, I say. The sooner they know who you really are, the sooner you can get past the boring introductions.

Pam glanced at the Long Islands sitting on the bar. "It's not very dick-like to buy a girl a couple of drinks."

I considered her premise. "I'm more of a casual dick, really. It's more about my complete apathy to people's problems than a need to be a douche bag. Trust me. I get into enough fights without needing to look for them." I brushed my hair out of my eyes and looked deep into hers. "What about you? Tell me something about yourself."

Pam smiled. She wanted to play along but was at a loss. "Um, like what do you want to know?"

"For starters, who's the other drink for?"

She hesitated and looked shy but held up her hand and showed off her ring. "My fiancé."

"Oh, I didn't notice," I lied. As I returned my money clip to my pocket, I reached around for a small plastic vial and screwed it open. I turned my back to her as I grabbed her drinks, carefully pouring the powder into one of the Long Islands and swirling the liquid to hide the evidence. Then I faced Pam again, holding both glasses in my hands.

"Bunny!" we heard, almost on cue. We turned and saw a broad-chested dude approaching us. He had a little more fat than muscle but it wasn't an unflattering ratio. He was only slightly taller than average, like me, so his eyes met mine perfectly. "What's going on?"

"Soren," said Pam, slightly flustered. "Hi. This is Dante. We were just talking..."

"About the Winter Music Conference," I finished. Pam's eyes darted to me quickly but she nodded. Given the subject matter and the present circumstances, it was sure to evoke a positive reaction. Especially since he was wearing a T-shirt that said "Ultra Music Festival 2012" on it.

"No shit?" he asked. "Are you going this year?"

"I always do. I'm from Miami and I know some of the producers."

Of everything I was doing, this lie made me feel the scummiest. Maybe it was because it was such an LA cliche. People left and right pretended to have connections they didn't. Just another kind of faker.

Soren raised his eyebrows in unison. "That's awesome, brother! I went a couple years ago!"

"No shit. Really?" The poor guy still didn't realize his T-shirt advertised that to everybody except him.

"For real. I deejay at the Echo on Mondays. We should talk!"

Soren raised his hand to shake mine. This was easier than I had thought. I returned both glasses to the bar and gave him a bro hug. I felt the shadow nestled deep inside him.

"He knows the bartender," said Pam. "He got us drinks."

Before I could release myself from the half-shake, half-hug, the girl snatched both Long Islands. The music kicked up in a steady beat and we were jostled to the side by a clumsy group of big women. When I finally turned around, Pam was handing a cocktail to Soren. I couldn't tell which was which.

"Good deal," yelled Soren above the noise. "Let's have a smoke on the patio and I can buy you one in return."

The guy placed an outstretched arm around his fiancée and pulled her towards the side exit, motioning for me to come along. Pam took a hesitant sip of her Long Island as they moved away.

Shit. What if they had the wrong drinks?

I sighed and tasted my rum and coke. I almost coughed as I inhaled the alcohol. It was even stronger than the last one. As I stepped away, I nodded thanks to the bartender who'd poured it.

The blonde with the big tits was selling sex. She made her tips by flashing her skin. The guy, he had a different game. He replaced flirting with hustle. But the main thing he offered, the thing that he could sell instead of sex, was a heavy pour. My choice of bartender was really just a practical application of my priorities.

Chapter 4

Layers of smoke greeted my face the moment I was on the patio. Technically, it was a skinny alley between two brick buildings. Despite being outside, the smoke hugged the ground ominously. It enveloped the resting patrons like a welcoming party from Hell.

In spite of that, it was a bit cool tonight. A welcome development after escaping the tepid confines inside. It didn't take much to sweat in there. Fresh air, or polluted air anyway, was a pleasant contrast. At least twenty other worn out people thought the same, and the tight space felt especially cramped.

Soren leaned against a painted wall that was thick with dirt. Everything in Los Angeles was covered in a sheen of grime. The smog wasn't noticeably bad—I mean this wasn't Beijing—but the lack of rain left the city a far cry from the cleanly washed surfaces I knew in Miami. People praise the sunshine in this city. Not so much the dust and brown grass.

Pam smiled and sipped her drink through a straw. She watched her fiancé produce and light a cigarette. He was a classic case.

"So you're a promoter?" he asked. He sucked heavily at the tobacco as he held a lighter to it again.

"Not me," I said. "I know people who run venues in South Beach and Downtown Miami. Friends of friends." I was purposely vague. It was just a cover story to make me interesting.

"You should look me up," said Soren, sounding a natural at his sales pitch. "I'm DJ Ingress. I spin minimalist post-electronica. It puts the crowd in a different place, man."

"What kind of places are we talking?"

"I have a residency at the Echoplex on Mondays. Swing by and see for yourself." Soren took heavy drags from his smoke and had a reflective moment. "I've always wanted to spin in front of a huge international crowd."

I motioned inside with my chin. "This is a big club."

"You need to know people, man." He lifted his broad frame away from the wall and shook his somberness away, holding up his cocktail in a toast. "To friends."

Pam and I clacked our glasses to his and we all drank. I kept a close eye on her as she sipped the Long Island, wondering if she had gotten the one with the powder. It would be a lot for her system to handle and the effects would be noticeable soon. She smiled at me.

"After we get married," she started, "Soren is going to work for my father and won't have as much time for deejaying. It would be great if he could get a chance to be a part of the Winter Music Conference before then."

The DJ rolled his eyes as she explained the bit about her father but was clearly excited about the opportunity in Miami.

"When's the wedding?" I asked.

"It feels like a lifetime away," he said.

Pam slapped her hand to his chest, as she had done to me earlier. "This summer, Soren! You promised!"

It wasn't even Thanksgiving yet. The two had plenty of time to fight and make up before then.

"I know, Bunny."

"I hate when you call me that."

Soren threw the cigarette butt to the ground and looked up and down the alley. Satisfied, he pulled a small joint from his pocket and lit up. I'd only known Soren five minutes and was already witnessing the third drug going into his system. That alone wasn't too strange. Everybody here fiended for something. People don't go to nightclubs to moderate themselves.

Still, Soren was different. I can always tell with them. A light touch, just while brushing past, is enough to feel the second shadow inside. I had bro-hugged the guy and the presence was unmistakable. Now it was only a matter of taking advantage of his need.

He passed the weed to Pam. She took a light hit and gave it back to him, then drank a large gulp from her glass.

"Hit this," he said. He held the frizzled paper between two fingers as he offered it to me. There was a chunky piece of metal on his finger. A ring gone bad. It looked like something you might pay too much for at the Renaissance Fair.

I shook my head casually. "No thanks. I usually go for the harder stuff."

Soren smiled. He still seemed very alert as he took heavy tokes and paced between the two walls. "I can help with that too," he said, "but this patio isn't private enough."

That was the last piece of the puzzle as far as I was concerned. He was one of them. A faker. Soren was a fiend, trying to exploit his senses and adrenaline any way he could. Dancing, drinking, smoking, spinning—he placed those pleasures above all other concerns, probably even Pam. If chemicals were his weakness, he'd be easy to exploit.

Those outside kept mostly to themselves, but there was a constant wave of people shuffling in and out. Doing anything illegal here would attract a lot of attention, especially from the bouncer standing outside the gate at the front. This was a bad spot.

Pam put her hand to her forehead. "Baby, I want to sit down." Our drinks were half finished but hers was hitting harder.

"Go ahead, Bunny."

She looked at the filthy concrete in disgust, put her hands on her knees, and leaned her ass against the wall. Her tight red skirt would have made it difficult to go all the way down.

"It's always something with her," said Soren in an annoyed voice. "It's Saturday night. I'm here till I get kicked out." He waved his hand dismissively at her. His heavy ring slipped down his finger, but he caught it and adjusted it back into place.

I took another sip of my rum and watched as Pam swayed to the side. She was getting groggy and her heels weren't the surest of footings. I put my hand on her shoulder to steady her. I was, after all, responsible for this.

"Maybe we should go upstairs and chill out for a bit," I said.

Soren let out a disgruntled sigh and upturned his glass into his mouth. "Every single time," he inflected. He extinguished his joint on the wall and returned it to his pocket.

"Here," I said, taking the Long Island from Pam's hand and pouring the remaining alcohol into his glass. He looked at me with a frustrated expression but appeared grateful.

"Thanks," he said. Soren stepped closer to me and lowered his voice. "You know, it wouldn't be so bad if she were a better fuck."

"Soren!" Pam yelled. One moment she was struggling to stand and the next she had summoned the strength to slap him in the face. His glass fell from his hand and banged on the concrete, somehow not cracking but tipping over and spilling nonetheless. Great.

Soren shot her an evil grimace and jumped at her. I put my arm across his shoulder and held him back.

"Dude!" I said discreetly, looking backwards at the gate.

The stout guy brushed my arm down but backed off, understanding that hitting her here would have sent him to jail. He exchanged a confiding look with me.

"It's just that she's always holding me back."

Pam began weeping as silently as she could manage.

Soren rolled his eyes again. "You see what I mean?" He put both his hands against the brick wall and leaned into it.

"No," said Pam, brushing her eyes. "I can dance. I'm fine. Let's go in." As much as she tried to reassure her fiancé, we both knew she didn't have it in her. She pushed me away and almost immediately lost her balance. Her ankle gave out, or she twisted it, and she slipped to the floor. I caught her and gently set her down as she struggled to remove her heel.

"Fuck this!" said Soren. With a sudden flare of temper, he rammed his head into the wall. The blow wasn't for show —his skull impacted the brick so fiercely it made a sound just as loud as his glass hitting the floor.

I let go of Pam and, as she dropped to the street, pulled Soren away from the wall. His forehead split open and blood dribbled down his forehead and nose. He started laughing. Then we heard metal rolling on the cement. Soren's ring was too large for him. It had fallen off.

"Chill out," I urged and looked down the alley. People watched us. We were a sideshow. Guys were chuckling. Women were horrified and trading judgmental glances at the floor. I realized Pam was lying on her back with her legs spread open, one knee resting against the wall, exposing her red panties to the entire alley. I felt guilty about that.

"We need to go inside," I told Soren. I looked him straight in the eye to get my point across. Once he nodded understanding, I released him. He scooped up his ring and headed for the door, leaving his fiancée in the alley.

I lifted Pam to her feet. "Come on, girl."

She was putty in my arms. "It hurts."

"Don't worry. We'll sit you down and take a look."

She hobbled unevenly with me while Soren went inside the club. I heard louder murmuring in the alley and hurried to catch up.

"My shoe," she said.

I looked back. One of Pam's red heels rested on its side by the wall.

"It's okay," I said, and pushed her inside.

Pam clung to me in a daze as I walked her up the dark staircase. She was soft against me, trusting me completely. All I could focus on was her boob pressed into my chest. What a dick I was.

At the top, I headed for the rows of seats in the mezzanine. Soren looked my way.

"I'll go clean up. When she settles down, catch up with me. I've got some snow."

He disappeared into the hallway. There was a men's room at the end of it that he'd be in for a while. Pam and I were alone again.

"Is he hurt?" she asked, putting up a meager attempt to fight me as I sat her in a cushioned corner.

I pulled in snug next to her. "It's you I'm worried about. You drank too much."

Her eyes lazily looked into mine as her face leaned against the seat back. "It must have been the pot."

I nodded and grabbed the edge of her skirt, pulling it down to make sure she was decent. She was dug in behind a table so she'd be safe for a bit.

"I saw you with some girls downstairs. I'll tell them to come up."

As I slid away, she gripped my thigh tighter than I would've thought her capable of in her condition.

"Don't go," she said with a longing in her voice.

I looked at her full lips and her big nose and her shapely legs and her hand resting on me and sighed. She wouldn't remember any of this.

"He used to be so sweet to me," she said.

I nodded. I knew all about it already. I didn't need the story but I offered her one.

"He's probably just had a rough couple of weeks."

The muscles in her forehead tensed and she wiped her wet eyes. "It's been longer than that. The first month of our engagement was perfect, but then he totally changed. He's been partying harder than usual and ignoring me."

I wanted to tell her he wasn't the same person she knew. I wanted to comfort her and tell her things would turn out okay, knowing she'd probably forget the whole conversation anyway. But that's why there was no point. What was important was that Pam would wake up tomorrow and be happier because of me.

"Too many drugs," she muttered, getting sleepy. "Three months already..."

I furrowed my brow. Did she just say what I thought she did? "He's been like this for three months?"

The girl's brown hair obscured half her face but I could see her eyes were closed.

"Pam?"

Her chest heaved as she breathed heavily but she was completely limp. She was asleep.

Chapter 5

My steps to the bathroom carried a determined intensity. No more pretenses. No more games.

The hallway was dark and painted black and red and had a small gathering of guys hovering at the end. The men's room door was open but the bathroom attendant stood blocking it. He was an old black man with scraggly white fur that grew unevenly across his cheeks and chin. As I approached, I realized he was sending the crowd to the other restrooms.

"Is my friend inside?" I asked. "With the blood?"

"He's fucking up my business, man," complained the attendant. "Get him out of here or I call security."

I smirked. This had worked out after all.

As I checked down the hallway, past some of the guys who refused to leave in case there would be something interesting to see, I noticed a single Asian girl staring at me.

She was short—tiny, even—and had pale white hair that hung just above her shoulders. The hair and her cream dress stuck out in the darkness. It was what initially drew my attention to her. Then I noticed the large doe eyes behind the bleached hair. They gazed at me intensely, almost unnervingly. Unsettling. And intriguing.

"Did you hear me?" pressed the black man. I turned and saw that his yellowed eyes meant business.

"No problem," I said and brushed past him.

The bathroom was lined with small white tiles. Old fashioned, but not in a trendy way. I was getting more of a hasn't-been-remodeled-since-the-Beatles vibe. The floor was chipped and uneven, looking as if the smog of the city had managed to seep inside and cling to every surface. It was a small space that afforded a few stalls, sinks, and urinals but was completely devoid of interest except for Soren, me, and the bathroom attendant.

Soren stood beside the sink. His head wasn't too bloody anymore, just some red along the hairline and circling the drain of the sink. He dug through a candy jar on the counter next to a row of colognes, cigarettes, condoms, and other trinkets the old man was selling. Soren had a big grin on his face when he saw me and threw a handful of wrapped mints back into the jar.

"I hate these fucking things," he said, "but now that you're here, we can get started." He pulled a small clear plastic bag from his pocket. He shot a glance behind me, then walked into the corner stall.

The bathroom attendant still blocked the open door. His

expression urged me to hurry. I held up my hand to ask for a minute, then walked cautiously to Soren as he snorted loudly. I pressed open the first two stall doors to make sure they were empty before arriving at the end. The guy had his pinkie in his nose as he finished another bump.

I didn't know Soren but I could tell he was getting worse. He gave no fucks about consequences. This was the second time in a five-minute span that he tempted jail time. He just kept pushing, trying to find more and more ways to top himself. And more people who would enable him. He held the baggy up to me.

I shook my head and leaned my side against the back wall. From my pocket I pulled out a box of smokes and produced a black cigarette. It was a clove, but not a normal one. It had a bit of my homemade flair to it. I lit up and inhaled the spice blend deeply. It tasted different from pure tobacco. The cloves and the sweet paper did a good job of mystifying the flavor. I found they masked my recipe the best.

"No. Not in here," said the old man, stomping towards me.

I pulled out a twenty and placed it firmly against his chest.

"It'll just be a minute," I promised. "Take a break."

The man was both outraged and excited at the same time. He made much more than that in a night, but it wasn't often he got a tip that large at once. I thought of it as paying for his lost time. If he was at all offended by it, he decided it better to back off. The old man picked up his tip jar and walked out of the bathroom. I snapped the door closed behind him, flipped the deadbolt, and turned around.

Alone at last.

I pulled out my pocket watch. It was 1:52 a.m. I was cutting it close with the train, but I could pull this off quickly. I returned the watch to my jeans to free up my hands.

Soren emerged from the stall, eyes wide that I'd gotten the attendant to leave. "You sure you don't want any, Dante?" he asked, flapping the small bag back and forth. "I owe you a drink. Take one bump, at least."

The constant pounding of the trance music was muffled in the enclosed space. This was as private as we would get in a club this big. I took a long drag at my clove and shrugged.

"Why not?" I stepped forward and offered him my cigarette. "Can you hold this?"

He traded it for the bag and didn't think twice before putting it to his lips. As he smoked, I put my fingers around the baggy and zipped the seal closed. I stared at the drugs in my hand.

"It must be fun to pretend you're something you're not."

Soren coughed and looked at the black cigarette in his hands. "What the hell is this? It's not pot but it's not just tobacco either."

I put the cocaine into my back pocket and smiled at his confusion. "You don't like it? It's perfectly natural. Illegal in the US now, even though it's not more harmful than a regular cigarette."

His face fixed to a weird expression. I couldn't pin it

down. Some mix of pain and pleasure. He inhaled the gray smoke that rose from the tip as if he could discern the ingredients.

"Well, that's not exactly true," I amended. "The effects are quite disagreeable for those hiding in another's skin."

As I spoke those words something clicked in him. He experienced a moment of clarity and realized many things at once. He knew his secret was known by another. He knew that I knew he was a shade. Not Soren, but inside him. The life of another, abusing the body to experience worldly pleasures that were otherwise out of his reach. He stared at me and realized that, not only did I know about him, but I intended to expel him back to his own world. To flush him from his host. It was time for Soren, the old Soren, to return and patch up any damage that had been done to his life.

The shade stared at me with coherent eyes. His tongue drooped out of his mouth, extended just past the bottom of his chin, and held in place. Blood from the cut on his head again flowed down his face. He raised my clove, the one I had sprinkled with white sage, and put the fire to his tongue. It sizzled and he grimaced slightly.

Something was wrong. He should have been dizzy by now. I had felt his second shadow; he was no different than the others. A common fiend. Not malevolent or evil incarnate—just a weak, desperate shadow of a man that once was. His vice was loading himself with chemicals and pleasure, anything that could make him feel again. And as high as he was, with the herb being absorbed into his lungs and blood, he should have been overloaded and collapsing, abandoning his host for good. Instead, he was somehow resistant. And angry.

"How are you fighting that?" I demanded.

He threw the extinguished clove to the floor and sucked his tongue back between his grinning teeth. Soren took a step towards me.

"Listen," I said quickly, perhaps with a tinge of panic, "if you just relax I won't hurt you."

The broad guy laughed and I suddenly regretted mixing up the Long Islands. I didn't have a lot of time to dwell on the mistake because Soren charged forward and planted his fist in my chest. I flew backwards in the air and collided with the wall, right next to the closed door. I slid to the floor and landed on my hands and knees.

He was stronger than the others, somehow. Different.

Soren ran straight at me, looking to crush me into the wall. But I wasn't helpless. I leapt up into the air and planted my feet against the wall behind me, then launched forward, over the head of my wild opponent. I hooked my arms and tried to catch his neck as I flew above, but he ducked ahead and slammed into the wall. I flipped around from the light contact and landed hard on my feet and waited to see if Soren would get back up.

Unfortunately, he didn't knock himself out. Soren picked up his wide frame and turned around. A trickle of dark red ran down the side of his face like a leaky faucet.

"You're just going to hurt yourself here," I said, holding my arms up to show that I meant him no harm. "Have a smoke and let's talk a second."

He approached me again, this time with more measure. I searched the stash of products lining the counter. I picked up a pack of Kools and lightly tossed it to Soren. He batted it away with his hand.

"Not a menthol guy?"

"Who are you?" he demanded, narrowing his eyes suspiciously. "What do you care if I drink and smoke and fuck in this world?"

"Soren might care."

He sneered. "I am Soren now. I deserve to live just as much as he does. Even more, since he is unwilling to fight for his place."

The shade advanced slowly, content to talk. He didn't care about the bathroom attendant outside. Or the bouncers. Or the police. In this bathroom, it was just him and me, and he was blocking the exit. I kept my distance by stepping backwards. It was a short-term solution.

"Why doesn't the sage affect you?" I asked. "You're nothing special, just a common shade."

Soren chuckled as he advanced but didn't answer. My back hit the wall.

"What gives you the power to defy me?" I insisted.

"Defiance *is* power," he replied, then spread his arms for a bear hug. He clamped down hard and pinned my arms to my side. I wiggled to escape but he wasn't weak and had leverage. I pushed off the back wall but he spun me around. My hip painfully skipped against top of the sink.

"Who are you?" he repeated.

I was in an awkward position. My ass was in the bowl of

the sink and the faucet was pressing into the small of my back. To add insult to injury, the motion-activated water cycled on and off sporadically. Both my arms were held and the wide frame of Soren almost smothered me as my legs straddled his chest. The only thing I had going for me was that my recessed position had forced him to lean forward and stand off balance.

My right hand was almost loose. I tried to swing my knees into his shoulders to slip his grip. He held strong and stared at me with frantic eyes, face awash in red.

I thrust my head forward and crashed it against his, near the same spot he had slammed into the wall. Pain flashed behind my eyes. His shoulders buckled. Soren released me and wobbled backwards for just a second.

It was enough.

In that single unassailed moment, I drew my knees to my ears and rocketed both of my feet out, extending my legs as far as they would go. I caught Soren square in the chest and propelled him backwards. He slammed through the door of the middle stall and tripped onto the toilet, hitting his head on the metal pipe behind it as he fell in a daze.

I rolled off the sink and kneeled on the floor, rubbing my aching back. Soren quietly groaned but remained still. I hoped he wasn't hurt too badly.

It wasn't supposed to go this way. Shades aren't overly aggressive. They shy away from pain. It hurts them just as much as it does anyone, even if it isn't really their body. The mix of chemical stimulation and the threat of force is enough to put them on their heels. If they don't abandon the world of the living that easily, exsufflation with white sage always does the trick.

I'm a scrapper from my days in Miami, but it's not something I relish when my opponent doesn't know any better. Now I had to hope Soren wasn't seriously harmed in this melee.

I plucked the half-smoked clove from the floor and returned it to my lips. It was wet. Probably piss and dirt, but I didn't care. I pulled out my lighter and worked the cigarette to give it new life. Then I stood up to face the wounded man on the toilet.

"How are you resisting the sage?"

I closed in and towered over his crumpled form. I repeated the question and he finally swayed his head to the side in an attempt to lift it.

"Who are you?" he asked.

I shook my head. He didn't want to tell me anything. I grabbed his face with my left hand and pried one of his eyes open. With my right hand, I brought the burning cigarette to within inches of his pupil.

"If you don't talk, you're not gonna like this next part."

He trembled but his silence was resolute. The truth is that *I* didn't like the next part. I didn't have it in me.

Someone pounded at the bathroom door. Shit. It was locked but there was a key somewhere. Someone had it. This incident had probably caused enough of a scene by now. That settled it. If my privacy wasn't long for this world, then the shade wouldn't be either.

"Okay buddy," I said as I put the clove back in my

mouth. I leaned Soren forward onto me and wrapped my arm around his neck.

"Who are you?" he asked again.

I pressed my arm into the back of his neck, constricting his air supply against the headlock.

White sage is usually enough for shades. The less coherent they are, the better. That's why I work clubs. They're already high out of their minds and exhausted. Half the job is done for me. But not all shades are created equal. Some are stronger than others. Or smarter. And sometimes I have to mix it up. Still, no matter how much strength they have, if they're asleep or unconscious and have the sage in their system, they have no recourse. No defense.

"...Who are you?" he repeated futilely.

Soren didn't fight much. He knew he was beaten. His grip at my arms weakened. His fists relaxed and he dropped his hands to his side. I heard a loud clanking of metal as something bounced on the tiles. I held strong and waited until he fell limp. Then, with a slow breath, I carefully let him go and rested his back against the wall.

"I'm Dante Butcher," I answered softly.

I opened his mouth and blew a plume of smoke into his face. It lingered and rolled with unpredictable activity until he sucked it in. I exhaled more sage and he took it in and out in ragged gasps. Soon, he was breathing evenly again. As I laid my hand onto his bloody forehead, I felt the second shadow leave him.

Soren would have a headache when he woke up, but he'd be okay. He'd be himself again. What's more, he wouldn't remember any of this.

It wasn't a black hole—he'd still remember most of the past few months—but he'd have no recollection of being possessed by something that wasn't him. He'd learn to rationalize some of the things he did that were beyond his control. I imagined a lot of profuse apologies to Pam and his friends and family, but he could rebuild his connections. He had his life again.

But these last few minutes—the fight, the banishment—completely gone. Expulsion overloaded the senses quite like blacking out.

Still, as I tossed the spent cigarette into the toilet between his legs, several things concerned me about Soren. He was taken for much longer than average. Shades weren't precise creatures. The bindings to their hosts were brittle and difficult to maintain. Fiends got tired or bored and often slipped out after a few weeks. Not Soren. Pam had told me he'd been this way for three months. Even more troubling: when confronted, he didn't run. Soren had stood his ground and acted like he had a right to this world.

I exited the stall and flinched at my reflection in the mirror. A scrape of blood ran across my forehead. I wiped it with my hand and drew a line of red across my face. That's when I noticed my hands were bloody, too. It was all from the gash on Soren's head.

I rinsed off in the sink and reveled as the cool water hit my face. It was refreshing. I grabbed a mint and popped it in my mouth. Since I was there, I sprayed myself with some Hugo Boss cologne for good measure. The attendant could take it out of the twenty.

Sharp raps on the door startled me from my calm. I jumped away from the sink and my foot kicked something on the floor. The small piece of metal slid along the tile and into the locked door. I sighed as the incessant knocking continued. Before I abandoned the sink, I spit the mint into it. Soren was right. These mints did suck.

I went over to the door and saw that the object I'd kicked was Soren's oversized ring. It must have fallen off when I choked him out. I picked it up, then clicked the deadbolt open. The old black man shoved his way in.

"Break's over!" he said, sharpening his eyes into a menacing mask.

I patted the bathroom attendant on the shoulder. "I got rid of him," I said, and walked into the hallway. He stuttered and pointed to the feet sticking out of the middle stall, but I didn't turn back.

I passed by Pam. One of her girlfriends was trying to rouse her. My job here was done. I strolled to the downstairs lobby and made for the exit.

In the empty hall, I pulled out my pocket watch and flipped open the cover.

You're getting sloppy.

"I had it under control," I said. "Besides, they're getting stronger. You should see that more than anybody."

She was moody tonight, but at least she was talking to me again.

Chapter 6

I emerged from the old theater into the dirty streets of Hollywood. The wide sidewalk housed metal barricades that guided stragglers in and out of the club, even at this hour. Along Vine Street, a couple of bright yellow cars waited. I glanced at the watch still in my hand and realized the train had just closed.

Fuck, I hate cabs.

As I pondered my options, a group of three girls and a guy came to my attention, mostly because the shortest chick was very animated. She was yelling at her friends. It was her. The Asian girl with the platinum hair from inside. They stood next to a taxi debating their next destination.

Something told me I only had a moment's chance, and I took it. I made my way to her.

Oh, it's going to be one of those nights.

I twirled the pocket watch by its chain. "Relax, you're an

adult now."

As I approached, the cute girl spouted obscenities in a language I didn't recognize. Her friends didn't look especially put off so I figured it was safe to go in. Maybe it wasn't the best idea to hit on a chick who was pissed off at something, but then again, I wasn't known for making good choices. And her tiny skirt hugged her tight body in a way that let me overlook annoyances like thinking and reasons.

"Don't want to call it a night?" I asked loudly enough to interrupt her tirade.

She turned around with half a look of disbelief on her face, but the other half held a smirk when she saw mine. That was the half I needed to court.

"Excuse me?" she asked.

"I'm just a white boy from Miami and I don't know what language you're speaking, but if I had to guess, I'd say you didn't want to go home just yet."

Her eyes narrowed in playful creases and she brushed white bangs away from her face. I had thought she was wearing a crazy costume wig, but it looked real from up close. She had a small hoop in her right nostril to accent her cute little nose. I also noticed she had silver glitter sprinkled on her face and neck that led down to her cleavage. It was an unfair trick that naturally drew my eye. I returned my gaze to her face without shame. It was what she wanted, after all.

"It's only two," was all she offered. She didn't look upset anymore.

I glanced at the other two girls. One was tall and one was thicker, but they were both pretty in their own way. All three had layers of makeup and fake eyelashes and high heels and were otherwise decked out for a party. It seemed a shame to cut the night short after all that effort. But the tall one looked a little wobbly. The guy with his arm around her looked bored. I guessed they were the ones who wanted to leave.

"I'm Dante. What's your name?"

She blinked coyly at me. "Eva."

Good. She was easy to talk to. "Well, Eva," I said with a confident rhythm, "I was thinking about getting a bite to eat. Why not all go together?"

It wasn't that I really wanted everybody else to come along—I just couldn't ask her to abandon her friends and hang out with a stranger. This way, we could all be friends. And if the couple got tired and wanted to leave early, so be it. Two hot girls were good company for the night, and I was still trying to get Soren out of my head.

Dante, heads up.

I ignored her as the thicker of the girls spoke up. "Let's go to K-town," she said. I already had the acceptance of one of the friends. I smiled at her.

Koreatown in Los Angeles is a funny place. It's the largest population of Koreans outside their native country, but it's also LA so they're still outnumbered by Mexicans. Mexicotown doesn't have the same ring and is probably superfluous in Southern California. Anyway, K-town has a little downtown center on Wilshire that's stuffed with restaurants and bars and tacky clubs. It's dirty and divey—and dangerous—but it's one of the few places in Los

Angeles where you could have a drink after two. Illegally of course.

Dante!

I spun around suddenly. I was in the middle of my groove and was trying to ignore the watch, but I'd learned to do that at my peril. She had a sense about things that I was still learning. So I flipped around and probably looked like an idiot. I didn't see anything at first. The clamor of partiers up and down the sidewalk blended together.

"What?" I whispered, not wanting to look like the kind of person who talks to a pocket watch. Not that it would stand out in Hollywood.

It's Soren.

I immediately saw him. The dude should have been passed out on the toilet. Or perhaps stumbling out to find Pam. Instead he was being escorted to a taxi by a white guy with dreads. Soren had managed to clean himself up but still looked dazed. I got the feeling he was just following the lead of the other man. As Soren sat down in the back seat of the car, his benefactor handed something to the driver, closed the door from outside, and rapped on the roof to signal them off. Then the stranger watched the cab merge into the line of cars trudging along Vine.

He was an average-sized man who had an impoverished look about him and wore a plaid flannel trench coat. I didn't even know such things existed or that there was a market for them. Satisfied that Soren was away, the man marched past me. I didn't get a chance to touch him to see if he was taken.

Not another one. Not tonight. Taking care of Soren was

enough.

I returned my attention to Eva and smiled. "Sorry, I thought I knew that guy." It was a weak save, and I could tell she'd been startled by my move. Shit. I wanted to touch her, but I didn't want to scare her.

"Let's go," said the Asian guy, opening the door of their cab and helping his girl get in.

You need to follow that guy!

I had to consciously fight off a grimace. I knew this was important. I could tell. Violet had taught me how to work the streets, but she'd never demanded that I make a specific move before. I didn't know what this was about, but it might have been one of my few chances to learn more about the girl in the watch.

Eva recognized my apologetic eyes and waved her friend into the cab. She stood as tall as she could in her heels and held her chin up, but she looked more cute than put off.

"Shit, Eva. I need to take care of something first. Maybe I could meet you in K-town?"

"I didn't invite you," she shot back. The glare of her large eyes reprimanded me and simultaneously pulled me in even more.

"Well, maybe I can call you sometime?"

She shrugged. "Maybe." Then she turned to get into the car.

"At least," I said quickly, "at least tell me how to find you."

She put her small hand on the door as she squeezed into the back seat. Her short skirt had trouble covering her thighs. She didn't seem concerned.

"Maybe I'll find you," she said and yanked the door shut.

I could only watch helplessly as the car pulled away.

I hope you're proud of yourself.

Chapter 7

I marched south on Vine, following the man in the plaid trench coat.

"I don't appreciate being cockblocked by a twelve-year-old," I murmured.

I thought I was eighteen.

"Yeah, well, I thought you could be an adult for once too."

Violet was eighteen, technically, if you counted from the day she was born. That's how most people keep track, I guess. But Violet was different, mostly owing to the fact that she was dead. Six years ago, when she was only twelve, she'd been killed under circumstances that were still a mystery to me. All I knew was that, two years after the fateful event, around the time I had first moved to Los Angeles, I found her.

It was serendipity, perhaps, that I wasn't in town for long

before I stumbled upon the watch at an antique store in the Magnolia Corridor. It was a cool trinket. It was old and looked it. As a bonus, it still kept good time. I was in for a bit of a surprise when I found out that the watch was haunted by a little girl.

Sorry, okay? She was cute.

"She was fucking hot," I corrected.

Whatever. This man's important.

I nodded as I twirled the watch around my hand. The man with thick dreadlocks did look sketchy, I'd give her that. He checked over his shoulder and turned west onto Hollywood Boulevard.

I hurried forward to keep up without making it look like I was chasing somebody. I assumed this scenario would result in having to expel another shade, but that was premature. I didn't know for a fact that he was even taken. I would need to confirm that first.

Violet was keeping something from me, which wasn't altogether strange. She was tight-lipped in general. All business. She didn't like to talk about her past. We'd done this dance for four years together, and I only discovered that she was murdered six months ago. I still didn't know the details. I just waited for her to open up or slip up. But whatever her problem was, whether trust or trauma, she'd always been a dependable teacher. And she never asked for anything in return. At least, not until now.

"So you know this guy?" I chanced.

There's something... familiar about him.

As I turned onto Hollywood, he was almost a block

ahead of me. I continued my brisk pace as the cool wind battered me. I had a long sleeve T-shirt on. That was enough to combat the LA chill for short walks. This November was cooler than usual, however, and I had no idea how far we were going. What was worse, my bright red shirt didn't exactly make me an inconspicuous tail.

"Is he taken?"

It's more than that...

I sighed. "You know you're being more cryptic than usual, right?"

Look. I want answers just as much as you do.

"Actually, I'm okay with just calling it a night."

This is important.

"Yeah, I got that." I shook my head and rubbed my hands for warmth. "Why is it I get the feeling that if I knew half of what you did, I probably would have ditched you a long time ago?"

Violet was quiet for a moment, but then she said what she always did. A few words, a poem, that stressed our strength together.

The path is rough, and simple feet step better with a shoe.

One's not enough; like lonely streets, they're better walked with two.

I sighed. The novelty of a talking watch had worn thin once I realized she only spoke to me, in my head. But she was an actual person, or had been, and she knew things I didn't know. She had been to the Dead Side and had somehow come back to this world by attaching herself to this watch. Then she had found me or I had found her—I wasn't sure which. I suspected it was a bit of both. And I liked the power.

I was always a little different, you see. I have a gift. Or a curse. I can see things. Not ghosts or demons or monsters or anything that movies render in CGI. Nothing quite so material as that. I can just recognize tears in the fabric of the world sometimes. I notice moments of singularity when others don't. I can feel the presence of the dead. Not as wandering spirits, but as a sort of second shadow within the very substantial people of the real world.

I'd left Miami when I was twenty. My goal was to get as far away from my batshit parents as I could. So I went to the opposite coast. I didn't really know what I was doing out here but I'd always felt drawn to the city. As Violet had said about the man I was following, the city felt... familiar. It was the natural result of my inertia. Then Violet came into the picture and I suddenly had an outlet for my quirks. I had a reason for being, even if there was no how or why. The girl in the watch took an instant liking to me and taught me to pay more attention to my talents.

Together, between the two of us, the lonely streets have never been livelier.

I gained some ground on the suspicious man. He walked ahead as we carelessly tramped on the marble stars of Hollywood legends. Laurence Olivier, Bob Hope, Buster Keaton, Nat "King" Cole, Liberace, Charles Chaplin, Ingrid Bergman—the sidewalk read like a who's who of a forgotten era, a time when having your name set in a star didn't mean you'd be covered in piss and blood and whatever else made up the sludge of the new city.

We walked past the beggars and drug dealers and prostitutes as well as the drunken club kids and bar patrons and police officers. Everybody was here but the tourists. They were the only ones who wanted to see the pink stars, but they came out during the day, when Hollywood was an entirely different kind of crazy.

At the intersection of Hollywood and Highland, the man crossed the street and headed south again. I ran ahead to catch the light of the crosswalk when he took a look behind him. I ducked within the sparse crowd as it crossed. The man with the dreadlocks might have seen me. I couldn't be sure.

"So let's get this straight," I started, mumbling under my breath as a group of guys passed me. "You don't know who this man is or if he's taken, just that something compels you to follow him. Is that right?"

Something like that.

I shook my head as I reached the south side of the street. That wasn't good enough.

"I don't mean to doubt you, but I can't just walk up to the man and shake his hand. If he was up to something shady then I'd basically be letting him know that I know. He's already apprehensive as it is."

Only moments before, the man had strolled confidently past two police officers on the street. Now he was watching his six as if he'd just committed a crime. He was jumpy. Maybe he had noticed me, after all.

You worry too much.

"You've never accused me of that before."

I kept my distance until I saw the flannel trench coat hunch into a crowd standing outside Mel's Diner. The establishment was bustling with business at this time. As if it were a commentary about the way things worked in Hollywood, there was a small line of hungry people waiting to get in and a bouncer standing at the door. He was more of a host really—a nice bald black man who didn't make any attempts to pacify angry guests—but it seemed fitting in this place. I nodded at him as I walked by.

The rest of the sidewalk ahead was fairly empty and I didn't see the man. I reached the edge of the building and turned the corner to check the open-air parking lot. No activity there either. Did he have time to walk this far?

I searched up and down the street with concern, then approached the window of the diner. There it was, behind the glass. The plaid trench coat.

"He definitely tried to duck us."

It's okay. Just stop acting so obvious.

"You're the one that's making me move too fast. He knows I'm following him. Maybe we should call it off."

No!

"This is what we do," I insisted. "We move slowly. We lay low. We don't jump into the middle of situations we don't understand."

You didn't call it off when you made a mistake back at Avalon.

I felt my face twitch due to indecision. Aggravation.

Even though you drugged the wrong person, you pushed ahead in a dangerous situation.

Fuck it. I slipped the watch into my jeans pocket. "I had it under control."

I greeted the host of the diner, who waited outside in a windbreaker, and shook his hand. He nodded me in even though there were other people in line. I ducked inside, leaving the fiver in his palm.

Chapter 8

I pushed ahead into the restaurant, not really knowing what I was planning on doing in there. I decided to give it a second to come to me.

Every single table was packed with recovering revelers. Some joined the waitresses in walking down the aisles and others made their way to the bathrooms. The bright lights took some getting used to but it was the smell of food that overtook me. Greasy as it was, I was suddenly ravenous.

The man in the trench coat stood next to the men's room. He must have been watching for me because we locked eyes for a second. Under the white interior lights, I realized how grimy he was. His well-worn flannel clashed with a brand new T-shirt for Dos Pizzas, a small area chain. As soon as he noticed me, he disappeared inside the bathroom.

"Dante!" I heard called out. It was my buddy Trent. He

sat in a booth away from the window with a Filipino couple, a girl and a guy, who I didn't know. I'd had enough of bathroom fights tonight—Trent gave me the opportunity to wait him out instead. As I approached his table he stood up and shook my hand.

Trent was a classic, educated white dude. He'd moved to Los Angeles from somewhere in Tennessee after getting a degree in Computer Science and was making good money in the tech industry. He had a strong jawline and muscled features but was a little older than me and worked too much to stay in real good shape, so he had put on a few pounds. His brown hair was trimmed into a crew cut that was just a bit longer at the front where he gelled it forward. The lack of long hair made his already large ears appear bigger. He liked to party on weekends and hook up with women so he was clean cut and always wore a button-up shirt. And on the nights when he didn't score, well, he ended up at Mel's.

"You didn't tell me you were going out tonight," he said.

"Yeah, well..."

"Hey, no worries. It's cool. You're just a dick like that."

I didn't argue as I slid into the booth next to the other guy. I nodded at him and the girl. "This is John and Cathy," Trent continued. "You remember them from the Fourth of July party?"

"Yeah," I said, even though I remembered very little of that party. "What's up, guys?"

"Just chilling," said John between sips of his coke.

I wasn't sure if they were a couple but they looked funny together. Cathy was a little heavyset and John was short and skinny.

"You let him call you a dick?" asked Cathy.

"You let people call you Cathy," I answered. "What's the difference?"

Trent laughed. "Exactly. Dante's the most inconsiderate true friend you could have. Let me give you an example of his dickery."

"There's no point," I protested. "I freely admit to it."

Trent ignored me. "I've known Dante for over three years. I ask him about his family sometimes. He's never once asked about mine."

"Why?" I asked with urgency. "Are they sick or something?"

"No. That's not the point."

"What is?"

Trent threw up his hands in frustration. "It's just something you're supposed to ask your friends once in a while, man."

I shrugged as if I didn't know what he was talking about. "That's cause you're from the Midwest."

"Tennessee's not the Midwest."

"Whatever. I'm a city boy. We don't ask people questions about their personal lives."

Trent and I laughed. The Filipino couple didn't know what to say. He decided to change the subject.

"So," said Trent, a smile crossing his face, "you went out hunting tonight?"

My face must have lit up at the irony. "You don't know the half of it."

"That's where you're wrong. I could tell you exactly what happened."

Trent leaned back as the waitress appeared and set a plate of eggs and bacon down in front of him. She gave Cathy pancakes and, shit, what was that guy's name again? Why was I always so bad with names? Anyway, he got a hamburger and fries. I told the waitress I didn't need anything when she asked and she shrugged and walked away.

Trent sprinkled salt and pepper on his food and kept talking. "It's the same story every time. You talked to some girls, maybe even got a number, but when the ugly lights came on you found yourself alone. So you decided to sober up and get some food."

Chicks. Trent talks about them a lot. You could say he's obsessed with them, but that would make it sound weird. Really, it's a natural thing. The bar scene is all about putting yourself out there and talking to people, friends and strangers alike. It's a social hunger that human beings feed on. The rush of meeting a girl, well, that's something different.

"Close enough," I said, inducing my friend to laugh out loud at his intuition. In truth, Avalon didn't close at 2 a.m. and I was hunting an entirely different prey tonight, but Trent didn't know that. And in a way, at the last second, his universal truth came to be when Eva drove off in a cab.

Damn. I could have been in Koreatown right now. Instead I was at Mel's Diner, watching Trent eat, waiting for a man with bad fashion sense to come out of the bathroom.

Sometimes I really hated this place. I hated not having a drink in my hand. Being told the night was over and that I had to wind down. It's not that I can't enjoy winding down, but for it to be forced on me? For it to be illegal to buy alcohol after two in a town as big as LA is ridiculous. Maybe it's a hang-up of mine. A product of being raised in Miami where places stay open till five or later. The funny thing is, I wasn't even twenty-one when I left Miami and I'd still found it easier to get an after-hours drink there. Now here I was, on my twenty-fourth birthday, and I couldn't buy a legal drink in Hollywood because it was 2:30.

I sat with them as they ate, making small talk and sneaking a slice of bacon, watching the bathroom. Guys went in and out but the dreadlocks never reappeared. I was beginning to think it was time to take a piss when we heard screams and a heavy fluttering noise. I turned to see a girl standing by the open front door, swatting the air above her as a large owl wildly flapped its wings in a rain of brown and white feathers. The rest of the diner erupted in hooting and yelling as the bird flew from one wall to the other.

This was weird. Normally I would've chalked it up to the normal chaos of the world, but it had been a strange night already. Owls were sentinels, watchers in the night that saw and heard all. What was this one doing here?

The large bird landed on a raised wall next to some booths on the opposite side of the diner. Patrons screamed and jumped from their tables in an effort to keep away. It was a great horned owl, a proud specimen with reddish-brown and white feathers. Next to its attentive eyes were large tufts that looked like cat's ears. Its head twitched one way and then the other.

This was strange behavior for an owl. Usually, a bird trapped in an enclosed space with this many people would fly as high as it could. Instead, the horned owl was comfortable in the presence of humans. It was unafraid. It landed close to them and almost expected to be left alone. I couldn't say for sure, but it was possible the bird was affected by a spirit.

Animals don't work like people. They can't be possessed, per se. They're much more similar to pocket watches in their ability to carry a foreign presence. Except animals aren't completely inert. And they're wild. While they can't be precisely controlled, they can be teased by forces they have no possibility of understanding. And their senses can enrich those on the Dead Side.

I grabbed the salt shaker on the table, unscrewed the top, and upturned the contents into my palm. Affected animals are always agitated. There's an imbalance that sets them on edge. It takes skill for a shade to satisfactorily guide them. It's like trying to animate a puppet that hangs from a single string. That's where the salt comes in. It's useless against people that are taken, but it's enough to shake any ties dug into animals.

It isn't a spell. Magic isn't real. There's just the material and the ether. What most people think of as spells are, if not complete bullshit, then a working knowledge of the elements layered with false ceremony and showmanship.

Like a doctor who waves his hands and says "hocus-pocus" as he slips an aspirin into his patient's drink. Salt draws out the transitional energies that most people don't know about. It effectively severs an already tenuous connection. So I cupped the crystals in my hand as I became sure that somebody was interested in me.

The horned owl spread its wings, lifted itself off its perch, and flew my way. If somebody did see me, I wanted to make sure they didn't get a good look. The bird extended its talons as it prepared to land on the wall beside our table, and I beamed it with a fistful of salt.

If the owl had acted wildly before then it was completely berserk now. It flapped its wings violently as it drew back and fell to the floor. It continued attempting to fly but looked more like a chicken racing across the floor on its side. Most of the diners were on their feet at this point. They scrambled to get away from the bird's impressive wingspan. Within minutes, the great horned owl recovered and escaped up into the recesses of the ceiling behind a fluorescent light fixture.

"Holy shit," screamed Trent. "That was awesome!"

My friends took their seats as the panic died down but I stayed on my feet. No, it wasn't awesome. That was already the third strange thing to happen tonight. First, Soren resisted the sage. Then, Violet had practically ordered me to take action for the first time ever. Now, the owl.

It was the Rule of Three.

Three is a special number. It isn't mystical, it's mathematical. Some people mention the mysteries of Pi and the definition of a circle and I tend to think it's related. Weird things happen in threes. It's like a loop encircling both worlds that brings them together. Instead of magic, it's some natural law that attracts certain events to each other. Like how celebrities always die in threes. It's eerie, is what I'm saying, but if you notice it, it's divine.

I marched towards the bathroom while everybody else focused on the owl. My foot crashed into the door and slammed it open and into the wall. Empty. Well, there was a guy in the stall with his pants down, but for my purposes the fucking bathroom was empty. And the window wasn't large enough to escape through.

I searched the restaurant and saw the buzz of people standing up and laughing and acting drunk and I realized the owl was a diversion. The man was gone. Probably slipped right by me while I was distracted.

I put my head in my hands. Shit. I had to get out of here while I was still buzzed.

"I'll see you guys later, okay?" I stormed by my friends after my sudden proclamation. I didn't know how else to ease out of the situation. A clean break was best.

"You're taking off?" asked Trent. "Okay, but let's go out next week. There's this new vodka bar that opened up downtown. I hear it gets packed up. It has a classy vibe so the crowd's a good ratio."

I smiled. "Attract the women, the guys will follow."

"And I do," he said proudly.

I shook my head. "You'd follow them to a community college knitting class if you thought it was a good hookup spot."

I left as he started a story about an actual class he had attended. I didn't even want to know the details anymore. The owl was already a memory to them. A photo opportunity to others. To me, it was a botched night. I needed to get out of here and make something happen. I stumbled angrily to the door, nodded at the host/bouncer, and stepped into the cold.

Chapter 9

As I followed the sidewalk, a couple came my way. They looked to be arguing. A douchey looking guy with diamond earrings who wore a scarf held up his hand to a girl in a green dress. She stomped away from him, insisting she wanted to have fun. She was Mexican and had short black hair in a sort of emo bowl cut, nice tanned skin, and a skinny waist despite pretty beefy hips.

I locked eyes with her right as I passed. There was something flirtatious attached to that exchange, as if she were looking for fun or trouble or thought they were the same thing. I almost said something but was caught up in the moment and settled on a confident stare and a strut.

"Hey," she said to my back. "Where are you going?"

I turned with a smirk on my face. "I'm getting a drink."

She raised a single eyebrow and crooked her red lips to the side, intrigued by the offer.

"Rachel," said the guy, now behind me. He pushed by and positioned himself between us. "I thought you said you wanted a milkshake."

She considered him with mischievous excitement. "Let's get drinks!"

The poor guy rolled his eyes.

"Yeah," I said, "let's go." To be fair, I was inviting them both. Rachel wasn't stunning but she looked fun. Besides, I really did want a drink.

"Where can we go?" she asked as she grabbed me by the shoulders.

The guy adjusted his casual dress jacket and scarf and kind of stood to the side, dejected. I could tell he barely knew Rachel and was trying to get her home. He was in a tough position. He didn't want to be the buzzkill, but he really didn't want to go out this late at night. So I upped the ante on him.

I tried to think of the busiest, loudest, most chaotic place that was close-by.

"We could go to Avalon. They're open until six."

Rachel's eyes lit up and the guy threw his hands in the sky.

Checkmate.

The rest of the night went quicker than I expected. The guy tagged along as he weighed the risk versus reward of the situation. Alone with the girl, he probably would have gone to the ends of the Earth. With me there, he dipped out after two blocks. The thought of just starting up at a club now without a sure thing was too much for him. Once we were alone, I convinced Rachel that drinks were more important than dancing and then we didn't even go to Avalon at all. It was a clever coup that I was proud of. She drove me to my place in the Valley, which solved my needing to take a cab. Then I put on some She Wants Revenge and poured us a couple of Havana Club and cokes that we only half drank before we started making out on the couch.

Rachel was spunky and playful in the beginning, then momentarily shy as the green dress came off, but then she sat on top of me and fucked like she was being filmed. Her breasts were small but her complexion was evenly tanned, and when she turned around I couldn't help thinking I had never quite had a girl so expertly work her ass like that on me before.

That's the great thing about one night stands. They're random and fun and they don't mean anything. We didn't hurt anybody. Rachel and I were two people who enjoyed our youth without being tied down. Unless that was requested.

One minute I'd been sitting in a diner with friends and the next I was carefully engaged in an interlude with a complete stranger. I hadn't even made the first move. I like to think I skillfully handled the situation once it was presented to me, but the truth is it was random providence, a single moment where two people with similar needs crossed paths.

In the end, the whole nightcap was so perfect that she didn't even stay the night. Rachel got a phone call and said she had to go. I'd only managed to put on my underwear by the time she typed her number into my phone and was out the door.

I collapsed onto the couch again. It was a good night and I would sleep well; the sun wasn't even up yet. I poured the rest of her cocktail into mine so that I almost had a full glass and brought it to my lips. For some reason, all I could think about was Eva.

Chapter 10 - Dream

The dream started the same as it always did.

I was trudging down a long barren street amidst the towering brick buildings of Downtown Los Angeles. I didn't know why it was always Downtown—it wasn't where I lived —but it felt like I belonged here. Like this was where I was supposed to be.

I was familiar enough with the neighborhood. I'd walked down these corridors and been to countless bars and other spots in the area. I knew it and it was recognizable, except everything was off. A little bit older and unkempt, but also twisted, if that was possible. There was a darkness that blanketed everything; it was as if a veil was tied around my head and all my senses were muted. Firm shapes appeared blurry, loud sounds were muffled, yet I could see the most innocuous wisps and hear far away mutterings as if they were all meant for me.

The most eerie aspect of this world was the light. Or more accurately, the complete lack of it. It felt like a dark day. A dusk. As if the sun had already bowed out but still graced the world with its trailing magnificence. Everywhere was the same, simultaneously bathed in shadow yet blanketed with this ever-present light that had no radiance. As for electricity and light bulbs and whatnot—they did exist here. But they fought against the oppression so fruitlessly that their influence was nothing more than a washed out whiteness. An overexposed black and white photograph with ghostly vacancy. It wasn't light because it failed to illuminate. It wasn't shadow because it was more of a presence than an absence. The hot spots clashed with the dark world but were neatly contained, often extending only inches from their source.

Truly this was a bleak place.

This world was dreary and suffocating and entrapped me in a haze; I moved through it with the grace of a hippo underwater. The buildings were mere shells and the roads desolate. It was a cryptic dance with a foreign tempo, and I always struggled to draw meaning from it.

Every time I dreamt of this place, I couldn't help but feel that I missed something. Some final trick that would pull the shade away and reveal to me the true wonders or horrors of what encompassed me. And it usually felt so close. But, like all dreams, I usually awoke at the most inopportune moment.

I pressed ahead with the sort of overdone effort dream worlds force upon us, where mundane actions require great bouts of concentration and still occur too tediously. Yet my steps were methodical and my labor was true, and before I knew it, I was walking down a strip I didn't recognize.

I was somewhere in Bunker Hill, but as with all things on the Dead Side, the surroundings were constructed not out of brick or stone, but from the remnants of the many memories that were trapped here. The world was an amalgam of the experiences of its inhabitants. It modernized itself as new souls took residence. Still, the occasional stubborn memory persisted, and in testament to that, I watched as a Temple Street Line cable car groaned past me guided by invisible wires.

This dream that was more than a dream was recurring; every two to three months I would find myself walking the lonely streets of a Los Angeles perverted by its inhabitants. Yet the dream was never the same. I always wandered, but as in the real world, I could choose to turn left instead of right, or get on the bus, or go into a building. Endless opportunities presented themselves to deviate from any pre-scripted conclusions, and I often took advantage of them and discovered new things. I learned about the city through surreal experiences I couldn't explain.

Except I was barely able to interact with anyone else. The muted shade over the world prevented me from breaking through and making real contact. And that was why, after years of wandering the gloomy corridors of the city, even back when I'd lived in Miami, I still couldn't, for the life of me, understand what any of it meant.

But this time I did.

As I arduously strolled down the sloped walkway and passed the aging wood balustrade of the St. Angelo Hotel, I heard my name called out. Foggily at first. Then again with certain clarity. Up the small steps, standing at the main entrance, was a little girl in a dress of horizontal red and black stripes. Her bangs and long hair blended smoothly between the colors of white and purple and black, and this hue was matched by her eyes. The young girl just stood there and fumed at me, then stormed inside.

There was no doubt it was Violet.

Chapter 11

"What's going on here?" I asked.

I had entered the St. Angelo and was in a thin lobby with high marble walls framing a set of three brass elevators. I wasn't sure if the solid architecture of the inside matched the ornate wood of the exterior, or if I was even in the same place anymore. Sitting on a large wooden reception desk was Violet, swinging her knee-high black boots freely as her legs hung in the air. I'd never actually seen her before.

"Welcome to my world," she said.

The girl wore a mask of depression over her outward features. A white cartoon skull smiled across the chest of her red and black dress. She had scores of black gummy bracelets and linked chains around her throat and arms. Her purple gloss lipstick complimented her eyes and hair, and she had way too much black eyeliner on her pale face. She was a skinny girl but had a chubbiness to her cheeks that could be the last vestiges of baby fat, perhaps the only pure and cute thing left about her otherwise goth appearance.

It was funny for being so overdone. Especially in this place. Many twelve-year-old girls go through a goth phase when they first learn to express themselves through style. They fight so hard to be unique and different that they copy others to a tee. Rebellion through conformity. It's an irony that takes time to outgrow. Violet never had that chance.

Who could really blame her for her dark disposition anyway?

"This is it?" I asked. "The Dead Side?" I moved more easily now, like I wasn't underwater anymore.

"Did you ever think otherwise?"

"I didn't know what to think. I mean, I understood *things*." I considered what it was exactly that I had thought. "You know when you're having a really weird dream but you innately just 'get' everything? It's like you're familiar with the backstory, but it only makes sense while you're asleep. As soon as you wake up all rationalization is gone..." I watched as the fuzzy world crystallized around me. Everything blurry was adjusting itself, coming into focus. It was as though my senses were experiencing HD for the first time. "How could this be real?"

Violet shrugged. "That's where you've got me. There's something about you that shares a closeness with the immaterial. I can't explain it. All I know is that, when you saw my pocket watch in that antique store, you could hear my voice when I spoke to you."

"If you live in the watch then what are you doing here?"

"Don't be stupid, Dante. This is where I live. My home isn't a little piece of metal and glass. The watch is just a conduit I attach to."

Violet revealed the brass watch in her hand. I instinctively reached for it in my pocket, but of course it was gone. I never had it in the dream. Now I knew why.

"It's a connection between our worlds," she continued. "A window. It allows me to be here and—"

"Talk to me up there."

"Yes," she answered. "I'm alone in this dreary place, but I can sense the old world through the watch. It keeps me content. But before you, I've never been able to speak with the living."

The living. It was hard to think of this little girl, the one I'd known for the last four years and could see sitting right before me, as anything else. "So you don't age, then? Even though you died six years ago, you're still a twelve-year-old girl."

She smiled dryly. "Sorry if that ruins my birthdays."

I didn't know much about Violet, but she had told me how old she was when she died. She never talked about her past life, but after a lot of persuading I'd finally gotten her to tell me her birthday. November twenty-second. The same as mine. Tonight. I never celebrated it much—I was out in LA alone—but I'd made it a habit to point the anniversary out to her. I don't know why.

I approached the girl and tried to put my hand on her shoulder. I wanted to comfort her. To tell her things were okay. That it was good to finally see her. But she swatted my hand away.

"Don't think you can sweet talk me and squirm out of this." A hint of anger twitched in her purple eyebrows. "I'm still mad at you."

I backed away. "What are you talking about?"

"That man. You let him get away."

"He saw me, Violet. I told you from the beginning that I was down for this, but I need to tread lightly around crowds."

"That was four years ago and you always work in crowds. Clubs wouldn't be clubs if they were empty."

"It's not the same. When you get in a fight in a club, you deal with security. In the streets, it's the police. I could get arrested. Or worse. I tried to be careful."

"You decided to joke around with your friends and get some pussy."

I gritted my teeth. It was jarring to hear the little girl talk like that, but she'd learned a lot since she died. Learned a lot from me. I got annoyed and tried to remember if that had ever happened in a dream before. But of course, this was something real.

"What was so important about him anyway?"

Violet almost answered but stopped herself, unsure of what to say. "Maybe I could've told you if you'd gotten him."

"Maybe," I said, "or maybe I'd be dead. Or maybe he would have realized what I knew. Which would be a trick because I don't actually know anything about him at all."

I felt warm all of a sudden, as though the front door had

opened and let a stale breeze in. It was a shock. But it was also somehow comforting. The heat energized me. It made me feel alive in this desolate place. And then I was unnerved. We appeared alone but we didn't feel alone, and I didn't really know why until I stepped back and focused on the spot.

In this strange limbo of absence and shadows, there was something in between, a faint glowing radiance that drifted past me. It looked like a ghost but not like a human. Like something I'd seen in fuzzy photographs of haunted houses on horrible cable channels. Except I knew those photos were fake. Spirits couldn't wander in the world of the material; they needed something physical to inhabit. But this place wasn't physical. And this presence, while having no form, was real. It seemed to move of its own accord. It glided by the elevators and into the back hall where it disappeared through the wall.

"What the fuck was that?" I asked.

Violet just rolled her eyes.

"I mean, I know it's a ghost, right? Can you do that?"

"I've told you before. When people get trapped here, they warp into all kinds of things. They forget themselves."

I nodded. "Sure, you told me that some spirits forget their names. Or they go crazy. Apparently others get really emo and dye their hair purple to match their name. But you didn't say anything about floating and moving through walls."

Violet narrowed her eyes at the joke and jumped to the floor. Her boots landed on the tiles with a solid thunk.

"Listen," she said, "I'm a girl. I died. But I still have a strong connection with the material world. I see it every day. I remember who I am. I remember my family—"

The girl stopped talking and put her hand to her mouth, then pulled it away quickly and turned around. She was obviously struggling with something personal and doing a poor job of keeping it under wraps. I knew she didn't want to get into it, though.

"That one," she continued, pointing to where the spirit had passed through the wall, "it doesn't even know that it was once human. It can't talk. Maybe it can't even think. It's mostly just energy now. A discarded sentience. My dad studied them a lot."

Violet stopped again, realizing she had brought up her family twice in as many breaths. She huffed out air in frustration and turned at me again.

"You mention him a lot, you know."

Her eyes shimmered. "No I don't."

But she did. Over the years I'd caught her making references to her father over and over. I suspected that much of her knowledge of possession and banishment and spirits was his doing. She never answered questions about him. But she did just say she'd never talked to the living through the watch before me. That and the fact that her father knew about the Dead Side could only mean one thing —that he was dead too.

"Were you killed with him?" I asked.

Her head snapped away from me. "What? Who said we were killed?"

"You've let it slip before." I waited for her to come clean. Her mind raced for an explanation. A way to change the subject. I brought a tender note to my voice. "Violet, I've known you long enough. You were the one who told me that most people who die move on. Getting trapped here is a sign of tragedy or unfinished work. It's an easy guess that you were murdered."

The girl pouted and walked to the elevator, poking her fingers at the brass door as if drawing an invisible picture that would make everything better. Her silence was confirmation that I was close enough.

"Or maybe, it was your dad who killed you?"

"No!" she screamed. "It was Livia. My father would never hurt me like that." There were tears in her eyes as she revisited the painful memory.

I'd tried looking up deaths of little girls named Violet before. Nothing fitting the circumstances ever matched. Maybe now, knowing she had died with her father and cross-referencing the search with the name Livia, I could find something that lined up.

For now, however, I had no desire to push her. I needed to cheer her up.

"Something's different, Violet. Something is happening. If you think following that guy in the plaid trench coat will enlighten us then I'll check into it. I promise. But you need to be straight with me. That owl last night was looking for someone. For me. I need to know what you know."

The girl leaned on the wall. "I don't know where the owl came from."

"Where's your dad? Is he down here with you?"

"I don't know. He's lost to me. I'm down here all alone."

"Can't I help you find him? Can't I help you find your way again?"

Violet shook her head. "You need to concern yourself with the world of the living. We don't belong there. In people or owls."

"And what about pocket watches?"

"It's just a connection. Maybe that will be cut one day too."

I smiled sadly as I looked at Violet. Would losing her be a happy occasion, a signal that she had finally moved on and found peace? Was it selfish that I enjoyed her company and appreciated the power it gave me?

"The path is rough," I recited, "and simple feet step better with a shoe. One's not enough; like lonely streets, they're better walked with two." I thought I saw a faint smile creep past her guard. I decided then and there that I was going to help her, one way or another, even if she didn't know about it.

"Why did you speak to me," I asked, "back in that antique store?"

"Have you looked around this place? Do you really need to ask why I would want some company or even... a friend?"

I smiled softly. "I mean, why did you tell me about shades and teach me how to expel them?"

Violet stared at the marble floor tiles and thought a moment. Her answer carried the innocence of a child. "I don't know. I guess I figured that people should go where they're supposed to go."

"And where is that?"

Violet raised her eyes to me. "If I knew, I wouldn't be here."

Chapter 12

Like all dreams, it wasn't clear if time had passed or if I just wasn't paying attention. One moment we were talking and the next the room trembled, threatening to dislodge the glass mirrors from the walls.

I sensed the disturbance but didn't know what to make of it. I had lived through several Los Angeles earthquakes before, and frankly, they were unnoticeable. Nothing but passing tremors. This incident had the same physical properties that a cartoon earthquake might. It was more foreboding, though. It wasn't clear why until Violet spoke up.

"Somebody's coming."

I turned to the door and noticed the heavy metal frame wiggling on its hinges. The glass panel, however, revealed nothing outside but the desaturated gloom.

"Get out of here," I commanded. Although I'd visited

this world many times, tonight was the first that it had solidified. That anything of consequence happened. Really, I was ready to expect anything, and I didn't want Violet to be in danger.

The little girl wasted no time and banged at the elevator call button. The shaking grew worse.

"What is it?" I asked.

Violet just shook her head.

A loud ding announced the arrival of the elevator as the brass double doors slid open. "You should come too," said Violet, looking concerned.

"Don't worry about me." The girl hesitated but I nodded her on. She stepped into the car and allowed the doors to close. That should keep her out of it.

The trembling came to a head all at once, thrashing violently as if to collapse the building, and then silencing so quickly it seemed to have been nothing more than a hallucination. A complete stillness filled the dense air and I was completely alone.

And then the front door swung open.

"Dante Butcher, you say?"

I trained my eyes on the source of the spectral muttering. A lanky figure materialized on the threshold. It was a sad imitation of a human with ratty patches of orange hair and skin blotched with scabs. He was both flesh and ghostlike at the same time and had the urgent twitches of a heroin addict. I'd never seen this man in my life before, but I had felt him. He was instantly familiar.

"Soren."

purest of environments. Little Aster McAllister quickly became a favorite of the household and was adored by her parents and grandfather. Alas, in 2004, the grandfather's health took a turn for the worse and he passed away.

By all accounts, the fairy tale life of Alexander's family was over at that moment even though it wasn't yet obvious. Alexander became distant and cold as he tried to take the reins of the business. Livia became frazzled at her husband's disappearances and had several breakdowns. Poor Aster was caught in an impossible situation and was often forced to take sides. Eventually, she drew inward into depression. She became increasingly disassociated from her life and began cutting herself, troubling her parents all the more.

This slow agony grew over the years. Livia visited several therapists and was on medication. She never recovered her old form but confessed to faking it for some time until, in 2008, six years ago, Livia McAllister finally snapped. She was ironing a suit for Alexander when the two engaged in a heated argument. The neighbors had reported some previous scandalous incidents, but this was to be the pinnacle.

When Alexander's back was turned, Livia struck the back of his head with the iron. He fell to the floor but was still conscious. His wife bent over his struggling body and bashed his skull seven more times until his form lay inert.

Livia started at the sound of crying and saw that her only daughter, Aster, was a witness to the event. Rather than try to soothe things over or plead forgiveness, the mad woman turned on her child.

Aster ran to the linen closet and locked herself inside. The doorknob was backwards and allowed this, and not unlockable from without, the closet had become a favorite place of safety for the twelve-year-old girl. Livia, however, could not quell her rage. She repeatedly banged on the metal knob with her domestic weapon.

Alexander's personal driver, who would ultimately call the police, heard the commotion, including the screams of the little girl promising her mommy that she would leave her alone. Livia was reported to have said that her daughter was against her and loved her father more.

Inside the closet, little Aster McAllister finally heard the doorknob crack away from its housing. It was unclear from the crime scene if she had made any attempts to struggle once the door was breached, but it was plain that Livia killed her daughter with two blows to the crown.

When police arrived, they found Livia McAllister raving like a lunatic. She said that she had freed her family, that she was the last, and stated something about moving on. They were exasperated words from a woman covered in blood. And while she no longer held the iron, she swiped a kitchen blade at any officers who approached her.

Livia's death was ruled a suicide even though one of the officers had fired a single shot at her. He claimed he was protecting his life but didn't want to kill the crazy woman and hoped to subdue her. When Livia fell to the ground, instead of allowing herself to be taken into custody, she slit her own throat and collapsed. Her ravings had ended.

Alexander's body was clearly visible to the officers in the hall as soon as they had arrived. They had known the woman was a danger and were cautious in their approach. The officer who ultimately fired the shot later controversially claimed he would have gladly killed the mother had he been immediately aware of the grisly scene in the linen closet.

While the paramedics were attending to Livia and Alexander, the police found the broken body of Aster in her battered hiding spot with a Kenmore iron lodged in her head.

Aster was pronounced dead at the scene. The authorities weren't able to remove the iron until later. Livia officially died during transport to the hospital. But what was most amazing, and definitely warranted further investigation, was that Aster's father, Alexander McAllister, had somehow survived the brutal attack.

Chapter 14

It was a perfect beach day. The sun ducked behind the clouds before it became unbearable but reappeared before it got too cool. Of course, the beach was perfectly supplanted by the pool in my apartment complex. It was large and had cute girls hanging around. Especially on Sundays. I sighed and put the thought out of my mind. There would be no pool today. I had things to take care of.

I strolled across the street and appreciated the short walk to the Red Line. Most people don't realize Los Angeles has a working subway. Probably because it's serviceable for some trips but doesn't exhaustively cover the city. I had read that there used to be more tunnels under LA but tire and automotive companies bought out and dismantled all the tracks in the thirties. It was the kind of big conspiracy that was actually true. In the end, the corporations were fined but the city was left more dependent on cars anyway.

As I walked, I thought about promises to little girls. I thought about Violet. I'd left her home. She didn't mind being alone as long as I spent time with her once or twice a day. It was normal for me to head out and do my own thing. Besides, I was just fact-finding. She wasn't needed.

The taken aren't as active during the day. I don't know why. Maybe the sunlight hurts their eyes, or maybe they're sleeping off the previous night's debauchery. There was a reason I worked the nightlife circuit. It was as simple as going to where my customers were. Or prey. Suffice it to say that the strange characters I passed in the California sun were good old regular Los Angeles crazies.

As I descended into the station on the escalator, the stagnant air deflated my mood. I had told Violet I would find the man in the trench coat for her, but I had another promise to keep. One I made to myself. And while I did my best to ignore it, the dark story of Alexander and Aster gave me shivers.

Sunday train rides tended to be the least eventful. People traveled for pleasure so there was a lower number of suspect passengers. A single aging woman announced to the entire train car that she was collecting donations before we set off, but besides that, everybody kept to themselves.

There were only a couple of stops in the Valley before the subway cut under the Hollywood Hills. A ten minute ride brought passengers to the beating heart of Tourist-town. Not bad, considering it would usually take that long just to find a parking spot. Downtown was twenty minutes further. That left me ample time to question my actions.

Alone time wasn't the only reason I had left the pocket watch behind. For this specific trip, I didn't want Violet to know I was snooping into her family. She kept her past preciously private, but I had to move forward regardless. Her father, Alexander McAllister, was still in a coma at Keck Hospital. I didn't know anything about the place but read that it was a state-of-the-art facility with cutting-edge technology, located near Union Station. It made sense that Alexander would be cared for at an esteemed location since he came from a rich family, but I still didn't know what to expect. Something tugged at me.

I hate hospitals.

I talked my way to the neurological ward, posing as a family friend. Walking through the serene halls sent chills up my spine. It was depressing to stroll past bed after bed of patients hooked up to machines that staved off their deaths. In truth, it was likely that several of them were already dead inside, and not in the way that most expected.

The dead don't operate like most movies portray. Shades require tangible vessels to substantiate their immaterial forms into our living world. Inanimate objects and animals are mere conduits and windows; they enable interaction but are not doorways. They aren't true escapes from the Dead

Side. I saw where Violet really spent her time. The Dead Side was her home; she only communicated through my pocket watch.

Humans, however, are another matter entirely. When people find themselves weakened, whether through harm or drugs or sickness, they expose themselves to certain spirits that have found a way to pass through. Many nights I hunt the fiends who get high and play in the minds of the reckless youth, but there are other kinds. As Violet had said, the Dead Side transforms spirits into any manner of twisted perversions.

There's a whole class of shade that thrives on sickness and decay. They possess men and women and break their bodies down until they're either expelled or their host dies. This kind is rampant in hospitals, no matter how nice or expensive, and it's often self-defeating to fight them. By the time it becomes obvious that these unfortunate people have decay growing within, it's usually too late to save them. I'd tried on occasion, and sometimes the patients underwent immediate complications and degraded. Or died. It was a facet of the dead that was unfamiliar to me and Violet. I figured, with a hospital staff working around the clock, it was better just to let their sad songs play out. But the tune grated my conscience.

I was relieved when I finally arrived at my destination. I stepped into the private room, alone with the dormant form of Alexander McAllister. The shades were drawn, creating a gloom that was brightened only by the displays of the medical equipment. Besides the lights and beeps and the white noise of the breather, it would have been a crypt in here.

I stood at the edge of the bed longer than I should have, afraid of what I might discover.

Violet had said that her father abandoned her. She said he was lost. Out of reach. Since he was here, was it possible that he was left behind? Was it possible that she was just waiting for her father to join her among the dead?

Then, like an idiot, I was smacked with the obvious, way too late. If Livia had been taken and tried to kill the whole family, that would explain why Violet was helping me banish the dead. Perhaps she wasn't in a hurry to see her father. She was on a crusade instead. And I was her soldier.

It was a sound theory but I had to collect the facts where I could. I may not have known anything about medicine, but I could see something that no one else in this building could.

I placed my hand on the quiet chest of Alexander McAllister. I closed my eyes and breathed relief when I felt no foreign shadow within him. The man was not possessed. Except for the grievous wound he had suffered, he was normal.

"Who are you?"

The words came from behind in a gruff voice. I jerked away from the hospital bed. In the doorway was a bald man in his mid-forties, yet still tall and strong. He looked like a former basketball player, especially since he wore cross-training sweats. In short, he looked mean and had large hands.

"Oh, sorry. I didn't know anyone was here."

The words repeated again in a thick accent. "Who are you?" He was Armenian, I thought. They have a sizable population in LA, and I'd been on one or two dates with Armenian chicks—but my expertise stopped there.

"I'm a friend of the family, actually. I knew his daughter V—Aster. I just wanted to see how he was doing."

The large man took a step forward. "He's in coma."

I nodded in agreement of the astute observation. But it was more than a simple statement. It was a suspicion of my motives. It was a dismissal of any further questions I might have.

"Are you a friend of Alexander's?" I asked anyway.

He sized me up. The Armenian man's face was made of sharp lines, a pointed noise, and taut lips. He took my curiosity very seriously. "Do we know you?"

"N—no. His daughter, I said—"

"What's she want?"

I stared momentarily, unsure how to answer the strange question. It was clear this man didn't work for the hospital, but if he had any association with Alexander, he seemed unaware of the details of his life.

"She's dead."

The large man snorted and puffed his chest out. "Time for you to go."

His request was so abrupt that I didn't know what to do. My inaction didn't do me any favors. I was becoming increasingly aware of the man's poor attitude (and possible intention to do me harm) when a shrill voice interrupted us.

Another man joined us in the hospital room.

"What have we here?"

This one, thankfully, was a mousy man with wiry glasses. He had gray-brown hair on the sides of his head and a mustache, but his crown was just as bald as the Armenian's. Clearly a businessman of some sort. He wore an old brown suit with a light blue shirt, no tie.

"You said you were a friend of Aster's?" he asked politely.

"Yes," I agreed quickly, "back—before..."

I found myself at a loss for words. It would've been easier to lie about being a friend of Violet's in life if she had ever shared anything with me. The older man must have noticed my hesitation, because he cut in.

"Yes, it was all very awful," he said. "It still pains me to think about it. I'm Mr. Glickman, the family attorney and agent holding Mr. McAllister's power of attorney." The lawyer handed over a business card with the announcement and I took a cursory look at it for show.

"Who are you?" repeated the large Armenian man, as if it was my turn to repay the favor.

"I'm Dante. I didn't know I'd be interrupting anything. I really just wanted to see how he was doing."

The lawyer waved his hand in the air. "Oh, it's not a problem. Don't let Bedros here scare you. I'm a lawyer so I prefer to garner information through discourse. This oaf is a bodyguard so you can imagine his intentions."

"I already have." Bedros grumbled like some kind of giant troll held back by a collar. I did my best to ignore him.

"What use does a comatose man have of a bodyguard?"

"Yes, yes, I know it's ridiculous," said Mr. Glickman. "Alexander was a kind man who didn't have enemies to speak of. His affairs in this matter, however, are ultimately his own. He continues to employ some associates through prior arrangements. It's his father's empire that follows him. Bedros here is a bit callous and will take offense at anyone besides myself or the medical staff approaching Mr. McAllister, but the whole thing really is quite harmless. Assuming, of course, that your business here is legitimate."

I couldn't tell if the lawyer was threatening me or not, but I'd about run this thread as far as I cared to for the moment. I took another quick look at Alexander.

"What's his outlook?"

"He has the resources to continue paying for life support, if that's what you mean. He's been popping in and out of a coma for weeks now and the neurologists are confident he could theoretically function properly one day —that is, the damage he sustained has been mostly healed— but we simply don't know enough about the brain to understand what's preventing his recovery."

Well, it wasn't a shade, whatever it was. Sometimes medicine was a mystery for purely scientific reasons.

Mr. Glickman's cell phone chimed and he answered it with a deft motion. "Please excuse me for one moment," he said and exited the room.

I took another look at his business card and slipped it into my pocket. Then I attempted to follow him out of the hospital room. Instead, Bedros stepped in my way.

"What you want?" he asked in clipped English.

"Now, now, Bedros," I chided, admittedly taking the situation lightly, "you heard the man."

He put his bearpaw of a hand on my chest as I tried to brush past him. Immediately, I sensed the presence within him.

Bedros was not Bedros.

"What you want?" he repeated.

The dude didn't have the common signs of the taken. He wasn't fiending for drugs or sensual pleasures. He wasn't sickly and diseased. By all accounts, he was a normal giant Armenian man in a track suit. I didn't really know how to deal with him so I did what came naturally to me in moments like these. I defended myself.

I swatted his arm off me. He reacted in kind and suddenly swung his other and connected with my face. As my head buckled, he rammed his fist into my gut. I fell backwards, reeling in pain. The blow would've had most people sprawled out on the floor but I wasn't most people. I could deal with his attacks, at least for a short time. The problem was, I didn't want to hurt him.

The large man drove a knee towards my face that was meant to crush my skull. I sidestepped it and thrust upward, grabbing his thigh and pushing him up and off balance. I didn't want to harm Bedros, but if he was a fighter I would give him a fight.

Holding him by the leg, I summoned all of my strength and swung him around. I spun in a half circle and released him, sending him flying into the building window that spanned the entire wall. His back hit the large pane of safety glass so solidly that it visibly rippled and still, unable to fully absorb the blow, cracked in a single line from the ceiling to the floor.

The man seemed to be embedded in the glass and remained motionless, watching me as I withdrew a sage cigarette from my pack and threw a pessimistic glance at the smoke detector above my head. Bedros smiled. He was curious about me.

Hospital rules on smoking weren't the only thing bothering me. Soren had defied me as well, but in a panicked sort of desperation that showed his fear. Bedros was calm and collected. Even inquisitive. What had I gotten myself in the middle of?

As I got closer and exhaled in the Armenian's face, it only seemed to amuse him and incite him out of his sloth. He broke out into bellowing laughter and made a heavy fist.

"What are you doing?" a nurse demanded from the doorway. "You can't smoke in hospitals, asshole."

We both stood there and absorbed her reproach like schoolkids. I quickly extinguished the cigarette and tried to mount a defense. "I—"

"Get out before I call the police," she said.

I took her up on her offer before Bedros could object.

Chapter 15

I held the cold bottle of beer against my swollen cheek. The pain wasn't too bad. With any luck, the bruising would be minimal. But Bedros had certainly given me enough to remember him by.

I decided that I had enough to do without poking into a little girl's private business. At least for today. Sunday was half over and I needed to get home to finish some programming. On top of that, I still had that promise to take care of. So I had exited the Red Line in Hollywood and found myself at a little pizza establishment, having a crappy slice and a Heineken.

Let me back up a bit. It wasn't the yellow tiles or red tables that I was looking for, nor was I seeking company with the sort of miserable patrons who went to a subpar pizza chain in Hollywood on Sunday afternoon. This location was interesting because it was only a block away from Mel's Diner—a connection which I didn't make until this morning. And it was a specific person I was after. Perhaps an employee. So after the kid at the counter handled the last customer and found himself standing idle, I grabbed my beer and approached him.

"Nice shirt," I said, pointing to the Dos Pizzas company logo that emblazoned the kid's chest. "Do all employees get them?"

"Perk of the job," he answered in a sardonic monotone. "You can buy one, if you want."

"Why the hell would I do that? You don't actually sell those awful things, do you?"

He kind of chuckled, just enough to show that he didn't care about anything too much, and said, "Not really."

I nodded and smiled. "Hey, I think one of my friends works here. Do you know a white dude with thick, mangy dreads? He always wears this worn down trench coat made of—"

"Flannel," he said, laughing. "That's Sal. Yo, that dude is crazy."

"I know, right?" I shook my head at the imaginary antics I pretended to recall. "Sal's so random. Does he work here? Like, maybe in the kitchen or something?"

"Yeah right. He takes a shit here, if he's lucky."

I raised an eyebrow at the confusing turn of conversation. I wasn't sure if we were both making stuff up or what, but somehow we had moved on to bathroom habits.

"Does he eat a lot of pizza or something?"

"Dude," said the dude, waving his hand as if it was obvious, "he doesn't eat a lot of anything. He's not an employee, he's a bum. He lives around here, in the back alley. He cleans the area up, and in return we let him use the bathroom and give him some pizza and—"

"T-shirts," I finished. He was a fucking Hollywood alley rat. What did he have to do with Soren?

"We can't take responsibility for the plaid, though," said the kid, chuckling to himself as he turned away to wipe the counter.

I held the bottle and what was left of the warming beer to my cheek again. If Sal did live on the streets then he could be anywhere right now. But there was a good chance he was close-by, in the back alley, maybe even tidying the place up. To be safe, I did quickly check the bathroom. Ironically, it was the last place I had seen him in, albeit in a different establishment. Maybe he had the same deal with Mel's. In fact, that would explain how he'd been able to skip the line. I doubted that homeless people were practiced in the art of greasing palms.

I left the abomination of crust on my plate and headed straight for the door. The kid at the counter spoke up.

"Uh, you can't take that beer—"

I didn't hear the rest because the door closed and I was outside. The rushing of cars flooded my ears as I checked the street. I was just a block south of the Mel's parking lot now, right where the man had disappeared. If I looked hard enough, something might turn up.

I had to hand it to Sal. There was less piss behind the

Dos Pizzas than other parts of the alley. Aside from that observation, I went up and down the asphalt and saw no activity. I emerged from the north end, right next to a grand Art Deco building, and found myself beside Mel's Diner. The other back streets proved just as fruitless. If Sal did live around here, he was nowhere to be seen at the moment. I had to settle for the virtue of patience today.

Still, as I walked back towards the subway, a thought came to me. Sal and Soren were linked. I didn't know how, but it was a fact. To get to one, I could find either, and whereas Sal was an unreliable drifter, Soren was much more predictable. I didn't know where he lived. But what did he say... DJ Ingress? He had a residency at the Echoplex tomorrow night. That set me up perfectly for a quiet Sunday night coding.

Chapter 16 - Monday

Echo Park is the new Silver Lake, which was the new Los Feliz. That is to say it's east of Hollywood and newly gentrified. Once one neighborhood fills up with cool, look for another adjacent to take the crown. Really, Echo Park is already getting a little expensive, but you can't go farther east without crossing a giant park, a couple of highways, and what people swear is a river despite the fact that it's molded out of cement and often devoid of water. I don't even know what's on the other side of all of that, to be honest, and I'm not the type to ask questions.

New vegan hot spots and wine bars crop up left and right in neighborhoods like this. Almost weekly. Yelp has a field day with these communities. But this seedy neighborhood had its own seedy establishment that had been around before cool was cool. The Echo and the underlying Echoplex always had a cutting edge music scene that featured local artists. Some might have called the line-ups pretentiously hipster, but anyone who walked inside would take that back. It may have been Hollywood Freeway adjacent, but there wasn't a whiff of that crowd in this club.

I felt bad for flaking on Trent a couple nights before so I gave him the heads up tonight. It was Monday so we didn't get out too late. Trent was perhaps overdressed in his long sleeve button-up. I just did my usual jeans with a bright-colored T-shirt. Since anyone out in LA could be a star or, at least, rich, dress codes were only used by some establishments in passively racist attempts to curtail trouble. This may have been a bad neighborhood but it was a friendly crowd, and the Echoplex wasn't the type of place to ask people to do more than necessary.

There was no line to get in and the sprawling basement had empty spots between the bar and the dance floor, but those two areas were packed. And it was hot in here. Pushing, shoving, and thrashing were the perfect recipe for sweat. So was the fact that this place hadn't had a working air conditioner in years.

The music was... interesting. I might've said cool if I'd wanted to impress a girl, but I've had stringent tastes for years now and I was just as well-off without post-mod-whatever-bullshit. But mostly, people in the Echoplex didn't care too much about anything at all and just laughed and drank and had fun. I couldn't knock that.

First stop was the bar. It was always the bar. Most times I couldn't have fun in a club if I didn't have a drink in my hand. It wasn't simply the state of drunkenness that I liked.

That was great for certain occasions, but really, just the act of drinking was pleasing enough. Tonight I wasn't on the hunt anyway; I was fact-gathering. So I had brought Trent along and decided I was allowed to enjoy myself.

Trent squeezed by some confused people to get a place at the bar while I scanned the room. It was an eclectic crowd. Lots of different types of people wearing lots of things: cool, funny, crazy, sexy. You'd have a hard time pegging this crowd into any single type, but you could at least get away with saying "low-key."

I didn't see any familiar faces until I noticed that Soren was the one on stage spinning the minimalist beats. That was good. We were a little early, but that was better than missing him. When Trent came back and handed me my Sailor Jerry and coke, I knew we could chill out for a while.

"Check out the muscles on the bartender," he said.

I peeked and the girl was a bit short like a gymnast, maybe in her late twenties, but her tank top showed off biceps that were bigger than mine. "Holy shit. I wouldn't know what to do with that."

"Shit, I would. Imagine what her ass looks like."

"Already did," I said. "Shit would break my dick off."

We clacked our plastic glasses together as was common with the first drink of the night and moved to get a closer view of the crowd. It wasn't long before I found her.

"Pam."

There was a brief look of confusion on her face before the recognition came. Then she smiled and jumped up and down in her flats.

"Oh my God! You came out!"

She hugged me and Trent had an impressed look on his face. I have to admit, I didn't mind her boobs pressing in to me, but Pam was engaged to Soren and wasn't really my type anyway.

"I forgot your name," she spit out quickly, as if pulling the band-aid from the wound cleanly were best.

I laughed. "It's Dante. Yeah, you weren't all there the other night."

Her cheeks flushed under the manic lights. "Sorry about that. Medical kush always does that to me."

"Heh." I generally thought the stuff was too strong too. She was wrong about it being why she passed out, of course, but I let her believe the charade. "This is my buddy, Trent."

"Nice to meet you," he said. "How do you guys know each other?"

"She's the DJ groupie," I answered.

"Stop," she said, playfully slapping my chest. "He's my fiancé. I could introduce you to him and his friends, if you want."

"Actually," said Trent, raising a single eyebrow and gulping the last of his vodka Red Bull, "I'd rather meet your cuter friends."

Pam pulled us both onto the dance floor as the music kicked up.

We met a pack of their people. A few girls. Some hot, some not. Trent went to work on them but I laid back. There was the odd boyfriend or two as well. Then there was Greg, a good friend of Soren's who fit in with us pretty well.

He had a way with meeting girls so Trent took to him. I think, personally, that an entire arm sleeve of tattoos is cheating. But the dude was chill enough.

Four drinks and two Michael Jackson remixes later, we cooled our sweaty bodies on the outside patio seats. Well, they weren't seats so much as a small set of metal bleachers, and it was really more of a parking lot cordoned off with steel guardrails than a patio. But it certainly was outside, so it had that going for it. The night air felt downright cold against my skin.

It was just me and Greg from the group for a while. After his set was done, Soren came out to meet us. The rest of his friends were at the bar or the bathroom. It had worked out for me that Trent was hitting on one of Pam's friends. That left me time to investigate.

"Thanks again," Soren said, shaking his head, "for taking care of Pam. I was so wired that night that I don't even remember any of that. I mean, I vaguely remember smoking a blunt with you outside and that is it, man."

It was a relief to confirm that he didn't want to kick my ass. I could tell by his demeanor, but it still felt good for him to spell it out. It was what I had expected, of course. Banishments were almost never remembered, usually wiping out the surrounding moments before and after.

"What the hell happened to you? Pam said you had to get stitches."

"I don't know. I must have passed out and hit my head on the toilet in the bathroom." Soren exploded into laughter. He tried to cover his outburst with his hand but failed miserably. "I woke up with the bathroom attendant yelling at me that he was going to call the cops!"

"Holy shit! Did he?"

"No way, man. I booked it."

Greg cut in. "I tell you, I'm supposed to be the crazy one. Growing up, Soren always had to talk me down. You know? But the stories with this guy lately." He shook his head and laughed. "Can I use your light?" I passed my lighter to Greg for the third time tonight. After giving it back to me, he continued. "It's too bad I'm never around for the truly crazy nights."

Soren nodded. "Sorry man. Maybe I shouldn't let you leave my side. Keep my head on straight."

"Hey," said Greg, offended. "Don't start treating me like the responsible one."

I had already checked out Soren and Greg and all their other friends. None of them were possessed. With any luck, the shade was just a hiccup in Soren's life and he could start putting the pieces back together.

"So I was bloody but fine," he said. "I had the presence of mind to wash my head off, but I was kind of dizzy and I didn't really know where I was or where I was going."

"You didn't see Pam?" I asked.

"Hell no. I'm telling you I barely realized I was at Avalon. I was struggling down the steps when some guy with dreads helped me out. He said he'd seen me spin before and was asking about booking me one night or some shit. But he could tell I was out of it so he helped me to a cab. I caught hell for ditching Pam from her friends the next morning, but it turned out she wasn't mad because she completely blacked out."

"There is a God," I said. Greg agreed. Maybe Pam getting drugged had actually worked out for the best. But I wanted to refocus the conversation on Sal. "So the guy just put you in a cab for no reason?"

Soren looked up at me. "Yeah. Well, no. He wanted to book me for a gig and was glad he ran into me. But I'm not really supposed to talk about it."

"What, like a secret party?"

He widened his eyes to stress the point.

Well, shit.

I was spinning around in my head how I was going to broach the subject again when Pam rushed out beside us.

"Oh my God! Jenny's making out with your friend."

"Trent?"

"Yeah, right in the middle of the dance floor."

"That's his move, if they let him get past the grinding."

I could tell from Pam's eyes they had done that as well. She turned to her fiancé. "We should have them come over to the house tonight."

"Sure," he said. Greg nodded.

"What's going on?" I asked.

"We're having a little gathering at our place," answered Soren. "Nothing too big but we have chill neighbors who don't mind the loud music. If you want to hang and drink, you guys are welcome to join us."

I raised my glass. "Why not?"

Chapter 17

We moved the party to the hills of Silver Lake. Small, windy streets with too many parked cars skirted old houses that creaked when they were looked at. The buildings huddled close together on their slopes, separated only by chain link fences. Soren's house was dark and uninviting. The yard was small but the crowd stayed out of it except for the occasional smoker. Inside, it was less serene. Furniture was shoved aside and people danced to Glitch Mob. A table with bottles of booze on it was constantly raided. They ran out of coke and ice so I resorted to drinking whatever liquor was offered to me straight up. In retrospect, I lost a little focus.

Principal to my losing track of time had to be the pot room. Soren led a few of us into his bedroom to sit on the floor and he produced a pipe. I made sure it was only weed. The dude was a lot more laid back compared to the night at

Avalon. But then again, that had been Nero, his second shadow. So we smoked and the yelling outside eventually subsided. The music remained on but drifted to a lower volume. And Trent was practically passed out. All clues that should have led me to realize it was late.

"One day," said Soren, "I'm gonna move out of here. Live in a proper Hollywood palace. I'll do my thing at the club and head back to a real party. With a pool. And a staff."

"Ice would be a start," I said, just to be a dick.

"Yeah. And ice. We'd be like royalty."

I yawned and stretched my shoulders. The base of the bed wasn't comfortable for long periods of time. "You're really planning on hitting it big with this secret party of yours?"

Soren looked to the others in the room. Nobody else was paying attention. "It's a start. But it's not just that. I've been an idiot. I'll party till I die, man. Believe that. But I need to take care of Pam too. She's put up with so much... You know?"

I nodded. He must have remembered some of the horrible things he had done to her when he was taken. He ignored her. Insulted her. Probably cheated on her. He must have blamed the booze or the drugs. Whatever his rationalization, he was trying to make it better.

"Something about her," he said, not really aware of the room anymore. "I was always a loner. Never knew my parents. Grew up in the system. I never thought I'd meet someone like Pam. And I've done nothing but fuck it up."

Soren stood up and pulled the drawer of his nightstand

open. "I gotta restock the bar or something." He emptied out his pockets—a wallet, some papers, his keys—and shut them in the drawer. Then he took his leave.

I snapped myself out of my daze and looked around. Trent wore heart-shaped glasses made of paper, like the 3D kind, except that these made all beads of light look like little heart halos. Pam's friend, I forget her name, was leaning on him, asleep. The only other person in the room was Greg. Although his eyes were wide open, he was entirely too high to see or hear anything going on.

The whole thing felt unnervingly similar to high school, to be honest, and there was something about the moment that threw me off. I'd even go so far as to say that, if I wasn't drunk and high and up to no good, I would have been ashamed.

Pretty sure that Soren had really just gone to take a dump, and knowing that we had to call it a night soon, I carefully stood up and went to the nightstand. I opened his drawer in what must have been clumsy belligerence because Trent noticed my rummaging. Luckily, he was in an awkward position with a girl lying on top of him; he didn't bother to maneuver his head to see what I was doing.

Soren had some receipts and coins and other junk in the drawer. I flipped open his wallet. A business card hidden behind a credit card caught my eye. It was a hard stock of paper, all black with white lettering: "Red Hat Events." The only other color was the red logo of the company. I had seen it on flyers for raves and such around LA. They were party promoters and threw electronica events. If Soren had recently lined up a new gig that he was excited about, this had to be related.

I slipped the drawer closed and patted Trent on the shoulder. Poor guy had to be in the office in the morning. At least he'd stopped drinking a while ago. When we stumbled out of the bedroom, we noticed the house was empty. I didn't bother searching for our host to say bye.

The only thing I remember about the drive home is that we were winding through the streets somewhere and the car made an awkward jerk. I asked Trent, who was driving, if he had fallen asleep.

"A little bit," he said.

Chapter 18 - Tuesday

The next day, late enough in the afternoon that I had outslept my headache, I got off the Red Line in Hollywood and marched down Highland Avenue one more time.

"It can't be a coincidence," I said to Violet. I spun the brass pocket watch by its chain as I explained everything to her. "The same block that Sal disappeared on is close to the back alley of the pizza place where he lives. Red Hat Events being headquartered there is telling."

You're saying he's a street soldier for Red Hat?

"Why not? They can't be the most reputable company. They run clubs and raves." It was a business that thrived on the illicit drug community without having paper ties to it. But surely they fed off each other.

It doesn't make sense.

I sighed uselessly into the air. Violet was the one who'd wanted me to aggressively follow this guy. I'd found out who he was, where he lived, and what his connection to Soren was, and she still had to pick me apart.

"I admit I don't know enough about Red Hat, but that's why we're here now."

It's not them.

"Okay. Who then?"

It's Sal. We're assuming he's taken, right?

"He has to be. That's why you noticed something off with him."

Right. Well, take it from me. If you get out of my hellhole and join the world of the living, you're not going to spend your days cleaning the back alleys of pizza places.

"So what? He's too much of a normal homeless man to have an ulterior motive?"

Something like that.

I nodded in that indignant way that said I recognized the plausibility of the statement but didn't really place much stock in it. No one could convince me that Sal wasn't possessed. It would only take a simple touch for me to know the truth. Finding him was the hard part.

We walked by the diner and cut into the block. The old Art Deco building that ran up the side of the alley was across the street. The words "Department of Water and Power" were emblazoned at the top of what must have been a historic structure. I was staring at the GPS on my phone when I realized Red Hat Events was showing up at the same address. That was strange because there were no markings for the events company, but I figured they must have been using the defunct site as an office.

I didn't have much time to ponder the matter, as it was, because at that moment a man emerged from the alley and turned to the building, walking through the large front door. He was notable for his plaid trench coat and thick dreadlocks.

"Fucking shit," I pointed out.

Sal turned straight at me. He knew he'd been spotted, just like at Mel's. I guess finding him wasn't the hard part after all. He ducked into the doorway.

I cut into the empty street and made a beeline for the building. Whatever happened, he wouldn't be getting away this time. I surely wouldn't be distracted by any owls. I rushed inside and saw the man impatiently pounding on the elevator call button. When he saw me enter, he abandoned that route and slipped into an access door.

This was a small lobby, empty except for the cute girl sitting at a reception desk. The solid red logo of a baseball cap spanned the front veneer of glass so I knew I was in the right place. But there wasn't time to talk to anybody. Without making too much of a scene, I slipped the pocket watch into my jeans and briskly followed Sal into the stairwell. The basement path was locked up behind a gate, but it didn't matter. I heard the man's feet slapping on the stone steps above. Matching his pace, I broke into a run.

The old Art Deco building was taller than it looked, or perhaps the stairs were too small. Sal didn't stop at any of the intermediate floors, and I found myself getting winded near the top. I heard the metal door to the roof pound open and I dutifully chased. Before I knew it, I stood on the tar-stained gravel that basked in the California sun.

Sal was the only other person on the plain rooftop. He had stopped running now. He turned slowly to face me, arms in the air.

"Why are you chasing me?" he asked, nearly in hysterics.

"Whoa, whoa," I said, putting my hands out to show him I had no weapons. I didn't advance on him. He kept his feet planted where he was, about ten feet from me. "It's Sal, right? I just want to talk."

"Are you police?"

"What? No, man." I had a dabble of a goatee on my chin and my hair was long enough to get into my eyes. I liked to think I didn't look anything like a cop. "I'm just a guy. They told me about you at Dos Pizzas. I was hoping you could tell me about Red Hat."

Sal was a dirty man. He twitched at times, he smelled something awful, and he had wild eyes that darted in all directions, but when I mentioned Red Hat I could swear that something registered in him.

"This... this building?" Sal lowered his arms to his side and became more relaxed. Maybe he realized he wasn't in trouble. He looked less jumpy, anyway. "I just ran into here to get away from you."

"No," I said. That wasn't right. "You were coming in here before you saw me."

Sal shook his head. "I clean the street. I live in the street. I don't have anything to steal."

He was just playing dumb now.

I stood there for a second and saw that he was done

explaining himself, so I withdrew one of my special cigarettes and lit it.

"Do you smoke, Sal?"

His eyes jumped between my face and the cigarette. "N —no."

I had found the only bum in Hollywood who didn't light up.

I took a step towards him. "How do you know Soren, Sal?"

The restless eyes narrowed and the homeless man didn't answer. He took a breath and sort of stood up straighter and taller than he had been. He slipped his hands into his coat and just watched me.

"Who are you?" he asked, finally breaking his study.

"I've gotten that question a lot lately, all by stranger characters than myself." I took another drag of the sage and confidently stepped towards him. "I'm just a guy who wants to have a conversation. Let's start with who you are and why you're here."

"I am just a bum, sir."

I chuckled at his change in diction. "Well," I said, continuing my casual approach, "perhaps we are both fakers."

"What we are, sir, are strangers. Unless you have a claim otherwise, my business here is my own."

"Why don't we get acquainted, then?" I held out my hand. "One proper introduction, and I'll be on my way."

Sal, or whoever he was, took a step backwards. He was unsure of my motives. He couldn't have known that I could see his true self with a touch—none had ever been aware of my ability before—yet the man still shied away from my hand.

I had to see who he was.

"Why should I be concerned with making friends?" he remarked.

I shot him a laser stare. "Because I've never been a good enemy to have."

He watched my hand with a frown, but made no move to shake it.

I threw caution to the wind. Only a few feet from the man, I lunged at him.

Sal spun and leaped over the parapet. Flannel coattails slipped through my fingers and waved in the wind.

"Wait!" I screamed, way too fucking late.

The man plunged into the sidewalk below with a wet thunk. I glanced down and pulled away reflexively, sickened by the splatter.

No. No. No.

He wasn't supposed to die.

Whoever I had been talking to, whoever was inside Sal, was a shade from the Dead Side. He had found a compatible host in the homeless man and was living his life for him by proxy. I've always tried to expel their kind without hurting the person. The victim. Sometimes things got messy or violent, as with Soren, but cuts and bruises were it. No one had ever been seriously hurt before. Definitely never killed.

I pulled the pocket watch into a tightened fist. "He's dead."

What?

"He jumped. I tried to touch him and he jumped."

I choked on bile. I felt it come up into my throat and fought it back.

You didn't push him, did you?

"No!" I yelled. "He jumped!"

I bent over and almost puked again. I couldn't get the image below out of my head. But something told me not to throw up. I couldn't leave my DNA at the scene.

Holy shit. The scene. I realized I was standing in the middle of what could be considered a murder.

You need to get out of here.

Yes. I stumbled to the door, fighting the knot in my stomach.

The cigarette, Dante!

"What?"

I realized I had dropped my smoke at some point. I saw it burning in the gravel. I picked it up and pressed it against the tar to put it out, then slipped it in my pocket. I looked around. Was there anything else?

Get out of here.

I slid down the steps, almost falling more than walking. I had to slip out, unnoticed. The back street was empty. With any luck, no one saw Sal jump. If nobody inside had heard anything then I could walk away as though nothing had happened.

At the bottom of the stairs, I took a forced breath and composed myself. I softly pressed the door open and entered the lobby.

The receptionist stood by the front, tears in her eyes. There was another man there, a short guy, pushing her away. There was nothing I could do except walk right at them.

"Watch out," said the guy. "Someone jumped."

I peeked out of the front door and my sight grazed the horrific display. "Oh my God." I looked around in not entirely feigned desperation and pointed at the receptionist. "Call 911." I exchanged the watch in my hand for my phone and pretended to dial the police as well. I stepped outside and put my cell against my ear.

I figured the guy was a bystander who had witnessed Sal's suicide. I didn't see anybody else in the road, and I tried to melt away without looking at the grim aftermath of what had happened up close. I crossed the street, spun around, and confirmed that my trail was clear.

Maybe it would be a good idea to avoid Hollywood for a few weeks.

Chapter 19 - Dream

The soft whiteness from the sky failed to cast light upon the physical denizens below it. The street was wet this time. Blurry reflections played on the shimmering surface. But it wasn't raining, or windy, or even cold; there was no weather in this place. It was all the facade of the dream. Things came into being and just were without origin.

I trekked down the old financial quarter on Spring Street. In place of renovated condominiums were old offices. Instead of a club with colorful lights and muffled beats, there was the Stock Exchange. I've always liked the early twentieth century architecture of Downtown Los Angeles. Wide structures of stone housed recesses for statues and the other small details that our age forgot. In the real world, the converted buildings were old and new all at once, an anachronism that I appreciated. It instilled a sense of history in the brick. But on the Dead Side, everything lagged behind. Not new. Not frozen. But abandoned. Decrepit. As if to make clear that, even in this place, time took its unceasing toll.

It was odd for me to be back here so soon. My visits were usually random and infrequent. The recent months had sparked a change in the pattern; this was only days after my last trip. That had never happened before. Still, whatever proficiency I may have been honing, everything fought against form and clarity just the same. Perhaps Violet had helped to crystallize my senses last time, but now I was alone.

I slowed as a whispering found me. It was my name, traveling along a hollow breeze. Something unnatural about the voice set me on edge. I looked one way, then the other, then back again, but I was ever alone.

Across the street, there was a cafe that seemed to be the area that held the least shadow. I desperately pushed myself through the haze of nothingness to reach it. Like a mirage, the welcome of the area collapsed as I approached, and I felt more vulnerable than ever out in the open.

Then a faintness—I hesitate to call it a light—appeared on the sidewalk behind me. I heard my name once more.

"Dante."

Though the surroundings were misty, the sound took a form that could cut glass. I reached for my trusty pocket watch, my security blanket, to give me guidance. It was no use. It wasn't there. I never had it with me on this side. And ever slowly, the presence approached.

I squinted at the form and it coalesced. It was doubtful

that I had caused the clarity, but it was no longer a mystery who was following me. Trailing me was the skeletal form of what was once inside Soren. Orange hair hung haphazardly on a head beset by rot. He bared black teeth at me as he closed in.

"Nero."

I turned and fled. I crossed Spring again and pushed down the opposite sidewalk. The lonely streets, ever empty, began to bustle with strange activity. A populace sprang up around me. A parade of cars and carriages smothered the asphalt. Pedestrians bounced me effortlessly between them as they hurried on their way. I now had the sense that I was sport, a helpless animal being surrounded by something greater than myself.

Behind me, with the ease of a skier on fresh snow, the fiend closed in.

I ducked under two men holding a roll of carpet. I squeezed in between the locked hands of a mother and her child. I pressed the back of an elderly man to force myself by. One by one I surmounted every obstacle in my path. I was a solitary salmon fighting the unbearable counter current. I was making headway.

But Nero was faster.

I got caught up in a row of women, two deep, who were caroling an old chant that was unfamiliar to me. They stood firm, their ghostly voices rising above my might, and I spun helplessly as I became encircled.

The figure of death and dependence marched closer to me. Nero shrieked and raised a withered arm to clasp my throat.

This was the most helpless I'd ever felt in my life, compounded by the fact that I couldn't wake up.

122

Chapter 20

Strong hands gripped my shoulders and carried me backward, through the throng and into the glass storefront of the nearest building. The fuzzy ground hardened into a staccato of tiles beneath my feet. Bold stone columns rose high, their impressive density supporting a massive ceiling. An array of shapes materialized into a series of haphazard solid wooden bookcases detailed with iron and steel. And on their shelves, books. Hundreds and hundreds of books. I was in a grand bookstore.

There was a red leather tufted chair. Beside it, standing straight with a single arm resting on it, was my savior. He was an old-world man of class and elegance, with a head full of jet black hair under an old top hat. He wore a well-tailored jacket the color of smoke. I was immediately struck by his sense of calm.

"Good morning," he said, ignoring my harried

demeanor.

My eyes darted from one bookcase to the other, scanning the aisles and the second floor banister and looking to the door for any intruders. I was still in shock. A mere moment before, I had been amidst a suffocating throng. This newfound silence was eerie. I didn't trust it. And I wasn't prepared to thank anybody just yet.

"What are you doing here?" I demanded.

"I'm always here," the man said in a measured voice. He lifted a wooden walking stick and rapped the alabaster head against his chest. Then he pointed it at me. "You're the intruder."

"It's a dream," I reasoned. I knew that didn't make this place any less real, but I couldn't readily be an imposition in my own dream.

"Interesting..." was all the man offered in return.

Now that the world had solidified, I felt I once again had my bearings and my wits. The situation seemed safe enough, and it didn't appear that Nero was coming inside.

I wiped my forehead and took a steady breath. "A bookstore?"

"The last," he answered. "There is great knowledge in these tomes."

"Who are you?"

The man smiled. "I've been called many things. My fifth wife preferred 'son of a bitch.'"

"So, a ladies' man?" I joked. He didn't relax his stiff posture and stood resolute in his coldness. "Is that what I should call you? Son of a bitch?"

"I am just a passing spirit. My name isn't important. You will likely never see me again. But him," he said, looking to the glass door, "he seems intent on meeting you."

I checked again to make sure the fiend wasn't entering. "I don't know what to do about him."

"Shades have a habit of finding you when you meddle in their business."

I nodded. "Seems fair. I did expel him."

For the first time, the man's stoic visage was allowed to appear impressed. "Ah, a rare talent."

"It's just science," I said.

"Isn't everything?" The man turned and paced casually. "These halls are filled with science. Even the fiction, stories passed down through generations, have truths to tell us. I have spent a great many years here in study, yet I have never found a story of a man who visits the dead when he sleeps." The metal tip of his walking stick made a flat note against the tile. "We all have our talents. Even shades. That," he said, pointing outside, "is a desperate one. He seeks to return to your world but is unable."

"I gave sage to the one he was bound to."

The man smiled blankly and said nothing. Had the spirit never read a story about white sage, either?

"He's trapped here forever now," I explained. "He'll never get back."

"It's likely you are correct. Most shades are fools. Others are smart and disciplined. He is still a threat to you for the time being, but I wouldn't be overly concerned. The crazy ones may be more violent—but it is the measured ones who prove to be more dangerous in the long-term."

I walked further into the bookstore. It was an area that felt warmer than any other place I'd seen on the Dead Side. If I didn't know any better, yellows and reds seemed to creep into the periphery of this desaturated place. Despite the comforting feel, there was a subtext to this conversation that I was missing.

"Is that what you are? A smart spirit? More dangerous than Nero?"

The gentlemanly figure turned. He shot me a look, not of one offended so much as of a man losing patience.

"You can't trust shades, sir. Their motivations are foreign to the living."

I scoffed. "Nothing's complicated about not wanting to be dead."

"Perhaps you underestimate the desperation inherent."

I strolled up to a small table where an original gramophone sat beside a pile of books. Taking a cursory glance at the pages, I tried to mutter as unassumingly as possible. "You're a shade."

The man smiled again. "And that is precisely why you shouldn't trust me." He sat on the leather couch, rested back, and crossed one leg over the other. "I wouldn't trust me, if I were you. Certainly don't take instruction from me. But you may note that I am giving none."

I nodded and leaned against the end table, facing him. This man was the definition of cool etiquette. He was polite and friendly and projected strong character. Everything he said made sense and appeared above board. But he had overplayed his hand.

"You said that shades can find you when you poke into their business." He looked at me as I spoke with a knowing expression. "One might wonder how you found me, but I've already figured it out. We crossed paths in the world of the dead because I chased you off a building in the world of the living."

He bowed his head slightly. "Bravo, sir. You have your man. I do apologize for acting like such a brute. I didn't know who you were and I panicked."

"And now Sal is dead."

"Well, let's not shed a tear for the unfortunates. I have little patience for madness."

"So," I said, acting cool in the face of his apathy, "you decided you would get to know me and my methods?"

The man removed his hat and brushed his hair along the part. "Turn about is fair play, but to the contrary, it was you who was seeking an audience with me. Was it not?"

He was right. Sal, or this man while inside Sal, didn't even know about me until I intervened in his affairs. Still, his business was illegitimate. That is what had attracted us to him in the first place.

"It was."

He nodded. "And what, pray tell, do you seek me for?"

"I make it my business any time the dead impose on the living."

"Do you now?" The man's dark eyes studied me intently. "May I ask why?"

I shrugged. My friends didn't know about my

moonlighting so I hadn't been asked about it directly before. I'd never really thought about the answer. "There's nothing quite like it."

"No illusions of nobility, then? You do it for the thrill. Because you can. Isn't that a little self-serving?"

"Says the man who just killed a human being to avoid being found out, then quickly changed his mind and decided to meet me anyway. Besides, I never said I wasn't self-serving. Aren't we all?"

The man responded quickly, dismissing the gravity of his actions. "Precisely. As for me, it is true. I am weak. I concede that, like everybody else, I desire to live forever. How is it that you do it, if I may ask?"

"Do what?"

"You said you were about to find me out. How would you have known who I was?"

Something else he'd never read about. I shrugged again. "Just a simple touch will do. I can see second shadows in my mind. Couldn't tell you how or why." I kept the part about Violet out of it.

"Fascinating."

I was unnerved by the man's composure. Shades, for obvious reasons, strove to blend in with the living. There were exceptions reserved for short-lived attempts at disruption, but Sal had been right to run from me. He'd known I was on to him. That something was off. Now he just pulled a one-eighty and introduced himself. Why?

"What's your business with Red Hat?" I asked.

My unnamed companion widened his eyes and stroked

his mustache. It was an outdated growth that drew too much attention, not exactly British magistrate but hipster enough all the same. "Take care with them," warned the man gravely. "Any frivolities you've had with the dead thus far are trivial by comparison."

"I've got it under control."

"Famous last words."

"What's your business with them?"

"They are an old company. Not Red Hat Events, of course. That is their newest incarnation. They started before your time—before my time even—as a millinery."

"What's that?"

He tipped the hat on his head. "A fine hat maker's shop."

There was nothing sinister about that. "Is it a front for a criminal enterprise?"

"The business? No, no, I suppose it is legitimate enough, as much as can be said for any in the nightlife industry. Red Hat is a means to an end, a vehicle of wealth and a structural hierarchy for a movement."

"What, do they want to take over the world or something?"

"No," said the man, forcing a laugh. "Nothing so sophomoric. They want what everyone wants." He looked at me and waited for an answer.

"To live forever."

He simply nodded.

The man was playing a delicate game. He had taken a risk by exposing himself to me and he was hedging what information he conveyed, for sure, but there was something more. He wanted something out of this exchange and I couldn't nail down what it was yet.

"Are you telling me that the entire staff is taken?"

"I am telling you that the structure is set up to propagate the dead. With your abilities and curiosity, it was only a matter of time before you found out for yourself. Not every employee need be possessed. Many can assist the cause simply by doing their job in ignorance. Many are just there to make money. But the ones in charge, the ones that matter, have lived a life other than their current one. They want to be rich. They want to be successful. And they want to find new hosts."

A dark cloud hovered over our conversation as soon as I understood the subtext of his words. "Soren."

The man nodded. "I was scouting for new troops. Red Hat recruits, you see. They look for strong, impressionable youths in good health. If they have been taken before, like your friend, then they've already proven viable receptacles."

"But he's not viable anymore," I countered. "I pushed white sage through his breath. He'll be safe, at least for a while."

"Whatever you think of your parlor tricks, they are only for the weak-minded. Like the shade that was chasing you outside. There is a set of elites who aren't dissuaded as easily. They can overcome your trifles."

There was something in his tone that sounded like... contempt. I began to get the distinct feeling that this man had no great love for Red Hat.

"What makes them so powerful?"

"That, unfortunately, is a question that even these books cannot answer."

I paced around the room, trying to find the catch. "So why tell me this?"

"I suppose every memorable dream needs a twist," he said, rising to his feet. "For my part, I am an agent of Red Hat in appearance only. I worked for them, at times, merely to apply a more critical eye to their activities."

"You were spying on them?"

"Indeed. This is a fact which may help you better understand my suspicion and behavior on the rooftop, and why I could not turn to the others for assistance. But here, outside the prying eyes of the Royals, we can be two men of discretion."

I narrowed my eyes. "Who are the Royals?"

The man in the old suit paused a moment, as if to afford the subject its proper reverence. "The monarchy of Red Hat. Powerful shades at the top of the food chain. Heed what I say. These aren't simple fiends like the orange-haired spirit that gave you chase. These are refined men and women, in touch with their craft, armed with a solitary mission. The Royals are a threat without scope. To take them on, you will need allies."

That was it, the opening I'd been looking for. Alone, it would've taken time and aroused suspicion to get the kind of information I was being handed now. Still, this seemed to fall into my lap too perfectly. Too easily. He had told me not to trust shades after all.

"Then why fight them? What do you have against Red

Hat?"

The man held his hands behind his back and stood with proper form. He answered the question as if he had expected it, and continued to carry his smooth demeanor throughout. "Their movement is a determined one that has destroyed countless lives. It necessitates the trampling of others. I, unfortunately, have not kept their footprints off my back. I wish to keep it at that."

It didn't surprise me that he wanted to keep some secrets. I was vague about my own motivations, after all. Our mutual caution was understood. It would be something to work around rather than overcome. In the end, whether I could trust this man or not, it would have been negligent to ignore him.

"What are they going to do to Soren?" I asked.

"First they welcome him into the fold. They befriend him, take over his routine, and then they control him."

"And you want to stop them?"

"Your friend doesn't concern me. You can worry about him as you wish."

"Fine, but stop calling him my friend. I barely know the guy."

"And yet you will be risking your life for his." The man set his walking stick down on the couch and approached me. "There is a private company party on the grounds of the Griffith Park Observatory this Friday night. Soren has been meeting with the promoters and will be a featured act. The choice presented to you is whether or not you wish to watch over him." The man extended a firm hand to me. "But know this. Your curiosity will not be well met. I am trusting that you will not mention my name."

"I don't even know your name," I said, clasping my hand in his.

He smiled, and then I woke up.

Chapter 21 - Wednesday

It was only midweek. That left me two days of idle time before the Red Hat party. I spent the morning in my apartment pretending to program but couldn't stop going over the recent distractions in my head. A hat store evolved into a party company run by ghosts? It seemed ridiculous and macabre, but there was something else troubling about it. It was the first time, in my four years of chasing shades, that I'd encountered any sort of true organization amongst their ranks. Did that mean that, all this time, I'd only been concerning myself with the scrubs?

I staved off my curiosity and ignored the internet for as long as I could. Once two o'clock hit, I knew I had to do something or risk losing all semblance of productivity. Since I couldn't readily address Red Hat at the moment, I remembered my other little project. So, on the pretense of grabbing a late lunch, I grabbed my Hamilton pocket watch and jumped in my car.

Los Angeles, much like Miami, is a driving city. The subway is great if you're going its way, but the sprawling neighborhoods of LA outrun the reach of the tunnels. Besides, it was sunny out and the middle of a weekday; it would be a fun drive in my Z. So I hopped on the 134 and headed east.

Eagle Rock is a quaint little place. More residential than anything else, with pockets of business along Colorado Boulevard and such. It's a convenient neighborhood because it isn't as far out as Pasadena, is a quick shot to Downtown, and hosts a damn good pastrami sandwich.

Before pleasure, however, I pulled my car up to the curb of an office building.

You're telling me you made a deal with a Red Hat agent?

I had put off the conversation all morning, but I decided to catch Violet up along the way.

"It wasn't much of a deal. He just told me about the party."

You can't just befriend random shades you run into.

"What, like if I happened to buy a haunted pocket watch in an antique store?"

That's different.

I couldn't tell if Violet was jealous or had a valid concern. I would've been the first to admit that I couldn't trust the man I'd met. As far as I could tell, though, he had asked nothing of me.

"Listen," I said, "you wanted me to follow the lead. Sal knew that Soren was no longer taken. He recruited him into the folds of Red Hat. Soren is the objective, not the shades I dreamt about."

Shades? Plural?

I sighed. I didn't want to worry Violet. I'd seen how terrified she was the first time it happened. "Nero. He was after me again. The bookstore was my only sanctuary." The man had done me a favor. Surely she couldn't blame me for talking to him. "Besides, I didn't see you jumping out in the streets to save me."

She didn't answer. I didn't mean to guilt her and I felt bad about saying that. Violet couldn't control what happened to me on the Dead Side. I pulled the key out of the ignition and sat in silence, wondering what to say without sounding cheesy.

Why did he jump?

"What?"

Why did the shade jump off the roof?

"He was running from us."

He could have retreated. Out of his host. Back to the Dead Side.

"He could have, but that takes time. A minute, maybe. I would've grabbed him. Identified him. That's what he was avoiding."

There's no way he knew what you could do.

"Maybe..." It didn't make a whole lot of sense. A shade being expelled, exsufflated with the smoke of white sage, would likely never be able to regain a footing in the same body. But at least there was a chance. With Sal dead, the chance was zero. "Was he just being vindictive?"

Or covering his tracks. If you expelled him, he wouldn't remember you, or that he was ever taken. But he'd remember some of the things he'd done. Sal might've been able to answer some of our questions.

I jingled my car keys in my hand. It was plausible. The dead didn't tell secrets. Well, not unless they became shades, anyway.

"Wait here," I said as I popped the door of the coupe open.

What are we doing here?

"You," I stressed firmly, "are waiting in the car. I have private business inside."

Chapter 22

The carpeted hallways were deathly quiet and the office complex appeared little used. I double-checked the business card in my hand. This was the right place. I entered a tiny closet of a lobby and greeted the receptionist.

"Mr. Glickman, please," I said, showing her the card he had handed me.

The woman, perhaps once a looker, had over-dyed her red hair to retain some sense of color. "Do you have an appointment?" She looked at me like I was a hoodlum, and I realized she was staring at my swollen cheek.

I scoffed. "He owes me one."

"It's okay, Margaret," came the mousy voice of the man from his office. He walked over to the doorway and waved me in. "I can see him."

I gave the secretary a playful wink.

"I am sorry," started the lawyer as he shut the door,

"about that business with Bedros. He can be a bit overzealous."

His enthusiasm wasn't what concerned me. The bodyguard was taken and I wondered what business he had with Violet's father. I shook Mr. Glickman's hand in greeting and confirmed that he, like Alexander, was clear.

"I suppose you want to see Mr. McAllister?" he asked.

"No. This time I wanted to see you."

The man widened his small eyes as he took his chair behind his desk. I sat opposite him. "Do we have any business? You're not pursuing legal action against Bedros —"

"No," I said, cutting him off, "but I'd like to ask about him."

"Well, I will try to accommodate, but I don't know much. The man is a holdover from McAllister senior, who did not employ me. Alexander is my client, but he was the one that dealt with Bedros, not me."

I nodded impatiently. The lawyer didn't think he knew much, and perhaps that was true, but I was completely in the dark. Even a pinhole of light would be a great help to me.

"Where can I find Bedros?"

"Where would anyone find a bodyguard?" he asked rhetorically. "I don't know the man's address, if that's what you mean."

"What threat is there on Alexander's life? Why does a bedridden man need a personal guard?"

The balding man shrugged off the question. "Alexander

McAllister is a wealthy man who is very protective of his fortune. His father, Finlay, left him an inheritance, you see. He taught Alexander to provide for his child, as his father had never provided for him." Mr. Glickman shook his head sadly. "It is tragic that the money can no longer go to family."

It was a sad story, but I didn't want to focus on Aster. If I couldn't get a line on Bedros then maybe understanding Violet's family would shed light on their business. "You're saying Finlay wasn't left with anything from his father but built up a fortune anyway?"

Mr. Glickman leaned back in his chair and took a deep breath. "It's a long story," he said. Seeing that I wasn't dissuaded, he continued. "I'm afraid the family's gains are ill-gotten. But have no worries, Alexander is nothing like his father."

Finlay and his sister Catriona led a maladjusted life. Their father was a profitable mortician in the early to mid-twentieth century, but the success came at a cost. The two children were left on their own much of their lives and had always struggled with the accidental death of their mother. Finlay was only an infant when it happened—his older sister was traumatized by the events and was never the same afterwards.

When their father passed away, it was up to the twenty-year-old Finlay to support the family. Unfortunately, their mad father, who had never truly showed his children love, left all of his fortune to a third party. Poor Finlay struggled to get ahead while Catriona broke down completely, eventually being admitted to a mental ward.

After years of struggling through financial hardship, the sociopathic Finlay resorted to a life of crime and quick pay-offs. He was a mildly successful gangster but lost sight of the fact that his lifestyle had led to isolation. In the end, even his illicit gains could not save him from the law.

In 1956, Finlay was imprisoned for racketeering. He lost all contact with his sister and fumed behind bars at the thought of living much of his life in a cage. The McAllister family was nearly wiped out and forgotten.

During his long sentence, reports from therapists, guards, and fellow inmates all indicated that Finlay made honest attempts at rehabilitation. His behavior became less erratic, he displayed true remorse at the state of his family, and he became more studious. After fifteen long years in prison, Finlay's sentence was commuted and he was set free.

He was afflicted with a troubled childhood, an untenable burden thrust upon him as a young man, and had his prime years of adulthood stolen from him. Finlay, released from incarceration but still in a shambles, resolved to correct his life.

At the age of fifty, only five years removed from prison, Finlay McAllister had somehow turned things around and led an affluent life. He established himself as an investor and was quickly married. His wife bore him a son, Alexander McAllister, but she died in childbirth. Refusing to acknowledge the setback, Finlay remarried. Unfortunately, his new wife was barren and he had no more kids.

The seventies and eighties proved decadent years. The former criminal finally had his family and fortune and lost himself in excess. He put his coarse life behind him and had no outward cares. Many years passed as Finlay enjoyed the twilight of his life.

When his son married Livia, Finlay encouraged the arrangement. When they bore him a granddaughter, he doted on her. Finlay stressed the importance of family to his son and always made a point that Alexander was heir to his fortune. He lined his son up as his successor and lived until 2004, dying when he was seventy-eight.

Alexander McAllister, without the same burdens that plagued Finlay's early life, became a respected investor in real estate. His life was perfectly scripted until the death of his father. That's when the rot of his marriage set in.

It was only four years later that Livia went mad.

Mr. Glickman's story was told with a craft that evoked the misery of the McAllisters. Even what was to be a happy ending with Finlay's rebound of wealth and focus on family would later end in tragedy. By this point, I knew about it all too well.

"A crying shame," said the lawyer, taking off his thin glasses and wiping his eyes. "Alexander tried to be a devoted father, but young Aster was a depressed little girl. I think he blamed himself. I recommended a child therapist but Alexander wouldn't hear of it. He was very stoic. Not the type to accept outside help. He's always been a very proud man."

An independent man, if not self-made. Alexander sounded like the kind of person that was used to handling everything himself. But he had no way of knowing about shades and the decay they instilled. A perfect life wrought into misery. I well understood the tragic side of that coin. It was the other that puzzled me.

"So Finlay was bereft of his father's fortune and went to prison a poor man, yet somehow came out and made his riches?"

The lawyer nodded solemnly. "It does raise eyebrows, doesn't it? As I said, the man was a gangster. I can't attest to the legitimacy of the money, only that what was built from it and passed on to Alexander was clean."

I nodded. Mr. Glickman was a lawyer. He would have attested that everything was above board regardless. But I hadn't seen anything to make me think otherwise. Was the son cursed by the sins of the father? "What did Finlay do to lose his inheritance?" I asked.

"I don't know," he said, shrugging. "Finlay's father invested it all into a regimental company for the war. Blue Bell, Blue Bonnet... something along those lines. It crippled the family. Finlay swore to pass on his wealth as it was never passed on to him."

"Only now there isn't a single McAllister left alive besides Alexander."

Mr. Glickman hesitated. "More or less," he offered, but there was a hitch in his voice.

"Who else is still alive?" I demanded. "Who is set to get the inheritance?"

The man scratched the brown hair that clung to the side of his head and had a puzzled expression on his face. "Those questions do not have the same answer. As Mr. McAllister's attorney, I can't provide you with the details of his will, but since she isn't a part of it, I can mention that Catriona is still alive."

Finlay's older sister. "Alexander's aunt? She's got to be..."

"In her nineties, I would wager."

That would make her Violet's grandaunt, or great-aunt, or whatever the terminology was. Violet had told me she had no living relatives...

"Catriona bounced around mental institutions and hospitals for the majority of her life. She's still mad, from what I understand, but much too old to be a nuisance. She's at Willow Gardens. They specialize in problem cases. But I won't recommend a visit. You wouldn't be able to get anything coherent out of her."

The man put his glasses back on and shifted in his seat. He was being cordial because I had been assaulted in the hospital, but it was obvious I was nearing the limits of his tolerance for easy information. Alexander's predicament, his life, read like an open book. All except for the business with his father, with Bedros. In my mind, the will was the key.

"Okay, Mr. Glickman. It makes sense that Catriona isn't seeing any of the inheritance money, but Bedros is sticking around for a reason. What's his stake in the will?"

The attorney rose to his feet. "The will is of little import now. Alexander is free to spend his money as he wishes."

He was playing with semantics now. "A man in a coma can't likely do that, can he?"

Mr. Glickman looked at me, befuddled. "You don't know?" he asked. "I thought that's why you were here. Alexander McAllister is awake."

Chapter 23

I sat in the metal patio chair with my back to the sun. The pocket watch was on the table, next to my soda. I was restless as the girl put my pastrami sandwich and fries down in front of me. I faked a smile, told her I didn't need any ketchup, and was relieved when she left me alone.

"So you have no idea who Mr. Glickman is?" I reiterated.

I've never heard of him. What did he say?

"He told me an interesting story." I wasn't sure how to broach the subject with Violet. The good news about her father was supposed to be a surprise. The only thing was, I didn't feel she was being forthcoming with me. As I dug deeper, I could feel the chasm between us widening. What was she hiding? From me?

I picked at my sandwich, but my attention was on the web browser on my phone. Eventually I stopped worrying about getting grease on the screen.

"Ever heard of Blue Bell or Blue Bonnet?" I asked.

No.

More denials. Why was it that I got more information about her family from everyone else? Violet was supposed to be on my side. The words of the man in the Last Bookstore came to my thoughts: you can't trust shades.

Google didn't bring up promising results. It listed day-to-day news in spades, as well as information about notable historical events. Historical day-to-day trivialities? Not so much. Violet's great-grandfather had left a good deal of money to a company when he died. I had no idea why. And neither did the internet. Maybe I was focusing on the wrong facts.

Does any of this have to do with Red Hat Events?

"What?" I asked. "No. I'm waiting for the party on Friday night to deal with them. I was looking into something else."

Why won't you tell me about it?

I stuffed my mouth with the biggest bite of pastrami I could manage to stall my answer. I chewed the thick strips of meat as I bided my time. Maybe showing Violet was better than any explanation I could come up with.

"It's not important," I finally said. "It's probably nothing."

Okay.

I took another bite of my sandwich.

It's just that Blue Bonnet sounds an awful lot like Red Hat.

I almost choked. What did the man in the bookstore say

about Red Hat? That it started as a millinery, a hat shop? The company had gone through various iterations, with Red Hat Events being the latest. I searched but didn't see anything about Blue Bonnet and uniforms.

But then it hit me. Blue. Blue was the wrong color. I scrolled back a page and saw the reference: Blush Bonnet. Blush is close enough to red, unless you're talking wine. I clicked through some pages before I found what I was looking for.

The Royal Ruby Millinery was founded in the nineteenth century. Nearing World War II, the frivolity of hats was wearing thin in the United States and Blush Bonnet Clothiers was born. They started out making dresses and women's wear, but transitioned to uniforms to assist the war effort. In fact, this was around the same time that Finlay's father had died. His life savings, instead of going to his family, served as a bastion for the millinery's young venture.

"How...?" I asked out loud but was unable to finish my question. I didn't even know what I was thinking. None of it made sense.

On one hand, I'd tracked Soren and found out that he was involved with Red Hat. Sal, or the shade who possessed him, confessed his motivations to me. Red Hat emerged as an entity that I needed to watch. I got that much.

But then, in a completely unrelated thread, I'd decided to look into Violet's family. I found out about Livia and Alexander and Finlay and Catriona. But Bedros was there. There was something suspicious about that.

Two paths to travel. Two completely separate tangents with different goals. How in the hell did they both end up tied to Red Hat?

I glanced hesitantly at the Hamilton pocket watch that rested on the table. It was the late afternoon, still within visiting hours. If I was going to figure this out, I needed to bring all the actors together on the same stage. I slipped Violet into my jeans and marched back to my car.

I didn't believe in coincidences.

Chapter 24

"You have no idea why we're here?" I asked.

I advanced through the neurological ward, pretending I belonged. Thanks to the altercation with Bedros, I had to keep an eye out for him and the nurse that had threatened to call the police. If they were around, I had to see them before they saw me.

I've never been here before.

"Maybe not," I said, "but don't you know why I'm here? Can't you feel it?"

The hall was clear. There were no signs of obstacles or complications.

Why would I know anything about hospitals?

I stopped cold.

I hadn't really thought about how to bring the subject up yet. I knew Violet wasn't being truthful with me, and I wanted to set her straight, but it wasn't fair to ambush her.

Not with news of her father.

"Violet," I started, taking a heavy breath and leaning against a white wall, "can we be honest with each other?"

She hesitated before she answered.

Of course.

I nodded, looking down at the watch in my hand.

"We've known each other four years. We're friends, right?"

Yes, Dante.

"Then why is it you never tell me anything about your life and your family?"

This time there was no response. I knew it was a sensitive subject. I'd always trod lightly in the past but there was a clear need to press now. I waited in the hallway, still on the lookout for any trouble, for the girl to answer. She didn't.

"Violet—"

My father isn't important to any of this!

"Isn't he?" I asked coldly.

What's that supposed to mean?

"I've been looking into it, Violet."

You have no business!

"Is it not my business to know what my friend's real name is?" I got a little heated, a little loud. A man walking down the hall eyed me strangely and I shrugged. I waited for him to pass in silence before resuming with a whisper. "Why are you keeping secrets from me?"

I could tell she was conflicted.

You might not like the real me.

Her answer hit me like a brick. Sympathy replaced suspicion. I remembered that she was just a little girl, only twelve years old. She had been through a lot. Seen her father struck down. Murdered by her mother. Of course she was haunted: she was a shade.

"I know your real name is Aster McAllister."

Stunned silence. I pictured the same little girl I saw in the dream with purple-white hair, staring at me aghast.

"That lawyer I met with works for your father."

...My father?

"Yes, Violet. He told me about your family, about your grandfather Finlay and his sister, Catriona. They were stripped of their inheritance because all of it went to Blush Bonnet Clothiers, another incarnation of Red Hat."

Red Hat. I never knew...

"You see how it's all connected now, Violet? I need to understand how Red Hat operates. But there's more." I peeled myself away from the wall and headed down the hall. "I know why you've been alone. I know why you can't find your father."

Dante...

"I know it must be bittersweet, Violet, but you need to be happy for him."

What are you talking about?

"Your father is still alive. Your mother didn't kill him."

You mean—

"He's been in a coma this entire time. Here. And now he's awake."

What? No, Dante. Stop.

I knew it was hard for her, but the girl had lived with this crutch for a long time. She needed to cast it away. Discover that she could continue without it. I kept approaching the hospital room doorway.

Please, Dante. Don't do this.

Not a nurse or a bodyguard in sight. I wouldn't be swayed.

For me.

I entered the brightly lit room, the same one with the crack in the window, and felt all the blood drain from my face. The bed was empty and all signs of personal possessions were cleaned out.

"What?" I asked, panicking. "He was here, Violet. I saw him on the weekend. I touched him and he was clear and—"

What did you say to him?

"Nothing. He was in a coma. But Mr. Glickman said he'd been in and out lately. He just told me he was awake now."

Who was awake?

"Your father."

Alexander McAllister?

"Yes," I repeated. "He was right here." I strained to think about what could have happened to him. "But there was another person here, a bodyguard. Do you know him?"

Someone who worked for my dad? I'm not sure.

"Bedros. A large Armenian man. He was taken. In good control of his host. You didn't know him?"

I'm not sure. My dad didn't explain his work to me.

"Well, he's dangerous, either way. I almost got it in with

him last time."

A glimmer of sun caught in the cracked window. Maybe the man was still here. Moved to another room. I scrambled to the door. "Nurse!" I called out, flagging down a guy behind a desk. "What happened to this man? Where is Alexander McAllister?"

"He was discharged this morning."

"But he was in a coma on Sunday." I was incredulous that things could change so quickly.

"It was induced," he explained. "He'd been in recovery for six weeks. After two days of observation, he was released under the care of a private physician. It was against medical advice, but we couldn't stop him."

"Where is he now?"

"I don't know, sir. Are you family?"

"A friend." I put my hand up as he started to explain patient privacy. "It's okay. Don't worry about it."

I walked away, as I always did, before I made a big enough impression to be remembered.

You should have told me.

I was almost back to the car when she worked up the courage to talk to me again.

"I'm sorry, Violet. I wanted it to be a surprise."

It was. That's my point.

"Don't start that with me. If I had told you what I was doing, you never would have gone along with it."

That should tell you everything you need to know.

I arrived at my metallic gray coupe and paused outside. I remained silent. I wasn't going to get sucked into another argument.

You said we were friends. If that was true, you wouldn't have snuck around behind my back.

"Every time I've asked you about your past, you've dodged the question. You never told me how you died. You avoid mentioning family. You even kept your true name from me. If you're gonna play the friend card, you have lots of explaining to do."

You're saying you don't trust me?

"I'm saying I don't believe you. I can't. Not after all the inconsistencies."

She didn't immediately say anything back to me. I unlocked the car door, threw the watch on the passenger seat, and pulled out my phone. Sitting down heavily, I released all my built-up pressure with a long exhale.

You could have really messed things up. Has it ever occurred to you that I might not want to see my father?

I watched the lowering sun and was relieved there was still plenty of time in the day. "Actually, no. I never considered that. If that's the case, Violet, then I truly apologize, but it's too late to back off."

What do you mean?

I dialed Mr. Glickman, annoyed that I had just seen him

in person but never got the address. "We're gonna visit him."

Dante, my father isn't a kind man. Can't we just forget about it?

"Impossible," I said as I held my cell phone to my ear. "This isn't personal anymore. Red Hat's involved and the man may be in danger."

The woman from earlier answered. "Mr. Glickman's office. How can I help you?"

"Put your boss on."

"Whom may I ask is—"

"Tell him it's Dante. And unless he wants another visit from me, he's gonna pick up the phone."

Chapter 25

The address I got was nearby. It was in the historic core of Downtown LA, amid a bustling series of storefronts ranging from jewelers to fine clothing stores. The air of class was apparent but forced on these dirty streets. Spending money didn't exclude one from the realities of the world. As such, designer shoes skirted homeless men, and the luster of beautiful facades was mired in the oppressive smog of the city.

The age of the buildings was apparent as well. Mostly brick and stone instead of metal and glass, these structures were from a different time. More care was put into the style and workmanship of the condo, even evident when I walked indoors. Having chosen this loft as his, I already knew something about Alexander McAllister.

The elevator rose to the top floor and I was left in a quiet hallway of carpeted elegance that only housed four front doors. My destination was the last one at the end. Ignoring Violet's repeated objections, I pounded my fist on the door.

"This should be fun," I muttered.

I heard the sound of shuffling but no immediate answer. The light from the peephole was momentarily covered and I heard some murmurs. Still, no one said anything. I knocked again. The talking stopped and heavy feet stomped closer to the door before it opened.

Bedros stood in front of me. He was wearing a similar track suit and was still as tall as ever.

"You," he said in his booming voice.

I took a reflexive step back. "Of course you'd be here."

"What you want?"

"I'm just here to see Alexander."

The big man slipped through the open door and barred my way. He didn't say anything—he just looked at me with a grumbling face. I took another step back, expecting him to attack again.

"It's all right," came a soft voice from inside. "The lawyer told us about him."

Of course. After my first visit to Mr. Glickman's office, he had probably informed his client about my inquiries. That's why he was all too ready to hand over the address when we spoke on the phone. Alexander McAllister was expecting me.

"Well, come on," said the distant voice. "Let's have a look at him."

Bedros creased his forehead and moved to the inside, motioning me to follow.

The loft had a high ceiling, spacious for the building. It was organized meticulously but had the musty smell of a tomb. The sun streamed in from high windows, but most of the lights were off and curtains were drawn over the main windows. For all the inherent pomp and luxury, these were depressing conditions to live in.

Bedros led me to an especially dark corner of the room where Alexander sat in a wheelchair, scratching a head of newly cut tan hair. He was cleanly shaven as well. The perks of not being a vegetable, I supposed.

"You'll have to excuse me," he said, beckoning with his hand weakly for me to come closer. "It has been some time since I've been myself. I still cannot manage to stand." The feeble man spoke in a whisper, as if the very act of conversation taxed him.

"It's fine, Alexander. Don't trouble yourself." I stepped closer and Bedros took up a post right above the man's shoulder.

"That's enough," he said through his thick accent.

Alexander McAllister looked slightly distressed. He regarded the current proceedings with a certain amount of apathy. To me, it looked as though Bedros was much more interested in what I had to say than he was. I would have preferred the bodyguard leave us alone, but that didn't look like it was happening.

"I'm failing," said Alexander, "to bring your name to my lips." The man coughed softly and returned his hand to his lap.

"My name's Dante. You didn't know me. I... I was a

friend of your daughter."

The man's eyes melted and he seemed to lose what little firmness his posture had. "I see."

"I..." I started, not really sure what to say. "I had just been checking up on you to see how you were doing. When I heard that you'd been discharged, I had to come."

The man nodded but his dull eyes showed no emotion. "Of course. How kind of you."

Alexander was colder than I'd expected. He didn't volunteer any information or even feign friendliness. He just sat and stared with a silent patience that must have been thrust on him by circumstance.

"May we talk in private?" I asked, breaking the silence.

"No," interrupted Bedros. I looked to Alexander for a decision but he barely blinked in response. Maybe my presence was an intrusion. I couldn't imagine what he would need to confront in order to get his life moving again. But there was something else. Something off. Something I was missing.

I felt I was losing him with every moment that passed. My inaction was spoiling my impression and my window was closing. Maybe I panicked, but I had no other cards in my hand. I reached into my pocket and withdrew the brass watch.

Alexander's eyes lit up for the first time. I spun the face around to make sure he got a good look at it. Then he predictably held out his hand. "May I?"

You better not.

I smiled casually and approached him. Bedros stepped

forward, hovering right over the sick man now, and I leaned in cautiously. As I handed Alexander McAllister the watch, I brushed his wrist.

There was no foreign agent inside him. No second shadow. He was free from influence, I thought, and then shot a glance at Bedros. Well, at least from within.

"Hamilton 940," he recited as he opened the case and spun it around. "Railroad grade. This is an antique."

"You recognize it? It was Aster's."

"I remember it well," he replied. "My father gave it to me. My child, she loved it so. She always had a heart for old things."

I watched with curiosity to see if Violet would speak to him. Of course, I might never have known if she did. I only heard her voice in my head. If she spoke to someone else, could I overhear? My test ended with disappointment. If Alexander heard his daughter at all, it didn't register in his eyes.

"Perhaps I could purchase this from you?" he asked softly, then broke into a fit of coughing.

I tried to put together words to respectfully decline. They didn't come.

Seeing my hesitation, Alexander spoke again. "My girl. She was such a troubled one. The years between toddler and teenager fly by. A great metamorphosis occurs. I think I failed to recognize her struggle. Or rather, I failed to acknowledge it. Looking back, of all of Aster's manic emotions, sadness always took precedence." Alexander rubbed the timepiece in his hands as if it could bring her back. In a way, it did, as a memory jogged loose. "The girl liked trains. I can't tell you why. The business didn't run in our family and we rarely rode them. But there was one time —I can clearly recall vacationing in San Diego. My wife and I took her down in a first-class cabin. Red carpet. White tablecloths. It was the height of pampering. Yet little Aster kept wandering off. I eventually found her outside, in the access path between cars. She wanted to be outdoors. To feel the wind on her face. When I found her, I was naturally upset, but her precious look swayed me. I stood there with her for the rest of the trip, and she clutched this railroad watch the entire time."

Suddenly, Alexander had the look of a man who couldn't afford sentimentality. Before I could say anything, he rescinded the offer. "On second thought, it would be too painful to have the constant reminder of a happier time. You can keep the watch." He gently handed it back to me, and I breathed a sigh of relief.

Now that I had appealed to his emotions and softened his demeanor, I hoped he would open up to me.

"Are you okay, sir?" I asked, trying to communicate the severity of my question with my eyes. Bedros watched me like a hawk. I tried to motion towards the bodyguard in a way that might be cryptic to a non-native speaker. "With everything?"

The man in the wheelchair took a long breath and nodded slowly. "I am as okay as a man in my position can be, son." Again, I couldn't draw any subtext from his words. He spoke plainly and seemed to either not be aware of or not care about the danger he was in. I was losing him again.

Finlay then. "Alexander, do you know much about your father's life?" The question appeared to aggravate Bedros. Alexander was a more difficult puzzle.

"Of course. He was always supportive of me, especially when I started my family." Alexander took a moment to recover himself. He strained just to breathe. "But so much of my life is a jumble now. It's hard to recollect specifics. Why do you ask?"

"How did Finlay acquire his fortune after getting out of prison?"

Bedros stomped forward. "Time to rest. You go now."

"But—"

"Time to rest. You go now."

I raised my voice. "Alexander. How did Finlay get his money?"

Bedros advanced on me. The man in the wheelchair lowered his head and shook it softly. "I know the rumors. They may be true. Unfortunately, that is a subject I am ignorant of."

The bodyguard placed his hand on my shoulder and nudged me. His second shadow was insistent. Determined. Desperate. He didn't want me asking these questions.

As I was shoved away from the tired man, my appeals became more urgent. "Alexander. Your money is in danger. You may be. Why is Bedros watching you?"

My protests were pointless. Alexander paid little attention to my meaning. It was all the favor he could muster by raising his head to me again.

"Don't worry about my assistant," said Alexander. "I hardly remember why I hired him, but my attorney says he's been by my side the six years I was in Keck. He's merely following the instructions of my private physician." The man rubbed his forehead and looked winded from the encounter. "I must agree with him about the rest. This exchange has exhausted me. I thank you for your concern and the memories."

"Yes," said Bedros. "Physician instructions. You go."

I swatted the bodyguard's hand from my shoulder and stepped away from him. He stood like a brick wall between me and Alexander. I sighed as I studied the nearly broken man. I couldn't help him by pressing his health. I kept several steps between myself and Bedros on the way out of the loft. As the large man closed the door, I shot a knowing wink his way, but his expression didn't surrender his intentions.

I held the chain of the pocket watch as I spun it in my hand, walking towards the elevator. Violet chose not to say anything.

This family was tough to read.

Chapter 26 - Thursday

The next day found me restless. I hit my programming deadline for the week. Players could now pay for the pleasure of earning experience quicker. Could you tell I was excited? The implementation was rushed but it worked. I decided to spend more time on the project next week to make up for it.

The Red Hat party wasn't until the following night, but being cooped up inside didn't feel right. Too much was turning over in my head. It didn't help that Violet was being especially tight-lipped. Not only was she mad at me, but she was intent on keeping her secrets. With Alexander under guard, I had one place to turn.

It was usually sunny in November, but the day was overcast with a haze that seemed a fitting portent for my destination. I sped north on the 5 in my Z. I-5 is what we would have called it in Miami, but the west coast likes to drop their Interstate labels. I had a bit of a drive ahead of me, about an hour and a half without speeding, and I was confident I could make good time. I always speed.

The city of Bakersfield was one of those last resort types of destinations that nobody should ever willingly subject themselves to. Work, finances, or complete apathy were the only valid reasons I could imagine for staying in the dreary place. While it didn't have the desert stigma of smaller communities like Lancaster, Bakersfield was bigger and should have offered more than it did. Instead, it was content in its mediocrity, and I found myself getting depressed just thinking about it.

Incarceration. That was another valid reason one might end up in Bakersfield. Although Catriona McAllister was technically a patient at the Willow Gardens Mental Health Center, as I saw the perimeter of fences and guard gates, I realized that it likely operated more closely to a prison. Like brother, like sister. Except Catriona had never recovered.

What are we doing here?

"You're talking to me now?" I asked snidely. The drive was pleasant enough but the city wasn't, and the only reason I was here was because of Violet's lack of cooperation. As I pulled into a parking space, I figured there was no reason to hide what I was doing. She already knew enough. "Don't you want to meet your only other living relative?"

No one else is alive.

"That's not true, Violet. Your grandaunt, Catriona, lives here." I walked on the long sidewalk leading up to the main lobby. Besides the guards that I'd seen, there were no other souls in sight, inside or out.

Please stop digging into my family. My life isn't important.

"This is what we do."

It was a mistake to ask you to follow Sal. I'm sorry. I should have just let you keep doing things your way.

"This *is* my way, Violet. Why you wouldn't want to save Alexander is beyond me."

You're right. If Bedros is a threat to him, we should expel him. We should be doing that instead of talking to some old lady.

I smiled sadly. Violet was only twelve. I wondered if she had ever known her crazy grandaunt. I wanted to give her the benefit of the doubt.

"I'm sorry, but we're talking to Catriona."

Chapter 27

I told the staff I had just married the grandniece of a patient and wanted to check in on the new family member. I was prepared to rattle off a string of names and associations to legitimize my visit, but the employees just nodded dismissively. After a short wait on a plastic chair, I was introduced to an administrator and led to the second floor.

"Mrs. McAllister never has visitors," he explained. "She can be a bit... incomprehensible."

I nodded grimly and wondered what an entire life in an institution would be like.

"Is she violent?" I asked.

"No, no, not at all. She had a history of harming herself but that was decades ago. She is mostly withdrawn and distrustful of reality. She needs to adhere to a strict routine every day simply to function. To tell you the truth, I have some worries about what a visit might do to her, but we need to consider the possible benefits as well. Friendship and warmth can be efficacious."

I started to have second thoughts about my purpose here. It was awkward enough in Alexander's loft to meet a complete stranger with little reason. Here, with a sick, old woman, was I justified? I decided that employing tact was paramount.

My escort unlocked a gate leading into a cafeteria. The emptiness of the halls finally gave way to sparse groups of senior citizens. He walked me through another door to a smaller, more intimate, lounge area. Here, an ancient woman sat with her back turned to the few other occupants. She was staring out of the only window, enraptured by the gray sky. The orderly pulled up a chair.

"Good afternoon, Cat." The woman made a faint noise, like a grunt, but remained still. "You have a visitor." The man motioned for me to sit and I did. "I'll be right next door," he said, "if you need me."

Catriona was ninety-six years old. The wrinkles on her face spoke of much suffering. Her long hair was thin and ghostly white. Her head swayed back and forth ever so slightly on her neck. She looked to be a woman near death, worn out—but not in ill-health. Her eyes, their green-gray color, were a comforting mix of piercing and assuring, and they slowly looked me over.

"Catriona," I started, unsure how to proceed.

"Pure," she barked out. "Pure. No one calls me that." She jutted her head one way, and then the other, before facing me again.

"I'd like to introduce myself. I'm a friend of the family."

"We're no friends," she answered. "The wicked have no friends. The wicked are not pure." Her eyes narrowed. "Are you Finlay's little boy?"

She was confused. Did she even know what horrors had befallen the rest of her family? I leaned forward to calm her.

"Are you Finlay's boy?" she asked again, drawing back. "Are you cursed? You stay away from me!"

"It's all right, Catriona," I said, sliding my seat backwards to reassure her. I looked around the room and saw a man sleeping in an old chair and another woman in the doorway watching me. She had an unsettling stare.

"Cursed!" screamed the other woman.

Some whispers came from the other room, then the administrator appeared and pulled her away. I took a breath and turned my head back to the man. He was now awake, silently watching me.

"No," I said to Catriona, "I'm not Alexander." The old woman didn't panic or make any rash actions, but she stared at me distrustfully. I sat and smiled, trying to appear patient. Friendly. "I'm not Alexander."

Catriona seemed content after a few moments and resumed her vigil of the sky. I thought she mumbled something but couldn't tell for sure. I checked the door again to see if I'd stirred up any trouble. Everything was quiet. The man on the seat had his eyes closed again.

"Is Alexander cursed, Catriona?"

She answered without her gaze leaving the window. "My mother always said she would give me her pearls one day.

When we found her body, they were missing. Years later, my brother gave them to his wife as a wedding present. She died giving birth to that boy. Those were my pearls."

I sighed inwardly. She was rambling, but not incoherent.

I felt fingers on my shoulder and spun around. A deathly thin black man stood behind me. His cheeks were sunken and his eyes looked like large white globes suspended in the air.

"Do you have a square?" he asked.

I brushed his hand off my shoulder. "What?"

The man sleeping on the chair woke up. "Who's smoking?"

"No—" I uttered, watching him try to stand up. "Sit down," I instructed, then turned to the skinny man. "And you, leave me alone." He stepped away from me. "Get out of here," I urged.

I waited until he left the room and the other man had closed his eyes again. Catriona hadn't reacted to any of it. When I turned to her, she was still admiring the sky.

"We like cigarettes here," she explained. "We trade them for pills."

I slid my chair to the side so I faced the entrance and took a deep breath. "What curse, Catriona?"

"The wickedness," she answered, "in our family. We hurt people."

"How?"

"I'm not crazy," she insisted. "I'm not well. My thoughts get jumbled sometimes. But I know things. I've seen things."

She had a conviction that made me believe.

"What do you see?" I asked.

Catriona moved her eyes to me again. "A familiar face."

I scratched my head in frustration. "We've never met before," I said slowly, to make sure she understood.

"I see an old watch," she said. "A vile thing."

I jerked back with a frown. I usually managed to keep a cool head, but her insight was penetrating. I pulled the Hamilton from my pocket. "This watch?"

"Yes. Why must you keep such an old thing?" The gaunt woman turned her head to the window once more. "I've left it all behind, don't you see, and I am alive."

She was mad, jumping between bouts of fear and disinterest, but her mind was still intact. She seemed to have powerful memories, however disjointed. Through patience and roundabout conversation, I was determined to get what knowledge of her family I could.

"Tell me about it," I said.

Catriona McAllister was the eldest of two siblings, already eight when her brother Finlay was born. She always said she was her parents' favorite and enjoyed a wonderful childhood with them.

Her father, Fingal McAllister, was a very successful mortician. He had an array of funeral homes peppered across the booming city of early Los Angeles. As his business grew, so did the family's wealth, and they moved to bigger grounds. Their ranch estate was built on a hill, and little Catriona loved to play on the paths that wound through the trees and opened into dazzling views.

As Catriona grew older, her father became more of a stranger to her. Fingal always paraded around clutching a pocket watch and talking to himself. He ignored his family completely except when he asked Catriona strange questions. He put a lot of pressure on her to be the obedient daughter, especially when her little brother was born.

That's when she started sleepwalking. Catriona would suddenly find herself in the middle of the yard, or in the study looking at pictures. One time, she found herself all alone in the nearby cemetery. Her dad yelled at her. Her mom cried for her. Everything was changing, and she didn't understand why.

One day, her mother went missing. After the police were called, they found the woman at the bottom of a steep expanse of tangled brush. Fingal said she had left the bedroom that night and never returned. Her death, people said, was caused by a misstep during a midnight walk. Without her around, Fingal added more staff to the house, and then everybody became a stranger.

Catriona tried to shut everything out. She tried to be alone. But she kept finding herself acting out. Sometimes she was the happiest child imaginable. Other times she wondered what it would feel like to jump from the same hill as her mother. She began daydreaming, and hearing things, and sometimes she pretended she was somebody else so she wouldn't have to deal with her problems.

As much as she came to despise her life and her father, Catriona loved her baby brother, Finlay. She had deep feelings about raising him right and took too much of his upbringing upon herself. She always preached to him about the importance of family. In the times when she felt most normal, they shared many secrets.

But there was another side to Catriona. Her name meant "pure" but she was anything but. She felt evil inside. Twisted. Sometimes she hid from her brother for fear that she would hurt him. She began to speak of a curse, and her father struggled mightily with her episodes.

Fingal McAllister was a different man after the years passed. His business became more urgent and he surrounded himself with scary characters. He offloaded his work to others and seemed to take less pride in the craft. He preferred to read or study in confinement, always talking to himself. In his late life, he became increasingly paranoid and isolated.

Catriona blamed herself. She suffered a quiet breakdown and became dependent on others to function. Although she was an adult when her father died, she had already undergone many procedures and taken many drugs in an effort to ease herself of the creeping fears. Her condition led others to believe she was unable to process that Fingal was dead. But she knew. She was secretly happy about it.

In some ways, it was fitting that Fingal had stripped his children of all rights to their inheritance. His secret business dealings took priority over love, and she cared little for anything that came from the man.

What absolutely crushed her, however, was that her brother stopped taking care of her. Finlay struggled to support himself and saw her as a burden. He associated with a bad crowd and eventually went to prison.

Catriona was permanently put under observation. She attempted to kill herself several times. Slowly, she abandoned those inclinations. She found the will to get out of bed. She found comfort in imagining what the next day would bring. She learned how to survive.

Time passed. People lived, families sprouted, elders passed on, and still, Catriona persevered. She was free from her family and her horror. In Bakersfield, of all places.

Catriona's story was muddled with wild observations and horrid expositions of her treatment. She focused on inane memories and glossed over key events. Eventually, however, I thought I had a thorough understanding of her life.

I removed my palm from Catriona's skeletal hand. I was sitting close to her now. Any fears she had of me had long since dissipated. The woman seemed to have inklings of the Dead Side and shades but held little true understanding. She wasn't taken now, but in all likelihood, she'd had brushes with ghosts in her difficult past.

"You are strong," said Catriona, showing a mouth devoid

of many teeth. "I can see that much. But do you know what makes that so?"

I thought about her question. The obvious answer was Violet. She had given me the insight to do what I did. She had instructed me. But even before I'd found her, back in Miami, I had the dreams. Violet had given me the knowledge. But did she give me the strength?

"Does it matter?" I asked, brushing off her point.

"It does. Even if you don't realize it, it does."

I looked down at the pocket watch and thought about Aster, clutching her father's possession. I thought about the violence she'd seen and wondered how far all of this had gone, and for what?

"I don't know if you know what happened to your brother's son," I started.

"Killed," she said. "That feisty wife of his went on a rampage."

I was surprised she knew. The woman spoke of it with such a lack of remorse that it threw me. "Alexander didn't die," I corrected. "He's awake, and I think he's in trouble." I drilled into her eyes and saw a recognition there. "You said he was cursed. What did you mean by that? What's after him?"

The woman contemplated me severely. Her eyes shifted to a coldness I hadn't seen yet, and she laughed. It was a labored display but she enjoyed it. When she had enough, she leaned forward in her chair.

"They said I was wicked," she whispered in a scolding tone. "I heard the same about Alexander's wife, Livia. But that's not the truth. Livia did what I couldn't do. She did what I should have done!" I pulled away from the woman but she grabbed me with a hellish grip.

"Catriona," I said, "she killed a poor little girl."

"She saved the girl from my life," she insisted. "Don't you see, young man? Don't you understand what the curse is? Are you prepared to face the evil?"

I gritted my teeth and sat firm against her spitting voice. She didn't scare me. She was just an old lady.

"The women of the family were poor souls. They were always the victims, daughter and mother alike. It was my father Fingal who murdered my mother. It was he who spurned us by destroying our inheritance. My brother Finlay was a criminal yet my sentence was far worse. And Livia, she wasn't an evil woman. She was troubled, but she killed her girl to save her from Alexander. She tried to finish him off to end the tyranny of the men!"

I was affixed to my chair throughout her diatribe. Catriona was a lunatic, broken from years of institutionalization and tragedy, but her madness was not without merit. Of all people, I knew that well. What if what she said was true?

"Alexander's the evil?"

The old woman released me and leaned back in her chair. "Now you see," she said, a sense of fulfillment returning to her.

I had always assumed that Livia was the one that was taken. That she had slowly degenerated until she turned on her family. But... what if...

I stood up in an instant, knocking the plastic chair backwards. "He was fine when I saw him," I insisted. "Normal."

Catriona smiled. "The McAllisters are many things, young man, but never normal. The world will be a better place when we retire from it."

I shuddered at her words. "I'll get to the bottom of it."

"The bottom is a scary place. I have been there many times." Catriona shook her head. "I fear your visit is a sign that I might soon be there again." The woman lowered her gaze to the pocket watch in my hand. "It has been so many years..."

"No, Catriona." I knelt down and put my hand in hers. "You'll be fine." I left the pack of sage cigarettes in her palm and patted her on the back. "You'll be fine."

Chapter 28

The walk back to the car was not a pleasant one. It started drizzling, which only happens a few times a year in LA. Everybody in the city panics at the first sign of water. Nobody knows how to deal with it. Without exaggeration, I would likely see at least two accidents on the highway on the drive back.

My mood may have mirrored the weather, but it wasn't caused by it. Violet had been lying to me. I finally uncovered enough of her family history to understand what had gone wrong in her life. For some reason, she'd refused to tell me herself.

It wasn't until we were well on our way that I broke the silence.

"You should have said something."

I clicked the wiper lever to trigger a single manual swipe. The rain was slow enough that even the lowest intermittent setting was too often, and I hated the sound of the rubber blades squeaking against the dry windshield.

He's my father.

I sighed. "I know it must have been very tough for you, Violet. Just thinking about you hiding in that closet as your mother bashed open the door..."

I stopped talking. It was coming out wrong. I wanted to show her that I understood—that I was trying to understand—but recalling vivid imagery wasn't going to help.

She began crying.

It's all my fault. I drove Livia crazy with my behavior.

"Don't say that. She attacked your father first. She saw what was in him."

It's too hard. There's too much death.

I just nodded. She was overwhelmed. I couldn't blame her. Catriona's testimony was tragic and heartfelt. It was a firsthand account of why I sacrificed my personal life to do what I did. What we did. Even if I had never thought about it like that before.

"It's okay, Violet. But you should have told me." I tried to sound as comforting as I could while also being instructive. The poor girl had probably never been taught right from wrong. "Livia wasn't taken. It was your father. She tried to kill all of you to keep you from the shade."

What do you want me to say? That my father's a bad man?

"I just need to know that you understand."

I get it, Dante. Don't you see that I'm alone by choice? I was never lost down here. I've been doing my best to stay away from him.

The patter of the raindrops on the glass picked up in intensity. I couldn't imagine what the girl thought of herself. Was she a victim, abandoned by her loved ones? Was she a runaway, striking out on her own? And where did that leave me? Was she afraid that I would leave her too?

"You and me," I said. "We should trust each other."

Violet didn't answer. We drove in silence and the traffic picked up. I was back in Los Angeles County, nearing the city. Most of the end-of-day congestion headed north, but the weather slowed the inbound lanes as well. I just needed to wait this out.

One day, Violet would come around.

Chapter 29 - Dream

It was day yet it was dark. The world a lucid blur. I was walking but, at the same time, floating. Everywhere, the softness of the world surrounded and prevented me from affixing a grip.

I was alone on the streets of Los Angeles again. Stone behemoths lined up like soldiers at attention, and I marched between their ranks in my own one-man parade. But there was no frivolity here; no applause or recognition would follow. These streets were mine alone, and I passed through the desolation without fanfare.

I knew where I was headed. There was only one place— one person—I cared about saving. The muffled nothingness attempted to stifle me so I pressed harder against the ether and made my way to Bunker Hill.

Grand Avenue. I stood across the street from the St. Angelo Hotel, its arched tower pointed at the black above.

The entire building almost appeared to shift on its sloped foundation.

The play of the dream was especially strong now. It was resilient as I was tenacious, and the world blended between sharp and soft, black and white. It was a struggle—without anyone here to help me this time—but somewhere in the gray I caught a handhold and forced my will upon this hell.

In an instant, as if it had been effortless, the Dead Side obeyed. It came into focus. Sounds separated from each other. Shadows solidified.

And there I was, standing in front of the hotel with a clear path up the steps and inside. Smiling, I wasted no time.

Violet stood on the marble tile, her foot sliding in place on its polished surface. The girl's head hung as she stared at the idle action. She was distraught. She didn't want to see me. She'd probably thought I didn't want to see her. But here I was.

"You can control it now," she said. "The focus."

I noticed the sharp red and black stripes of her dress, the white skull patch etched on her chest, the little buckles on her black combat boots. I'd seen them before, even clearly, but that had been Violet's doing. She had pulled me in. This time it was me.

"I've had practice."

"A good teacher, you mean." She raised her head and brushed the purple-white hair from her face. The same color was in her eyes, eyebrows, lipstick, and even accented by her pitch black eyeliner. "I've been trying to help you," she said with quivering pupils. "To help people."

I smiled at the girl and nodded. I didn't know where I would be without her. Violet was conflicted and I didn't fully understand why, but I wanted to help.

"Like lonely streets," I said, "they're better walked with two."

The twelve-year-old girl turned away momentarily, overcome with emotion.

I waited patiently for her to say something. I had trouble myself, to be honest. I'd never known Violet to be someone that needed affection and approval. For too long I'd talked to the voice in the pocket watch without understanding the child behind it. I was twenty-four years old and a bachelor—what did I know of support?

"Whatever it is, Violet, it's okay."

She wanted to tell me something. I examined the high walls of the lobby to give her time. Large, marble slabs encased us. A mirror with an intricate frame hung behind the reception desk. Its reflection of the room wiggled slightly. Just a minor shake, a reaction to an invisible tremor, then nothing.

Violet was still looking away, her attention on her past. But I was in the moment. Something was not right.

The floor trembled. Not visibly, but I felt it in my feet.

The front door chattered on its hinges. And then the whole building started shaking.

I turned to the door. "Not again." It was Nero, no doubt. That fiend would not rest until it had dealt with me. I clenched my fist and waited. "Get out of here, Violet."

There was a faint feeling of air bristling against my face, as though the pressure outside was creeping in. Then, as before, the door flung open. The skeletal shade had returned.

"Death comes to all life," he hissed through black teeth, and entered.

Nero's haggard body was more decrepit than the passage of a few days allowed. His orange hair had almost all fallen out. One of his eyes had glazed over. His movement was more erratic and his legs and arms more emaciated. He was weakening, no doubt, but his ghostly power was still frightening.

I stood my ground to allow Violet's escape. I had controlled the world this time. Focused it to fit my needs. Maybe I could prevent Nero from suffocating me in his muddy grasp. As he approached, I summoned my courage, ready to meet his might.

"This needs to stop, Nero."

"Neros," he whispered in a raspy voice. "My name is Neros. And there is only one end to this."

I paused at his correction. Had he changed his name or had he always called himself Neros?

Before I mounted an offense, Violet charged out in front of me. I clutched at air as I tried to stop her. Too late. The shade that was Soren raised his cadaverous arms as the girl approached.

No. I wouldn't let her sacrifice herself.

Neros lunged, but the girl grabbed his chest and stopped him in his path. It was as if he jumped into a pane of glass. He wiggled, unable to move further. Enraged, he placed his clawed fingers around her neck.

"No!" I yelled, leaping forward. But Neros jerked as if he'd touched a power line. He released his feeble grip and shook violently in the little girl's arms.

I froze as a warm glow overwhelmed the fiend. His body became soft, his expression distant, his jaw lax. I watched in awe as the light became blinding and illuminated the room.

"Give me life," he stubbornly said.

And then I realized this dilapidated shade wasn't a man anymore. Not physically, of course, but not in spirit either. It clung to life because it was the only thing that gave the fiend sensation. Even its name, Neros, was not a name at all. It was Soren spelled backwards. A sad imitation of something it desperately wanted to be.

"I..." said Neros, locked in radiance, "I'm scared..."

"You're free," said Violet, then the light was no more.

A peace overtook me, stunning my senses by depriving me of sight and sound. Then, slowly, the world faded in. The room was quiet again. Still. Violet and I were standing close to each other, same as before. Where Neros was, only a faint glow remained. An aura.

The warm luminescence pulsed in intensity and began to move. It floated by me like a jellyfish riding a smooth current. Eventually, it faded out completely.

"What did you do?" I asked Violet with reverence.

"Nothing you wouldn't have."

I didn't know what to say.

"Bravo, my dear," came a familiar voice from the still-open door.

Violet, one moment triumphant, suddenly turned around in panic. "Father!"

I looked at the stoic figure on the threshold. It was a man in a fine suit with a black mustache and wavy black hair. In his left hand, held over his shoulder, was a walking stick with an alabaster rose.

"Son of a bitch," I whispered.

"My proper name, Mr. Butcher, is Alexander Ambrose."

Chapter 30

The well-dressed man glanced around and cleared his throat. "May I?" he asked, motioning himself inside. He made a show of cordially removing his top hat. When no one answered, he let himself in anyway, and the door fell closed behind him. Then his hat resumed its place on his head.

"Who are you?" I demanded.

A smirk crossed the man's face. "I have just told you, sir." He pushed past his daughter carelessly and approached me. Violet averted her gaze, trying not to call attention to herself.

"I mean, why are you here? What do you plan to do?"

"To lay my cards on the table," he answered. He lowered his wooden stick to the floor and the metal tip clicked on the tile. "Let's face it. You were on the verge of discovering me anyway."

"Livia recognized you," I said, narrowing my eyelids. "She attacked Alexander McAllister to defeat Alexander Ambrose."

"Ah," he said, frowning, "I see that you already have found me out." He clicked his tongue several times, as one might do to a child. "One step ahead of me."

"Tell me then," I said. "What do you want from me?"

"I've told you that shades can find those that poke into their affairs."

"But why did you save me from that fiend last time?"

"Bah," he said dismissively, "I doubt that I prevented any grievous damage. The fool was weak, as even my daughter has proved."

"Leave Violet out of this," I warned.

"Is that what she calls herself these days?" The man turned his head partly to face the girl but she looked away. He chuckled. "Things in this world are not often what they seem."

I studied the calmly composed gentleman. He was the sort of person who exuded power so much that he didn't need to prove he had it. It was in the way he spoke, the way he dressed, and it was apparent in the casual attention he gave everything.

He locked eyes with me but spoke to Violet.

"Why are you helping this man, dear?"

The young girl fidgeted and crossed her arms over her chest.

"Oh come now," he demanded. "It has been six years since we've had the pleasure of speaking, and now you are mute?" The man turned to face her. "Why are you helping this man?"

"Because he's good," she answered indignantly. "Because I can."

The man laughed softly. "I notice you didn't affirm that you were good." The man was amused with himself.

"I'm better than you," muttered Violet.

I'd never seen Alexander Ambrose get upset before. In the little time I'd known him, it was apparent it didn't happen often. But now, his cheeks flushed with anger and he set his jaw.

"How dare you!" he boomed. His voice carried a mystical reverberation that echoed off the high walls. Violet cringed at the sound. "You will not speak to your father that way."

"Hey!" I yelled, rapidly losing patience with the man's cryptic arrival. "Leave her alone. She's just a little girl. Just another tragic victim of your careless meddling, like Sal and Livia." The man turned to me and I drew my face close to his. "She's not even your daughter, you twisted fuck. Aster was Alexander McAllister's daughter. She was killed because of you. And now a broken man woke up from a coma and found himself all alone."

Alexander Ambrose took a measured breath and regained his cool. The heat left his face and gave way to a faint smile. That smirk, that crooked smirk, widened—then broke out into a walloping laugh.

"Ha, ha, Mr. Butcher! So you are one step behind, after all."

I shot a puzzled look at the man and backed off. I didn't try to hide my confusion. I didn't try to play cool. I just wanted to know what the hell was going on.

"What are you talking about?"

The man beamed, amused by the proceedings. By my consternation. After a moment, he broke his silence. "What did I tell you about trusting shades?"

"What is he talking about, Violet?" I asked.

The girl lifted her head and tears were in her eyes. Lines of black eyeliner ran down her puffy cheeks.

"For starters," said Alexander, finally showing mercy, "her name is Viola Ambrose, and she was born in 1902."

I swallowed something wrong. I choked. It became difficult to breathe. But I could see in the girl's eyes that he wasn't lying.

"You're not twelve," I said to her, each word a dagger. "You're a hundred and twelve."

Chapter 31

Viola Ambrose was born just after the start of the new century. It was a time to shake off old attitudes. The Victorian mindset that had consumed England was dying a slow death and the industriousness of a new America was coming to a head.

Alexander Ambrose was a railroad man. Having devoted twenty years of his life to the Southern Pacific, he was well regarded and well-off. His young wife had taken ill and died, but Alexander dutifully raised Viola as a single father. Her hair was still black then. The two were close, and he never remarried, at least not in this life.

Alexander Ambrose was a man of moderate success, pulled up in class by his hard work and relentless drive. Even though he was of poor beginnings, he put on a show of nobility. He always dressed and spoke the part. More importantly, he was a man who could be trusted to his word. His reliability earned him promotions and a promising career.

His prized possession was his custom made Hamilton Watch Company 940, given to him by respected associates at the railroad. By all accounts, Alexander and Viola Ambrose had their futures well assured. Their success was self-made. So it would be with their undoing.

One early fall morning in the year 1914, Alexander sealed his modest house, turned the gas on, and reclined on his sofa. Viola, sitting beside him, clutched her father's pocket watch, as she often did. The girl was only twelve at the time and she trusted her father implicitly. Alexander spoke of the future. They held each other. As she nodded off, he recited a comforting rhyme.

"The path is rough, and simple feet step better with a shoe.

One's not enough; like lonely streets, they're better walked with two."

Viola succumbed first. Alexander, holding the lifeless form of the only person in the world he still loved, waited in peace.

The bodies were dressed and presented at a respectable, if small, funeral. The Hamilton 940 was hung from Alexander's jacket and the girl had a purple flower placed in her hands. When the time came to put them in the ground, the greedy mortician, a man by the name of Fingal McAllister, spirited the pocket watch into his possession before he let the ground take them.

The Dead Side was not an easy place. Father and daughter wandered it together, fighting to keep their wits about them. Viola was scared but she had her father to protect her. He seemed to know what to do; she had to believe there was a reason for it. And there was, as Alexander proved to have connections in the beyond.

Strange meetings occurred. Their new partners did not take kindly to Viola's appearance. She was not, it turned out, in their designs, but Alexander stubbornly refused to accept any outcome that abandoned his daughter and impressed his fellow shades with his conviction. In the end, they begrudged him the vice, and the father, for his part, kept Viola away from their proceedings.

All did not go well. Some on the Dead Side were disappointed in Ambrose. He was unpracticed and unable to cling to the world of the living. Desperate for success, he redoubled his efforts.

As Alexander attended to business, Viola dreamed of her old world and soon found that she could inhabit the familiar workings of her father's timepiece. Originally a secret, the revelation of this news excited her father and his cohorts. As Viola watched the world of the living through Fingal's watch, her father was given a unique conduit between both worlds.

So it was that, after more than a decade on the Dead Side, Alexander Ambrose overcame the obstacles needed to possess Fingal McAllister, an overworked family man with a wife, a little girl named Catriona, and a newborn son, Finlay.

Alexander, now in possession of a new life, began instructing his daughter to inhabit Catriona. These attempts met with initial success, but Viola, not gifted with the growing talents of her father, always struggled to hold herself inside her host. Catriona was strong-willed and a pure soul and fought for her independence. Worse yet, the agitation caused to the family by these events shone a light on the suspicious circumstances, and the mortician's wife became dangerously interested. Alexander Ambrose, unknown to his innocent daughter, staged her death to appear like an accident.

Alexander's new life did not go as he had hoped. In return for his reincarnation, he owed a great portion of his wealth to his benefactors, his associates from the Royal Ruby Millinery. Those in positions of power dubbed themselves the Royals, a select few with monstrous abilities but subtle designs. Fingal's business proved useful for promoting their illicit empire. Bodies could be hidden. Grieving families could be assessed. Alexander's work was immensely needed. His company expanded, but he found that ever more of his time and efforts went to the cause and very little benefited him. His work garnered little respect. His ascendancy to the Royals never happened. Alexander discovered that, in freeing himself from the shackles of his previous life, he had only entered the service of another.

Leading to more distress was his inability to cater to Viola's needs. He pushed her to join him amongst the living but had only succeeded in driving Catriona mad. He had little time for his real daughter, much less Fingal and Catriona. After twenty years of hardship, something needed to change.

Alexander Ambrose knew he had indebted one lifetime to Royal Ruby. Perhaps it had been nigh time to see that contract completed. He gave his pocket watch to his son, a new man, and after some grooming and preparation, Alexander Ambrose found he could do the impossible: he bound himself to another living person.

Powerful shades had jumped bodies before. At least, in a more opportunistic fashion. But Ambrose used the same trick that had brought him to the living in the first place. Viola's trick. The pocket watch once again served him and strengthened his grip on the living. Finlay was Alexander's new host. The old Fingal, devoid of any will left within, quickly lost himself and passed away soon after.

The Royals had created a new flagship company, Blush Bonnet Clothiers. As his final act of duty and per the terms set, the totality of Fingal McAllister's empire went to the new venture. Alexander Ambrose was left behind by the Royals. Seen as weak. As an outsider. But at long last, he was free.

Unbeknownst to Blush Bonnet, Alexander had continued on in the world of the living. Binding to hosts is extremely difficult and often happenstance. The ability to bind to others, well, that is nearly unheard of. Alexander was never meant to have brought Viola into the fray and her peculiar bond with the physical pocket watch had allowed her father to learn more about possession than most men. So Alexander lived a secret life, but a free one, as Finlay. The line continued. And the Royals had no cause for suspicion.

The new life was rife with challenges. Catriona was a handful and was eventually committed to an institution. Financial wealth proved more difficult than Alexander had supposed. To make ends meet, he was forced into a life of crime. Viola Ambrose contented herself with remaining on the Dead Side and only communicated with her father through the pocket watch. It was an empty life for both of them. And then Finlay went to prison.

Not wanting to be subjected to the rigors of confinement, Alexander Ambrose abandoned his host to the fate he had dealt him. Again amongst the dead, he reconnected with his ill-tempered daughter, but the bleak world crushed his soul. He had ambitions to once again leave that place but his conduit, Viola's pocket watch, was locked with the prisoner's possessions and isolated. Without it, his foothold was missing. So Alexander

Ambrose, never content to allow his fate to be dictated to him, practiced his talents.

Shades don't operate on tangible quantities. The machinations of the world are ill-defined. To skirt the impossible, one needs only the ambition of man. And Alexander Ambrose was nothing if not ambitious. After years of study, he discovered he could possess bodies other than the one he was bound to. It was erratic. Only sustainable for short periods of time. But it allowed him to practice his craft in secret. Slowly, the man once thought incompetent outgrew his reputation.

So it was that there were two parts of the same man: Finlay McAllister, serving an interminable sentence but living his own life again, acting to better himself and working towards rehabilitation, and Alexander Ambrose, jumping into the bodies of his gangster acquaintances and setting up his fortune.

Viola, at a time when she had the opportunity to be closest to her father, found herself ever the afterthought.

Finlay McAllister, having been a fine example of a prisoner and serving fifteen years, had his sentence commuted and was released. He recovered his pocket watch, the gift from his father, and exited the institution. He was prepared for a new life. He never realized how truly his wish would be granted.

Ambrose, seeing the host he was bound to set free and reunited with the conduit that was his stepping stone, reclaimed his place within the man. Finlay benefited from Alexander's elaborately executed crimes, which he had committed while possessing his gangster puppets. He had embezzled hundreds of thousands of dollars from Blush Bonnet in an attempt to have his fortune repaid to him. Upon his release, he had immediate access to a store of savings.

He was affluent but he was old, the best years of Finlay's life having been wasted in a cell. With all his knowledge and all his power, Alexander was determined to keep everything he had built. He quickly established himself as legitimate, found a wife, and had a son as a successor, whom he named Alexander. He did think of his daughter, Viola, but his wife died in childbirth. Still, he remarried to try for a daughter, but his second wife proved barren. Finlay grew older, gave in to the excesses of his lifestyle in the seventies and eighties, and had no more kids.

It was at this time that Viola Ambrose first considered that her father was a bad man. Not an evil man, or a dastardly one (since she had known little of Alexander's darkest dealings), but at the very least, an absent father. Viola realized, on her own and without guidance, that her place wasn't among the living. Finlay McAllister carried the watch less and less over the years, and this suited Viola well.

It wasn't until 1996, when Alexander and Livia McAllister gave birth to Aster, that Ambrose began to take notice of his family again. In particular, seeing the little girl grow up before his eyes, he remembered the pact he had made with Viola and how they would be together. Alexander found times to return to the Dead Side, when he could, to rekindle their relationship, but it was hard going. The poor girl was broken in many ways. She had never had the opportunity for a normal life. Even in death, she was largely on her own and had to make sense of circumstances by herself. But Alexander was her father, and she loved and needed him. He began plans to bring them together again.

At seventy-eight, in 2004, Finlay's health suffered a turn for the worse and he died unexpectedly. Alexander was forced to possess Finlay's son rather suddenly and his wife, Livia, took notice of the change. Whereas once they were a perfect couple in love, she found herself trapped with an entitled stranger. She was a strong woman but it drove her to the edge, and she sought council from Catriona.

Over the years, Alexander convinced Viola to once again take up residence with the living and possess Aster. He promised her love and attention. The perfect family, reunited once again. He gifted the girl the pocket watch. He claimed not to need it anymore, and her use of it might avoid the incidents that plagued Catriona. Viola begrudgingly obeyed but remained distant. Even with the timepiece, she continued to struggle with control. She didn't feel fit for her new life. Aster McAllister drew inward, became depressed, and began cutting herself.

Livia's marriage was quickly failing and her senses continually tested. Seeing her daughter become dissociated over the years finally broke her. In 2008, believing to catch her husband in proof that he was possessed by a demon, she struck him on the back of the head with an iron. Alexander Ambrose was caught off-guard and succumbed to the attack. He was beaten to within an inch of his life as he lay helpless on the floor.

Viola, who had always sulked about quietly, saw the entire act firsthand. She saw another life destroyed. She blamed herself for failing her father. She blamed herself for failing the McAllisters. But most of all she blamed her father for meddling with the living.

As the little girl sobbed, Livia turned to her and said that what was happening wasn't tragedy but salvation. They were prisoners of demons and would be free in Heaven. When her mother came after her with the iron, Aster McAllister locked herself in the linen closet.

If possessing bodies is not a clean experience, then vacating them is downright filthy. It is possible, of course, for a shade to exit the living, but it isn't an immediate process. The binding is tenuous, unpredictable, and mysterious.

All that said, as Livia banged on the closet door, hitting wood with metal, Viola had sufficient time to escape to the cold comforts of the St. Angelo Hotel. Viola Ambrose was a child, powerless to save herself against the madness of the mother who meant to destroy her. It would have been normal, even expected, for her to have fled the brutality that descended upon Aster.

But Viola, though only a girl of twelve, couldn't bear the thought of her counterpart being slain by a mother she loved. Had she left her host, Aster McAllister would have opened the closet door and experienced firsthand the cruel smiting by her own flesh and blood.

When she had first died, her father Alexander had shown her mercy by doing it peacefully with gas. Now, unable to look after the fate of his daughter, this death would involve no such kindness.

Viola Ambrose did not think herself brave when the door splintered and broke open. Nor when she stood firm as the iron fractured her skull. She simply closed her eyes and knew that the nightmare would be over soon.

On the Dead Side, Viola and Alexander argued for a long while. Everything had been set up perfectly, but her refusal to accept her new life had raised Livia's suspicions and ruined the plan. Alexander was just doing what anybody would have done in similar circumstances. People didn't matter, only they did. There weren't such things as good and evil. He would find a way back with or without her.

In the end, their split was mutual. Alexander no longer needed his daughter to return to the living, and Viola didn't get proper parenting whether she followed him or not. Aster's death sat at her feet and she wouldn't add another, no matter the cost to herself.

Her father stormed away in the heat of passion, unsure how to proceed in a great many matters. Whether this was a blessing or a curse, Alexander McAllister had survived in a coma. This left Ambrose a stronger link in the world than any other could provide, albeit through a host that was comatose. Alexander once again resumed inhabiting other bodies temporarily for his own means. After time and retrospection, he also reconsidered his feelings for his daughter and looked for her. Surprisingly, she was absent.

The little girl had decided to act on her own for the first time in her life. Instead of being the victim of abandonment yet again, it was she who had left her father. She took up private residence in the St. Angelo Hotel, a spot only she was familiar with, and kept her head down. She clung to the pocket watch, if only to keep it from her father. Viola Ambrose had no more family, living or dead, and she was reborn as her favorite color, Violet.

Along the course of the living, a forgotten Hamilton pocket watch found its way to a little antique shop in Burbank...

Chapter 32

My beleaguered psyche was devastated by the time Alexander Ambrose finished his account. I could barely muster the strength to face the floor.

Here was a man, standing before me, guilty of crimes of supreme evil. He was a man that had stopped at nothing for his own selfish gain and likely had greater designs ahead. It seemed that this man, above all, deserved the brunt of my vengeful attention.

But the quiet sobbing of a little girl tugged at me harder than the devil ever could.

I'd always thought of Violet as my sidekick. My little sister even. Now it was hard to get past the fact that she had betrayed me. She was the very incarnation of what I fought against, under my nose the entire time.

How had I been so blind?

I tried to rationalize the deception. She'd only been a kid

listening to her father. She didn't know what she was doing. She had tried, in the end, to do the right thing. But all my excuses rang hollow.

Alexander Ambrose stood tall and proud over my hunched form that leaned against the wall, and only the guilty tears of my friend mattered.

"You told me Pearl was an accident," muttered Violet, under her breath.

Alexander furrowed his strong brow. "What?"

"Fingal's wife," said Violet, raising her voice. "You told me she fell down the hill by accident."

"Ah," replied the man, a morose look on his face. Perhaps he'd gotten carried away in his exposition and revealed too much. He had likely mentioned facts that Violet herself had never known. He'd told so many lies over the years that he probably didn't even realize what it was she was supposed to believe.

"You monster," I said. "How could you have done all this to those people? To your own daughter?"

I stood up feebly as I addressed him. I had no strength. Or will. All it took was his cane to hold me at bay, the alabaster rose at my chest.

"Tut, tut, Mr. Butcher. I have come to you to confess the past with the purpose of putting it behind us."

"You expect me to believe that?"

"I do," he answered. "I will not pretend to be a noble man—pragmatism has always defined me—but a checkered past will either force a man to take stock of himself or continue on his way to destruction. I have shattered lives. I have lost my daughter. My prizes? Suffering at the hands of the Royals, withstanding a prison sentence, and bearing the agony of coma."

I considered them both. Violet's expression showed that she thought he was just as full of shit as I did. The girl had worked over the years to show remorse. I didn't know her intent, I had to admit, and she had continually lied to me, but she had stopped killing people.

"What's your business with Alexander McAllister?" I demanded.

"He is a susceptible man and he is rich," he replied. "I should know—I made him both of those things. I admit I have watched him. Purely for his benefit, of course." Alexander must have seen the disbelief on my face, so he explained. "You must have noticed I have not taken the man. Does that not lend me a spatter of credibility?"

"I know about Bedros," was all I answered.

"Yes, of course. Your touch. The Armenian was an associate of Finlay's, by which I mean, mine. His watchful eye has done much of my work for me. Although you must excuse him. He is quick to judgment and action alike, and he had you pegged for a thrall of Red Hat. You will find the man completely harmless from now on."

"Harmless?" I asked incredulously. "He's supplanting the life of a human being. He's next on my list for expulsion, if you don't mind." I added the last part in a tone mocking the polite indifference of Ambrose. He actually seemed amused.

"Of course," he said. "By all means, you are certainly welcome to try, but the sage that you find so efficacious against the addicts may do you little good against the Armenian. And I am afraid he is well past my advice on the matter."

I thought the situation over. It would be great to not worry about Alexander McAllister anymore. If Ambrose truly cut him free, if Bedros backed off, then half my worries would be solved. I didn't even need to consider how to approach the man again or introduce him to Violet—his true daughter was far from my reach, and I had no more business with him.

But it seemed too easy. I had looked in on the family too far to just let it go that quickly, especially since I only got the confession when I was on the verge of discovering it myself. It's easy to apologize after getting caught—the true merit of a man lies in what he does beforehand.

"You killed a man," I said, my confidence against the man growing. "Just two days ago, to avoid being caught. That doesn't strike me as someone who's turned a new leaf."

Ever formal, Alexander conceded my point with a nod as if we were debating politics. "My morals have never aligned with most, Mr. Butcher. I have already admitted that killing Sal was a mistake, but ultimately he was just a tool in a larger project."

"And what kind of tool am I?" I asked indignantly.

The man smiled softly. "A hammer, Mr. Butcher. For the first time in a century, I have met another man who would go against the Royals. It is true what they say," spoke the man, looking to his daughter and then back at me. "Misery acquaints a man with strange bedfellows."

The lobby of the St. Angelo Hotel drew silent as Alexander Ambrose waited for my answer. Violet, drying her face, maintained her balance of animosity and fright. I had been told not to trust shades, and the events taking place supported that maxim, but I could have used a tool or two myself.

"Go on," I said.

"You've got to be kidding me," berated Violet. "After everything he just told you, Dante."

"At least he told me."

The girl's look pierced my heart. I felt subdued on the inside, unable to continue, but my practiced countenance remained firm.

Alexander proceeded to explain his plan. "I have already admitted to being in league with Red Hat as a means of spying on them, but I owe them no affiliation for previous favors. In fact, the Royals know nothing about who I truly am."

"Who are they?"

"The more powerful of the shades who control the company, many having lived at the time of the Royal Ruby Millinery. Make no mistake, sir, they are your enemy. Not the company. Certainly not me. I will stay out of your affairs save to assist you against the Royals."

"You can't trust him," said Violet.

Alexander did not appear miffed. "I do not ask for trust. I have laid the truth bare for your sole discretion, Mr. Butcher. Keep your actions to yourself. Involve my daughter or do not. It is entirely up to you. Just know that a hammer striking nails into a wall makes a great deal of sound, but unless you are hitting the studs true, your work is for naught."

The man had charisma. No one else could sound a convincing ally so soon after confessing to murder.

"So where do I strike?" I asked.

"I would recommend surveying the scene first," he answered. "You have a party to go to, Mr. Butcher."

Chapter 33 - Friday

A thick rain fell on Los Angeles through the morning. It was the season for it, but weeks could pass before it happened again. This type of weather, the type that blots out the sun and lingers more than a day, is not a staple of the city. It happens once or twice a year. But it never feels native.

LA is meant to be mired in dirt, caked in its own decadence. No rain or snow or gloom; the constant sameness disguises the passage of time. The unending sun serves as a source of pride to the city's inhabitants. It also prevents their rebirth. There is no pause for reflection on the lives led under the spotlight. The sun rises and sets, like divine clockwork, and we power ever forward.

Being from Miami, I'd always found moments like these to be a gift. It was the rain that stripped us of our pretenses, that beleaguered us with our own helplessness. This mortal coil had a grander design than I'd ever ventured to explain. And why try? It wasn't for me to set all right with the world.

I didn't need any master plan. For the most part, I'd always settled for the washing away of the dirt.

I lay in my bed staring at the dark ceiling, listening to the patter of drops die down. The pocket watch sat on my nightstand. I knew it was there but I kept my gaze off it. My thoughts, however, were not as tightly under my control. I had stripped away all of Violet's past deeds and reacquainted her with her father. What more evil could I have wrought on her?

I left her quietly and jumped into the shower. Defining the past helped little to predict what was in store for me tonight. The unknown was ahead. Like the city, if I was to face it, I could use a cleaning.

I let forty-five minutes pass before I was back in my room, renewed. It was brighter in here. I could see the sun gaining strength between the vertical blinds. I trudged over to the window and drew it open. The clouds were set to give way and the earth, to dry. It was to be a normal Southern California day after all.

So much for reflection.

"That's the one," I said to Violet, pointing at my laptop screen. I was sitting in the living room now, pillow behind my back, leaning towards the coffee table. It was a meager workstation, but it was the only one I had, and it sure beat a cubicle.

This is the worst plan ever.

"I can't just stroll into a private party," I reasoned. "Not one run by Red Hat. They're professional event organizers. They also happen to be run by a secretive cabal of shades. I think the security's bound to be tight."

So you're going to disguise yourself as someone from the catering company? It sounds like something from a bad detective novel.

I shook my head. I agreed that it wasn't ideal but Violet couldn't offer anything better. It was a silly argument, but it allowed us both to stall the inevitable conversation of trust and betrayal until later. It was enough to process that Violet was really Viola Ambrose, the daughter of my enemy. The fact that she was ashamed of her past scored points with me —I just didn't know if it was enough. I decided that distracting myself was all I could handle right now.

"You would have me just walk up and, if I get caught, play dumb? Just tell them I thought the party was open to the public?"

There's always a chance of getting caught. You're less likely to explain it away if you're wearing a fake catering uniform.

Her argument was sound. The image of me trying to talk my way out of that brought a smile to my lips. It reminded me of an *I Love Lucy* situation, and one copied by every sitcom ever since. But it didn't solve our problem.

I had known about this party for days. Instead of preparing for it, I'd spent the week digging into Violet's history. Now the moment was upon us and I felt unready.

Between Red Hat and Alexander McAllister and work, I was stretched too thin. It was likely to lead to mistakes where they were least afforded.

"So then we need to go to the Red Hat offices," I offered. "We need to see if there's a way we could schmooze ourselves into the party."

After what my father did to Sal, we shouldn't go anywhere near there. Besides, what if you just make your intent on sneaking in more obvious by bothering them?

"And Soren?" I pointed out. "He's a guest of honor. Maybe he could score us an invite."

Maybe.

It seemed easy enough, except he hadn't told us about the party. In fact, I had to go through his wallet drawer to discover his secret gig in the first place.

We probably don't want him to know you're there, though. It might change... What are we expecting to happen anyway?

"Shit, I have no idea. The Royals are placing themselves close to Soren in hopes of possessing him without much notice. That requires a change in his lifestyle and circle of friends. This party is a start to that."

What if they mean to take him tonight?

"We can't rule it out. We need to be ready for anything." I leaned back on the sofa, abandoning the research into the service companies at the party. "One thing's for sure, he will have contact with Red Hat agents, maybe even the Royals. Trailing him will get us a list of people to watch."

I picked up my cell phone and scrolled through my

contacts until my finger rested on Pam. Violet had a point. What I did best was blend in with the other partiers. Showing up in the garb of an employee would hinder me more than help. Better to keep things natural.

It's a risk to let him know.

I knew it was. I didn't want to do it, but I couldn't show up with nothing.

Before I could call her, I heard a firm knock on my door.

No one visited me. Not unannounced, especially. I had no family in California. I wasn't dating anyone, and if I were, they wouldn't show up without a phone call or there wouldn't be any more dates. No. It had to be a mistake. Or a solicitor. I remained seated and waited for the person to go away.

Instead, they knocked again, this time louder. I sighed and got up, in a mind to not be very polite to the person handing out flyers or trying to sell me magazine subscriptions. Without much thought, I swung the door open. A large Armenian man towered in the hall.

I nearly jumped but didn't want to alarm him. Really, I didn't want to show him that I was alarmed. "Bedros," I said coolly.

He pulled his hand from behind his back and presented it in front of him. I'm not proud to admit that I flinched. Then I saw he was offering me a glossy black envelope. "With compliments. From Mr. Ambrose."

I almost laughed. I was a bit embarrassed about the flinching thing, but it was more than that. This gruff man's attempt to be genteel was unnatural. Just as it was for

Bedros to be an ally. He should be trying to smash my face in. I should be putting him in a headlock. Still, the man harbored no hostility towards me at the moment. While I didn't reciprocate the feeling, that grudge was best left for another day. I took the envelope.

Bedros gave a curt nod and walked away without another word. He didn't even gloat.

Back on the couch, I opened the envelope with the delicacy of a child on Christmas. Inside was a rectangular flyer on thick stock, twice as glossy as the wrapping. A small red bow was tied around the bottom and held a ticket the size of a business card, in the shape of a red hat.

It was a formal invitation to the party.

Still think the catering thing is a good idea?

"Still think your father can't offer us anything?"

It was a petty retort. I regretted bringing it up, mainly because the topic skirted dangerously close to admitting that the two of us had a lot to talk about.

In truth, I wasn't comfortable with Alexander Ambrose one bit. Case in point: he'd sent his goon to my front door. No one had ever come to me like that before.

I hurried to the closet and retrieved a hammer from my toolbox. I know Ambrose said I was a hammer, but the real world didn't run on metaphors. I pounded a single nail in the middle of the doorframe, above the front door. Then I scooped Soren's horseshoe ring off the coffee table and slipped it in place. In the old days, real horseshoes were hung in thresholds to ward off spirits. I was hoping the ring at least worked on Armenians.

Chapter 34

Griffith Park is a funny place. It's the Central Park of Los Angeles, more or less, except that it's much larger and more sprawling. The park contains mountains, hiking trails, the famous Hollywood sign, the Greek Theatre, and the Los Angeles Zoo. Still, despite its size, it is easier to miss than its New York counterpart. It doesn't sit in the middle of Downtown flush with skyscrapers; it's offset from the city proper a bit, extending to Hollywood and Burbank and lining the Valley.

The scope of the park is impressive. In places it appears feral, more like a state park than a municipal one, but if you keep to the roads it's easy enough to navigate. Near the bottom edge of the grounds, sitting on the top of a mountain and facing the LA Basin, is the Griffith Park Observatory.

This public science center is an Art Deco wonder.

Besides the planetarium shows, everything is free. Accessible to the public is, among other things, a Tesla Coil and a pendulum that swings with the rotation of the Earth. The large domes, intricate tiling, and mountainside grounds create pure architectural splendor.

And tonight it was all closed for a private party.

On the road below, a guard checked my invitation just to drive farther in. I found a parking spot with some difficulty, and it was still a fifteen minute hike to the peak, during which I passed another security checkpoint on foot. There were lots of trees and natural paths that avoided the street. I silently took note of which routes were clear in case I would need to sneak out. From my passing observations, no staff members were guarding the forest.

The sun was nearly set and the sky was filled with an otherworldly pink that blended into a deep blue overhead. Not a cloud on the horizon. The view of the city, washed clean of the smog by the recent rain, was breathtaking. The air was clear and the streetlights began to glow: the magic of the night was upon me already, even before I heard the music.

Techno winded through the trees and descended the mountain to the ears of those climbing the steps. A series of blue lights around the observatory lined the large courtyard and revealed the packs of people standing on the grass. Although I could see the event in the distance, it still took another five minutes to wind around the street to reach it. There, a man in a suit patted me down and checked my invitation. Easily enough, I entered as a guest.

The trance music was deafening.

This was an industry party, for sure. From their styles of dress and their attitudes, I quickly pegged several musicians, promoters, and donors. It wasn't just Red Hat either, but their associates. There was enough here to appear legitimate, at the very least.

As I stepped through the crowd, I brushed my shoulders against the throng, searching for second shadows out of habit. Again, despite my initial expectations, everything was above board. Not a shade in the house. That set my mind at ease. I'd been afraid I was walking into a wolves' den. Now I just hoped I could find the predators among the prey.

I slipped the Hamilton watch into my hand.

Well, we're here.

"Mmm hmm," I hummed under my breath.

Now what?

"Isn't it obvious?" I asked, watching the crowd swirl before me like the rough seas. "It's time for a drink."

I found the bar and ordered a Bacardi and coke. The selection wasn't my fault—that was the only rum they had. And if that was weak, the pour was even worse. It was hard to work the bartender at a place like this, too. Either they had been told to skimp on the alcohol or they didn't know what a proper drink tasted like. I finished my cup in the same area while I got a lay of the land, then ordered a double the next time around.

Don't you think you should go easy on the rum?

"I've—"

Got it under control?

I smiled. She was familiar with my methods by now. I wanted to give her a snarky reply but there was a cute girl standing next to me and I didn't want to explain about my talking watch. Still, Violet had a decent point. It wasn't that I couldn't handle my drinks—but it was quickly getting dark.

The courtyard was divided by a stone spire. The DJ, and the thick of the crowd, were on the opposite side. After I sipped my drink down enough so that it wouldn't spill, I entered the fray. On the makeshift stage were two guys spinning on old-fashioned turntables that sat in antique suitcases. Their music was spooky and sampled old radio shows and the like. It was experimental in a way that Soren might have liked, better than his stuff even, but DJ Ingress was nowhere around. I kept wandering.

The inside of the building was closed off. That's what I was told, anyway, when I approached. It seemed believable since I doubted the museum could handle this kind of crowd. No one visibly went inside, either. But since I found myself with nothing else to do, I decided to double-check.

The side of the grounds had a line of port-o-potties, each attracting a pilgrimage of worshippers. I strolled past to the walkway running along the observatory and climbed the stone steps. There was no security in sight.

The building had multiple levels and paths surrounding it, all outdoors and freely accessible. As I headed to the back, some small groups walked by me. The strong smell of pot flooded my nose. Of course. The music was fainter here and there was less added lighting due to the event. This was the perfect place to chill out away from the crowd.

Just in case Soren was somewhere out here, I circled the grounds.

"It's still early," I said, swinging the watch.

That means we might have three hours of DJs to wait out.

"Nah. No way Soren is headlining. They'll put him up first."

Or last.

"Maybe, but he'll be around otherwise. That's when we need to be watching him anyway. I was hoping there would be another DJ booth somewhere, but that doesn't look to be the case."

We were alone near the back railing, on a thin walkway set against the building and the sheer edge of the mountain. It made for a beautiful view. I leaned against the railing, listening to the muffled music, rubbing the chill air away.

It's good to be on the hunt again.

I winced. That sounded dangerously close to a lead-in to a conversation I didn't want to have.

"What are we doing here?" I suddenly asked. The unspoken nagging doubt was the only distraction that came to mind. "This doesn't feel right."

I sighed and studied the moon. Maybe I was getting jumpy for no reason. Granted, I didn't take Alexander Ambrose directly at his word—there was no way he was being completely straight with me—but I would've come to this party with or without him. As the man had said, I was close enough to discovering everything. Why, then, did I feel like I was being played?

I heard a giggle below me. To the side of the building, the way I had come, there was a walkway leading down the mountainside. Not all the way; it was just a gated path with a view. I noticed two girls hopping up the steps.

I approached them as they reached the walkway. The girls were Asian, and I had seen them before. I was particularly interested in the short one wearing bright yellow. I was on the level above them and they were going the other way, so I had to call out.

"Eva!"

The straight platinum hair spun around and her doe eyes were wide open for a brief moment. Then the recognition hit her and she smiled.

"Dante!"

"Good memory," I said. I waved to her friend, not sure if I had ever caught her name. "What are you ladies doing out here?"

Maybe it was because I was standing on a platform just above her, looking down, but she seemed shorter and skinnier than when we had last met. Not in a bad way, though. The tight yellow dress she wore hugged her form well. Her cleavage and legs competed in showing more skin and the moonlight caught a shine on her lips. I was immediately struck by how beautiful she was. I wanted her more than ever.

"I," she said, pausing to place emphasis on herself, "was invited." She looked up at me questioningly. "I didn't know you were in the biz."

"You don't know anything about me," I answered with a

smile.

She stood still and batted her eyelashes playfully. "I know you probably crashed this party like you wanted to crash my little K-town shindig."

It was true I had wanted her to invite me, but then I never would've hooked up with Rachel. I thought things worked out for the best. "What were you afraid of? That I was dangerous?"

"No," she said. "Where we were going, they don't let white people in. White people talk to the police." Her friend giggled.

"I'm the last person that would shut down an after-hours drinking operation."

"They don't know that. For all they care, you could be an undercover cop yourself."

I nodded smugly. She wasn't making this easy. "Who said I wasn't?"

Her girlfriend started walking along the overhang, towards the staircase that would lead them up to my level. Eva followed her slowly.

"I didn't know there was anything here worth keeping an eye on," she said.

I walked along the upper rail, in step with her. "From where I'm standing, I'd disagree." Eva tried to hide her pleasure at my compliment, but I caught her forming a slight smile. She continued parading behind her friend. I finished the rest of my cocktail in a single gulp and set the plastic cup on the concrete railing. She was sexy, and the banter was fun, but I wanted to get to more important matters. "What is it that you do, Eva?"

She looked at her friend as she started up the staircase. "I'm a... promoter... at Korean clubs." The friend said something in the language and they both giggled. I stopped and waited for them at the top of the steps. The girls were having an interesting time of it in their high heels.

"Any places I would know?" I asked. They just giggled again.

At the top of the staircase, I held out my hand to the friend to help her up the last step. She accepted, but as I tried to do the same for Eva, the friend stumbled and pressed against me. I caught her and she leaned into me, staying for a moment. By then, Eva had already sauntered past me, shooting me a glare.

"Liz is drunk," she said. "It's shameful. Koreans are the Irish of the Asians. They should be able to handle their whiskey."

I had to think about that for a second, but it was hilarious. "A girl who knows how to drink. I like you more already."

Liz kept leaning on me for support as I escorted them back to the front courtyard. I wanted to disengage with her so I could get closer to Eva, but I didn't want to look like a dick. It was bad enough that I was one. Still, I suspected that Liz wasn't as drunk as she was acting and that they were having fun with me.

By the time I had gotten Liz to stand up on her own, Eva disappeared around the corner ahead of us. We hurried to catch up but the crowd was thick. I couldn't see her. Liz grabbed my hand and pulled me towards the bar.

A different DJ was spinning now, some bald Mexican dude who wasn't wearing a shirt. The beat was harder and more disjointed, with some dubstep influences, and the crowd was more active. I still didn't see Soren anywhere.

As we pushed to the bar, Eva was already coming back with three plastic cups half filled with liquor.

"Chivas," she said, handing them to us.

I wasn't the biggest fan of scotch, but this wasn't the place or time to object. I held my glass up to match the girls.

"One shot," said Eva, and we downed the oversized drinks.

My mouth burned with a pleasant heat. We all laughed. I knew I was on a job, but I'd always been able to do two things at once. Besides, being at a party without finding fun was worse than work. Liz took the empty cups away. I saw an opening and put my hand on the small of Eva's back to pull her closer to me.

Unyielding and with a great sense of momentum to it, the feeling struck me like a train. As my arm brushed against her, I could feel the foreign presence that resided within her. The second shadow. Eva, this beautiful, fun girl, was taken.

She caught my momentary shock and looked at me strangely. "What is it?" she asked.

"You're..." I started. I didn't know what to say. The realization didn't sit well with me, but I had to play it off. I couldn't let her know that I knew. Not here. Not now. "You're so small," I said, looking her over. "I bet I can pick you up."

I grabbed the girl by her hips and lifted. Her hands clutched the back of my neck. I was never wrong about this kind of thing, but something in me hoped I'd made a mistake. As I spun around in a full circle, her small feet trailing in the air, there could be no denying it. She was one of them. Before I released her to the ground, I took one last breath of her platinum hair. As our cheeks lightly brushed, I privately cursed my hidden talents.

Just this once, I wanted to be normal.

She giggled as Liz returned and they both shared a devious exchange in Korean. Each of them grabbed one of my hands and dragged me to the dance floor.

Maybe it was the whiskey, or maybe it was being sandwiched between two pretty girls, but I let the music take me over.

Chapter 35

Two skinny black dudes shared a set, and then a guy with sunglasses and a cowboy hat took over. This was the only stage at the party and the DJs only had twenty or thirty minutes each to make an impression. It was a lively time, one I began to enjoy rather than observe. Dancing and drinks led the night toward its end, and I had still not seen Soren.

It's now or never.

Violet had put up with me long enough. Perhaps, after what had gone down on the Dead Side, she'd given me more leeway than usual. She didn't start complaining the second I was hitting on a girl. But even I conceded I was stretching the limits of what was reasonable. I couldn't dance with Eva all night.

I herded them to the side of the dance floor. It was a cool night—not uncomfortable—but our bodies were slick with sweat all the same. I needed a chance to stop. To think.

The girls wanted to walk to their dark path and smoke a joint.

"I'm looking for a friend," I said, shaking my head. "He said he would be here."

"Come on," said Liz. "Don't you want to go somewhere quiet?"

I did. I really did. But I changed the subject all the same.

"Eva, do you know any of the DJs spinning tonight? Have you heard of DJ Ingress?"

She shook her head. "I'm more customer-facing. I don't deal with the musicians at all. Most of them are jerks anyway. Let's go. It'll be quick."

The problem, I decided, with working at parties was that I could never cut loose. Not completely. "How about I catch up with you later?" I offered.

They tried to convince me some more, then Eva got a little hot and complained. I thought her little tantrum was cute. It reminded me of the first time I had seen her, yelling outside a taxi. It wasn't anything serious, just part of her personality, and her friends were used to it. Liz calmed her down. They eventually left me by the dance floor, and I again set myself to searching the crowd.

It was a loose event: no rigid structure, no corporate announcements, no middle management leading team-building exercises. Thus far, for all I could tell, this was just another party thrown by Red Hat Events. Sure, maybe all the guests were connected to the company in some way, but I didn't see anything sketchy going on. It made me think.

I toyed with the antique watch in my palm.

You think she's a Royal?

"What—Eva?" The thought hadn't even occurred to me. "No way. Her second shadow didn't feel especially strange... although I couldn't place her pleasure."

What, you can feel what kind of shade they are now?

"...I don't know. I mean, she's drinking and smoking out. But she's not just looking for an easy fix. She doesn't strike me as a fiend, like the shade that was in Soren. Then again, I don't think she's masterminding anything."

Would you be able to see if she were?

The thought put a sour taste in my mouth. "Trust me. After recent events, I'm not taking anything at face value."

That's when I noticed John standing in the crowd. He was an older Chinese man, in his forties, who I regularly ran into in the nightlife. We weren't friends. In fact, sometimes it felt like just the opposite. I didn't know what he thought of me exactly, but his motivations were easy enough to peg. Our needs often overlapped. Still, I always had the feeling that I had to watch my back around him.

I approached him from behind, not announcing myself until I was upon him. "Still fighting through the economic downturn, I see."

John flipped around. His face was pockmarked a bit and his hair was short in a crew cut, but otherwise he wasn't very memorable at all. He dressed plainly, except for a blue and white windbreaker. The man always appeared unassuming; in fact, it was his business strategy.

"What do you want, Butcher?"

"I should have known I'd see you here," I said, yelling a little louder than I liked. The music was pumping and the crowd was really going for it. I motioned my head to the side and John followed me a bit farther from the speaker system. "You get around," I said. "I was wondering if you'd heard of a DJ playing tonight. Ingress?"

John eyed me coldly. "I don't run the shows. I supply them. You always ask too many questions, anyway." He looked around a bit, then reached into his pocket and produced a baggy of pills. "What do you want, Butcher?"

"Is it always about drugs to you?" I asked with a smile.

He didn't see the humor in the remark and put the bag away. "Get out of here, man."

"Why?"

"You're bad for business," he answered. "Trouble follows you."

"John, you know those guys always threw the first punch."

"Hey man, I'm a lover, not a fighter. I stay away from drama. I don't need that bullshit."

"Listen," I said, catching his arm before he turned away, "who's running this party? What else is going down here besides this dance floor?"

"Fuck you," he said.

"It's an easy question, John. Where's the Red Hat management?"

The dealer looked around again, then put his hand in his pocket. "Seventy-five bucks."

"Seventy-five? Don't you know this is a down market?"

"Hey man," he said, holding firm, "do you think any of these assholes pay attention to Wall Street?"

I smirked and begrudgingly pulled out my money clip. This was John's way of getting his back scratched too. I handed him the cash.

"There's a side entrance, by the cafe. It's closed off for some VIPs but pretty quiet. I heard about someone interviewing in there, but you'll probably just find some groupies having sex with their boss."

"What boss?"

"I don't know. You asked for Red Hat management, right? I don't know their names, but they're the only ones with access to the inside of the observatory."

I nodded as he slipped two pills into my palm. For seventy-five bucks, I should've gotten three.

"I think you forgot one," I said.

"Nah," he returned, "that's a special price, just for you. Because we're friends." He stormed off.

I stared at the capsules in the palm of my hand. "Well fuck you too," I muttered under my breath.

Chapter 36

I wandered to the side of the building I hadn't been to yet. There was a similar path around the observatory that circled to the back, but there were also some steps down to a lower level sitting flush with the mountain. That's where the restaurant was. A makeshift gate closed it off. I watched it for a while from a distance. No one came or went.

I passed by the regular path and headed to the back, glancing in the likely direction of Eva and Liz. I was too far to see them on this side. It was for the best—I'd been distracted enough tonight.

I waited as a couple strolled by, whispering in each other's ears. Then, when I was alone, I approached another staircase that was cordoned off. I didn't see anybody watching it, above or below. As quietly as I could, I descended to the outdoor cafe.

Rows of plastic tables and chairs filled the platform.

Glass windows revealed the same inside, but the doors were locked. Everything was hushed out here. Nobody was around. Even the techno music seemed to lack access to this restricted area and did its best to quiet itself. Without a crowd for cover, I felt strangely out of place, and I knew acting with temerity here would spell danger.

As I snuck around the dimly lit plaza, I noticed a man in a suit near the front of the building, away from the cafe. He appeared to be guarding a door. I was betting it was unlocked.

The second he sees you, he'll raise the alarm.

"No way," I said quietly. "This is a party, just like every club we've worked. People will always believe you're an idiot before they suspect any wrongdoing."

But these guys are smart.

"Some of them, maybe, but that guy? If he was smart or important, he wouldn't be standing next to a door." After staking out the scene for an acceptable length of time and not seeing any activity, I lit a sage cigarette.

Just be careful.

"When am I not?"

The man in the suit spied me before I wanted him to, but I approached him with the confidence he would have expected from a drunk.

"You can't be here," he said.

"Yo," I started, ignoring his comment and talking in a whisper to draw his curiosity, "have you seen two hot chicks walking around out here?" I looked back and forth as if they were just around the corner.

"No one is out here. You need to go."

I took a drag from my cigarette and looked him over. The dude was about my height but I could see his biceps through his jacket. He obviously worked out and could handle himself in a fair fight, but he was a young guy, and we all had our weaknesses.

"Sorry, I know, but the thing is, they said they were desperate for these." I flashed him the pills I had bought. "They didn't have any money, if you know what I mean."

The guy smiled. I had disarmed him of any suspicion, at least. "Good for you, but you're gonna need to get your blowjob somewhere else."

I chuckled and leaned against the wall, close to him. "If only. You should see these chicks. One of them is a spinner, a tiny body with an even tinier dress. She has amazing lips. And the other, she has curves for an Asian chick. I think her boobs might be fake. The small one has pale skin and the other has kind of a permanent tan. Let me just say that I slipped some peeks and I haven't seen any tan lines yet." I looked to the bouncer and leaned in. "You sure you haven't seen those girls wandering around? They said they were gonna be at the cafe."

The guy raised his eyebrows and relaxed his strong features. "I would know if I'd seen those two chicks."

I nodded. "You wouldn't believe it. So get this. They didn't want to give me a blowjob. Said they were too good for that or something." I rolled my eyes, a bit too much, I thought. I was having fun describing Eva and Liz as nymphomaniac groupies. "But I think they're lesbians or something, because they told me, if I gave them the molly, they would kiss and touch each other while I watched."

"I don't know," said the guy. "It sounds like you're giving your stuff away too easily. Just to see them make out?"

I slid along the wall, next to him. "Without their dresses on."

He kind of bounced his head up and down as he considered the trade. "Still..."

"They're not wearing any underwear."

"Well shit," he said. "Why didn't you mention that?"

I smiled. "You sure you don't mind if I wait around for at least one smoke?" I pulled out my pack and offered him one before he could realize he hadn't invited me to stay. "Listen, dude, if we tell them you work here, I'll bet they'd let us both watch."

The guy pondered my offer quietly. He pulled the cigarette to his lips and I lit it.

"But no touching," I stressed. It was almost too good to be true, and I didn't want him thinking I made up the entire situation. I gave out enough to entice him but dialed it back enough to be plausible. "They made me promise."

He smirked and took a drag. "No problem. I get paid to keep an eye out, anyway."

We laughed and settled in to our smokes.

Cigarettes aren't a great habit. I don't like the health ramifications, but I've done worse. To be honest, I only smoke socially or for utility. There's a kinship among smokers. Even more so, now that it's going out of style.

Smoking is the last vestige for men to have quiet moments with each other. It's a way to do something without doing anything at all. And, especially in times like this, smoking is a way to kill some time without asking for any other pretense to fill the void.

"This is a nice place," I said after a minute had passed. "Have you seen that Tesla Coil inside?"

"I've never been here before."

"No shit? You should check it out before you leave. Maybe they'll let us turn it on."

He shook his head vigorously. "Can't do it." The guy cleared some phlegm from his throat. "The big dogs are inside tonight. It's closed to the public."

I noticed his every mannerism. The way he talked. The way he smoked. I could tell he was one of them without even touching him. The question was, how strong was he?

"Different pay grade, huh?" I asked.

"You know it."

He coughed after his answer. "What kind of cigarette is this? It's pretty harsh."

"Yeah," I agreed. "It's a clove. From Indonesia. I think they're illegal now." I laid down the standard peer pressure stuff. Trying to make it sound casually cool. "Pretty good, huh?"

He inhaled again. "I guess."

After I'd given my pack to Catriona, I made a new batch. Since I had trouble with Soren and Bedros seemed immune, I upped the ratio of white sage in the recipe. It was more obvious now, but discretion was only valuable when the subterfuge worked. Alexander Ambrose had called me a hammer. Sometimes, to get the nail in, you needed to pound harder than usual.

The bouncer took a hasty step away from the wall and caught himself. He tossed the cigarette and shook his head rapidly, as if he was snapping himself awake.

"Watch it," I said, "you don't want the big dogs to see you slacking."

He leaned forward and put his hands on his knees for support. He spit on the cement. "Hey, listen. I don't see these lesbian sluts anywhere."

"Well, if they were sluts then they'd also be liars."

"What?" he asked, turning his head to look at me for a second. "Why do you say that?"

"How many times have you ever seen someone admit to being a slut?"

"Right." He tried to chuckle and let his head fall again. "Okay then, I guess you should go."

I nodded but remained leaning on the wall. I glanced up and down the stone platform as I finished my cigarette. Save for the muted beats in the distance and the occasional coughing and spitting, the area was silent.

"About that," I said, approaching him. "What if I were to go inside instead?"

The guy's face became muddled. He struggled to stand up straight. "That would be a bad idea."

"Why is that? Who's in there? The Royals?"

He stiffened and latched on to me, pressing me to the wall. "Who the hell are you?"

I stayed there for a moment, watching as the bouncer used what little strength he had left. Then I casually swiped his hands away. Without me supporting his weight, he buckled to his knees, coughing.

"I'm just a guy," I answered. "Why does everybody always ask me that?"

The dude struggled to remain upright. He didn't say anything.

"I'm sorry to inform you that Red Hat may have overstated the type of life they could offer you."

"You mother—"

The man collapsed. I rolled him over and leaned him against the wall, to make it look like he was sleeping. He would probably wake up within minutes, devoid of the stranger.

"Finally," I said to Violet. "Something came easy." Then I slipped inside the observatory.

Chapter 37

It had been a while since I'd visited the museum, but the high marble walls and fancy tiles were familiar to me. As I entered the hall, the faded music outside re-energized and echoed through the chamber. There were speakers inside conveying the outside performance, although the source of the music was still farther away. This was good. I could identify Soren's post-modern techno in case he started a set.

The museum was dark, only lit for mood. Maybe John was right. I'd only find people fucking groupies in here. But I had to check. And everything here was empty. This wasn't the main part of the museum with the displays, but this was where Red Hat had chosen to have the entrance. They had to be close.

I walked lightly, making sure my sneakers didn't make a sound on the old tiles. It was strange walking in a public area like this when it was abandoned. Shut down. I felt like a cat burglar searching for treasures. There was something cool about that. It made it feel more like a mission. But then, it also made it more dangerous.

Speaking of missions, my thoughts strayed to the video games I worked on. I wondered if I had a life bar hovering over my head somewhere. Maybe I should look for some gold coins or something to collect.

I heard some laughing ahead and immediately pressed myself into an alcove. Two guys, maybe three. I peeked out but didn't see anyone. Then I heard footsteps from the group dispersing. A door closed. I waited but no one came my way.

Fuck. What was I doing here? What was I supposed to say if I got caught? The drunk routine wasn't likely to fly inside.

After seeing I was safe for a bit longer, I resumed my careful advance down the hallway. Still no people in sight, but the music was getting louder. It sounded as though the audio was coming from my flank. As I walked by a door, I pinpointed the source.

The door was skinny and made of wood, with a detail outline of antique brass to match the doorknob. It was snug in its marble frame, the product of an era when precision mattered, so I couldn't see if any light was on inside. I pressed my ear against the wood. The music was definitely coming from within.

I peered up and down the empty hall and took a breath. I had to enter. Everything I'd done so far would be wasted if I didn't open the door. But I just stood there, thinking of the consequences of announcing myself.

Soren could be in there right now.

I nodded as I slid the Hamilton into my pocket. She was right.

Her point made no difference. I didn't open the door. Someone else did that for me. It swung past me and a stout man with a large belly and a bushy mustache stood on the threshold. He wore black leather pants around his tree trunks of legs. A white wifebeater clung to his enormous mass. There was some kind of weird metal jewelry around his neck. He looked like a Mexican old-timey circus strongman. The sort of dude that would play the bad guy's henchman in a Hollywood production. Scratch that. He loomed over me like the next challenger in *Super Punch Out*. And he was not pleased.

His bushy eyebrows crinkled over his face in befuddlement. Then his eyes darted past me and his mouth began to open in the formative stages of a wide scream.

He was about to call out to the others.

I charged forward, barreling my shoulder into his round gut. Immediately, the second shadow within became apparent. My focus, however, remained on dislodging the large man from the floor. His weight pressed soundly against me—but he wobbled. I'd caught him off-guard. He only managed a "humph" before he lost his footing and collapsed backwards. KO.

The strongman's back crashed into a coffee table. It was made of old wood and had a metalwork binding, like an antique trunk. The table was wide and low and solid. His back crunched against it and it didn't buckle in the slightest under his weight. Several laptops on the table didn't fare as well. His body smashed one and knocked another off like an explosion had gone off. It was a hard landing. He didn't get up quickly is what I'm saying. Flawless victory.

I glanced out the door behind me and didn't see any reaction to the sudden commotion. With that piece of good news, I pulled out a cigarette and shut the door.

"What are you doing in here?" I asked, inhaling the smoke calmly into my lungs.

This was a small sitting room. Just enough space for a low table, four velvet chairs, and a buffet sideboard. The carpeted room had a padded warmth to it that contrasted with the metal chandelier.

The man was splayed out over the table with his arms hanging over his head on the other side. I stepped around to look at the LCD screens and saw video streams, multiples on each monitor, of the party. Security video. He'd been watching the DJs, the bar, and the exterior. I couldn't see all of it because at least one of the laptops was under him.

As he stirred, I unplugged the nearest computer and tied his wrists together with the power cable. Up close, the metal band around his neck wasn't as crude as it had looked. Solid but with an intricate design etched into its mass. The weirdest thing was that I couldn't see how it came on or off.

"You're security, huh?" I blew some smoke into his face. "Except you weren't standing by the front door, so you're important."

He growled and I pilfered another cable. That's when I

noticed there was no other wiring in the room besides the power cables for the computers and speakers. The video surveillance and audio feeds must have been streaming over Wi-Fi. Pulling the cables didn't even turn the laptops off, as they had their own batteries. As the man began to grumble louder, I turned the dial on the speakers to increase the music volume. Infected Mushroom, an Israeli psytrance duo. Nice.

I bobbed my head to the beat as I tied the cable to his left foot. When the strongman saw what I was doing, he pushed against me with his leg. I tried to force his feet together, but his ankles were too wide to grip. He found the agility to sit up. Bound hands careened towards me. My arm blocked the shot but I was pushed back. The strongman lifted his massive frame off the table. Maybe not so flawless after all.

"You fucked up now," he warned.

I flicked my cigarette to the ground and ran straight at him. Instead of going for the gut again, I jumped over his lowered arms. My foot hit his chest, on the slope right on top of his belly. I pressed down hard and took my other foot to his shoulder, running up the large man like a staircase.

His arms clamped around my lower leg. It halted my momentum and I fell forward. My hands clasped onto the metal chandelier above us. With one leg caught, I rotated my body and wrapped my thighs around his neck. I ended up sitting on his shoulders, straddling his head. Good enough.

As he swiped up at me, I squeezed my legs together. I

tried to put pressure on the man's thick neck, but it wasn't easy. He was a strong guy—even his neck muscles were ripped. My legs had trouble finding a lock, and his metal jewelry didn't help.

Meanwhile, I was hanging on the chandelier with both arms, pulling my chest and head above it. Not only did I use it to keep from falling, but it worked as a shield against his prying fists. More than once, his knuckles banged hard into solid metal.

Clang. Clang. Clang. At best I was wearing him down. Why did life bars have to be invisible, anyway?

It was a bizarre scene. The pivoting chandelier threw spots of light across the walls. If I wasn't there, it would have looked as though the strongman was dancing, lurching with the high tempo beat blaring through the speakers. Adrenaline surged through me and I enjoyed the show.

The man was harried but far from defeated. He tried a new tactic: moving away from the chandelier. I used all my upper body strength to counter his pull, twisting his head sideways. Then I saw my opening.

I swung backwards hard, jerking his shoulder down and shifting his balance over the table again. With his hands still tied together, he failed to catch himself. The big man fell hard again. I was tugged down with him, and the chandelier with me. It pulled the plaster from the ceiling before I released my hold. Then we crunched to the floor. We both yelled in pain. The dislodged light fixture above hung precariously on its electric cable, swaying chaotically in an out-of-control dance.

As the electronic music shifted into dubstep, I pulled another laptop cable free and wrapped it twice around the man's neck. He had part of his weight on top of me by now. I had to fight hard or be smothered by him. With his back on me, he kicked violently. His strong legs shoved the coffee table towards the door and gave us more room to wrestle on the floor. Personally, I think I had better odds with the Ultimate Fighter.

I pulled desperately at the cable under his chin. His hands, side by side in a knot, heaved at his neck. I'd finally gotten a hold. The strongman was in trouble.

And then, instead of being cooperative and passing out, the man lifted his head as high as he could and slammed it into mine.

Critical hit. I was rocked with a boxer's blow. The same move was banned from MMA for being too destructive. One moment, the upper hand was mine, the next I was waking up in a daze. I hadn't been out long, just a second or two, but I had been out. Once, when I was younger, a guy had sucker punched me and the same thing happened. When I came to a split second later, I was still on my feet. To others, I must have just appeared hesitant. This moment was similarly brief because the Mexican strongman was only just removing the cable from his neck.

I grabbed the laptop on the floor next to me and shut it in the same motion. The man, still on the floor, turned to me. With both hands, I swung the computer and connected with the crown of his head.

He fell back. I sprang to my feet and tried to run past

him. Again, the big man caught my leg. I kicked at him as my hands clawed forward, trying to grab the table and pull myself away. It was no use. He was too powerful.

Instead, I gripped something else. The cable tied to his foot. As he tried to yank me back, I quickly tied the other end to the leg of the heavy wooden table.

Searing pain ripped into my calf. The dude fucking bit me. I shoved his head away with my other foot and he twisted me around. Then I rolled toward his face but past it, over his head.

As my back hit the corner of the small room, the Mexican slid forward to protect his aching head from any more blows. We instinctively rolled away from each other like oil and water. We both retreated to safety.

I rubbed my leg and pulled up my jeans to reveal a bleeding wound. It wasn't that deep—my bone had prevented too much penetration—but it hurt like a bitch.

On his end, the big man placed his bear hands, now freed from the cable, on the low table and lifted himself up. He spun around and sat down on top of it for a minute, panting hard. He was exhausted. So was I.

We sat there, at opposite ends of the tiny room, panting heavily, just out of reach of the other. It was like a boxing match when the bell has rung—we both respected the lull before round two began. No one made a move against the other. No one bothered to say anything. This fight had surprised us both, and neither fared well.

For a moment it seemed we were done. We would both recover, stand up, shake hands, and be on our way. But those paradoxical actions were common in fights between friends and brothers. Not this kind. Not with these people.

The strongman put his hands on his knees and lifted himself up with sheer will. I pressed my feet down and slid my back up along the wall. My left leg seared with pain.

"You're tough," he said.

I nodded to accept the compliment. "Listen," I rasped, "I'll tell you what. I'll lay off if you turn around and walk out of here right now."

He smiled. The door was behind him now. I was trapped in the room, and he had no intention of letting me go.

"What are you looking for?" he asked through his thick mustache.

My leg buckled as I put pressure on it. I almost fell but leaned back against the wall again. I didn't want to give him the satisfaction. He was standing, so I had to be too, no matter how hard that was. I didn't think anything was broken, but pain shot through the limb every time I used it.

"I'm serious," I warned. "Take this chance to get out of here."

The man's amusement came to an end. He reached down to his lower leg and pulled out a small machete from a zippered sheath. Was there such a thing as a small machete? Maybe it only looked puny in his massive hand.

"Seriously?" I asked, still gasping for air. So much for boxing metaphors.

The Mexican struck swiftly. He took two bold steps towards me. On the third, his bound leg still tied to the table tripped him up. As abruptly and wordlessly as he had intended to pounce on me, his head slammed into the floor.

I set my jaw and put my weight on my foot again. Ignoring the pulses of agony, I jumped up and grabbed onto the dangling chandelier. The strongman rose to his elbows as my weight came down and ripped the fixture from the ceiling. The heavy piece of metal landed with a solid thunk on the man's back and head.

I rolled away and knelt on the floor, watching him for some time. He didn't move again.

After some labored breaths, I lowered the volume so I could think. There was nothing in the room that could help me. The remaining video streams were standard security stuff. There were no documents or anything else to suggest who these men were. As far as I figured, I had just walked into the wrong room.

I sighed and rubbed my forehead. This was crap.

The only thing to do was to move on. I left the big man sleeping and exited the room, closing the door softly. Unfortunately, it took only five paces to notice the man standing in the hallway, watching me.

"What the—" I exclaimed.

Approaching me was the Mexican strongman, wearing the same white wifebeater and black leather pants and metal necklet. Like every fighting game ever, it appeared that I needed to win two out of three.

I balled my hands into a fist but thought it might be better to run.

"How'd you do that?" I asked.

The silent man stopped in his tracks as the door behind

me nudged open. I turned and saw the same man I had just fought, beat up and bloodied, emerging from the room.

"Fucking twins," I groaned, shaking my head. One of them had been hard enough to beat. Now I had a double team to deal with. And no matter which one I faced, the other was right behind me.

So much for my life bar.

Chapter 38

I regained consciousness on the floor of the makeshift office, on my stomach. My head hurt. I wondered how long I'd been out this time. One of the strongmen sat in a chair that straddled me. His large foot rested on my back. I couldn't feel the second shadow within him, through the boot. The sole was probably thick enough.

From what I could see, the laptops had been set up again, barring one that was beyond repair. The bent chandelier sat discarded in a corner. The other three chairs were evenly spaced around the low table, set up for a conference of sorts. I had the feeling I was on the agenda.

My hands weren't tied or anything. And I was alone with the Mexican. For a second, I considered trying to fight again, but all that had done last time was piss the strongman off.

"Hey listen," I chanced, sounding as sincere as a half-assed liar could. "I'm sorry about the whole bringing-the-chandelier-down-on-your-head thing. It was a dirty trick."

"Not me," he said gruffly. "That was my brother, Eladio."

"Oh. Well who are you?"

"I'm Emilio."

Original. I hoped they didn't have a brother named Ernesto. "Of course. Well, I'm still sorry. We kinda started off on the wrong foot."

"That's Eladio. He's not as reasonable as me. He likes starting fights."

I smiled through my pain. This twin wasn't as intent on harming me, it seemed. I figured some favor with one of the two would help in my position, so I played along. I wasn't sure I could've done anything else anyway.

"That's good to hear, Emilio. Really, this whole thing is a misunderstanding. That's what I was trying to explain when your brother jumped on me." Emilio sort of grunted. I wasn't sure if that conveyed understanding or if he had something caught in his throat, so I continued. "You and I, we can talk things out, right? We don't like to fight."

"Oh, I like to fight."

"You just said—"

"I said Eladio likes to start them. That's his thing. Picking fights. Then I'm inevitably drawn into them. And that's what I do."

"What's that?"

"Finish them."

Wow. He'd set that line up perfectly. I wondered how

often he got the joke off that smoothly.

"You mind if I sit on one of the chairs?" I asked. "This is getting uncomfortable."

"You shut up," he commanded. Then he returned to vigilant silence.

"So much for being the reasonable one." I wiggled around awkwardly to get a hand to my side. "This is new," I whispered, reaching for the Hamilton watch—but it wasn't there. My pockets were empty. "Come on," I complained. "Where's my stuff?"

The man's boot pressed into my back. "Listen, are we gonna have a problem here?"

I sighed. This wasn't a problem. It was a mess. But I waited it out patiently, trying to keep Emilio in his happy place. It wasn't too long before his brother returned to the room. He was bloodied and beat up and had bumps that weren't supposed to be there. Obviously he shot me a hateful stare. Behind him was a small man in a cream-colored button-up vest.

I studied the man, hoping the new development was fortuitous. His black skin was a dark espresso. It complemented his metallic red oxford shirt, its stiff collar unfolded and worn high, hiding the man's neck. His pants and vest were off-white and had a meticulous cut to them. He had wiry gray curls on his head that seemed to migrate down his cheeks and neck. All around, his hair was trimmed short, his nails were manicured, and—except for the absent tie—he was a display of modern chic.

"No, no, no," he muttered, carrying himself around the

girth of his escort. "This won't do. Get this man up off the floor."

I didn't wait for the big man to remove his foot. I immediately shoved myself up. It annoyed him, but lying prostrate didn't do anything to ease my temper.

Eladio continued his menacing glare. The man in the suit, however, watched me with civil curiosity, or curious civility. Or maybe he was just a professional. He held up a hand and I leaned over the table to shake it. He did not reciprocate. I realized the motion was meant to signal me to sit down. I nodded and did so. Then he clasped his hands behind his back and paced behind the opposite chair. It was a cramped room but his small stature gave him enough space to appear comfortable.

"Listen," I said, after nobody spoke. "I—"

"You are Dante Butcher," he said with his back to me. Only one arm was behind him now. He was studying something in his other hand. "You live on Fair Avenue, apartment 7405." He turned around and waved my ID in his hand. That's when I noticed my money clip, keys, smokes, and cell phone were on the table, next to a party invitation and an antique pocket watch. Check out my observation skills here. He tossed my driver's license into the pile. "Butcher. That's a good working class name. A straightforward name. From a family that served its community."

I gave him a funny look. Was this some kind of interrogation technique? "Centuries ago, maybe. Trust me," I said, "I like a good steak. Meat and potatoes are my two main food groups. But I can't stomach it if I visualize the animal it came from."

"Men can do a lot of things they never thought possible when under duress."

"I don't know, dude. I'm pretty squeamish about medium-rare."

The short man smiled. "Perhaps you have other surprising strengths. For instance, you gave Eladio a challenge, and you're only a third his size."

I almost provoked the man, made a joke about how he was small but obviously the strongman's boss, but I decided against it. I didn't know what to say so I just nodded.

"You'd be surprised at the things I know," he said. "I make it my business to know things. In fact, it is literally a business. Yet I don't know why you are here."

Emilio was sitting down and scrolling through my cell phone, probably looking at my contacts. I had Pam listed in there, not Soren. Emilio's brother, Eladio, stood to my right sniffing my pack of cloves. He seemed bored with them and put the box down.

"I'm not going to bullshit you," I said. "I didn't just sneak in here to get the VIP treatment. I was looking for someone." The black man's eyes were active, flicking about from this to that as if he could see my story from all the angles. But while his face was expressive, his mouth was silent. I decided to keep talking. It was working out so far. "I was hoping to find a Red Hat producer. You see, I'm a DJ. I spin old school breaks and hip hop, that kind of stuff. I thought, you know, I could sneak in, impress you, maybe get a job."

The man quietly studied me for a few moments. Eladio grumbled by the door while his twin watched idly, tuned out of the conversation. The black man looked to the other two, then back to me, and then picked up the pocket watch. "This is a railroad piece," he said, opening the cover and studying the timing mechanism. "An antique in nice condition. Did you know that, Dante?" I just watched him. His statement wasn't all that revelatory. My fear was that he knew more about the watch than he let on. "I've always liked railroad men. They're a direct breed. They lack the time for anything else." He stepped back to the table and placed the Hamilton down gently. I tried not to show my relief. "Railroad men say what they do and do what they say."

The man sat down in the chair across from me and just waited. It was clear he didn't believe my story. Hell, it was clear that Eladio hadn't bought it. The truth was, I had no idea what to say to him. I'd been looking for Soren, nothing more. I didn't know if I had expected to find these men in the middle of a pagan ritual sacrifice, with Soren tied down to a stone altar, or what. But now I felt ridiculous. Woefully unprepared. I'd wasted all week looking into Violet when the obvious threat was here. The invisible enemy may be more dangerous than the apparent one, but you still need to watch them both. I had failed to give proper attention to Red Hat.

If I was going to give him what he wanted, maybe I could make it a trade.

"Can I at least get my stuff back?"

After a brief thought, the man nodded curtly. I stood up and the strongmen flinched. They were ready for trouble. The black man didn't move at all. I took the watch back first, then put my other belongings in my pockets, including swiping my phone from the hands of Emilio.

I've seen this man before, with my father.

That was confirmation enough. I hadn't touched the man yet, but I'd be surprised if he wasn't a Royal. Perhaps even the owner of Red Hat Events.

Thing is, that was a long time ago, but he doesn't look much older.

"I was curious," I admitted aloud. "About different things. About Red Hat. I wanted to see how you did things. But I'm mostly here to watch over Soren... shit. I don't know his last name."

The lack of information didn't prevent the man's eyes from lighting up as soon as I had mentioned the name. It was clear I immediately captured his interest. "I know Soren," he admitted. "The last name isn't important. How do centuries of history reflect upon the individual? I'm sure a butcher who doesn't like the sight of blood would agree. I'm of the opinion that men should always know each other by their first names. Matters are more personal that way."

"Yet I still don't know yours."

He flashed his teeth in a smile, but said nothing. The man nodded and signaled to the door. "Excuse us." I wasn't sure what he meant but the security detail exited the room as quickly as their bulky frames allowed. When they closed the door, the man in the vest turned to me again. "Thank you for being truthful. That explains how you got an invite. Where is Soren?"

I started. "I was planning on meeting him here."

"Dante, don't squander what goodwill you've earned by lying again."

"It's the truth. I got tired of waiting for his set to start so I took a look around. Are you saying he hasn't shown up yet?"

The man shot his jaw forward as he mulled over my question. "I'm saying that he missed his slot completely. I had to fit in someone to replace him. He hasn't returned my calls. I didn't know there was anyone else at the party who knew him."

"Isn't that the way you wanted it?" I asked. I wasn't sure why. I still didn't know how much I wanted to reveal to the mysterious man. He didn't answer my question and his expression didn't betray his feelings.

If he was telling the truth, why hadn't Soren showed? Had he learned the truth about Red Hat? That was almost impossible. Something else had to cause him to forgo his dream of being a DJ. Maybe Pam had finally won out.

"Look," I said. "I can find him. I'll just take off and let him know that you're asking for him."

"Would you now?" he asked. He was suspicious, obviously, but he wasn't in a position to say why. He knew what Red Hat's secret was. So did I. But he couldn't broach the subject without giving it away. "And would you also pay for the chandelier?"

I choked on my answer for a second. Any repairs to this place had to be expensive.

"Don't worry about it," he teased. "My insurance will cover it. But we still have the problem with Soren to deal with. We had a contract, he and I. Reneging on agreements is distasteful."

"Can you blame him? You don't exactly have his best interests in mind."

The man studied me intently. No doubt he wondered exactly what I knew. "There are two types of people in this world, Dante. Those who *know*, and those who don't." He eyed me carefully as he spoke, searching for any acknowledgment of the subtext. I didn't reward him with a response. Still, instead of appearing weak, he opted to remain composed and in control of the situation. "Soren is my employee until I hear otherwise. That means he is under my watch for the time being. I'll tell you what. I'll let you work off the damage you caused. Find Soren, talk to him, and come by the Hollywood office. I take it you've been there?"

My eyes lowered to the ground unintentionally. I blinked and met his gaze. Trying to appear normal but fearing I failed. "Sure."

"Bring him there and ask for me. No tricks. I just want to talk. A sit-down in my office. You can sit with us, if you like. To ease your mind."

"And what will the three of us talk about?"

He smiled casually. "The conditions of his employment. Full disclosure. Then the choice is his. And yours."

I wasn't sure what to say. I didn't know what he meant by full disclosure. He wasn't planning on copping to possession, was he? It didn't matter. I was cornered and I wanted to get outside into the crisp air again. I nodded in agreement.

He turned to the door. "Emilio," he called out. The door opened and the uninjured strongman grunted. "See to it that Dante is escorted off the grounds."

I felt trapped in the room. I wasn't sure if I was ever getting out. Hearing this order, I stood up anxiously, swinging the watch on its chain. "I'll let you know," I said weakly, inferring I would look into Soren for him. I didn't give the man another glance. I rushed by the large Mexican and started down the hall. To my surprise, the black man followed me out.

"Aren't you forgetting something, Dante?"

I turned and saw the man in the cream-colored outfit extend his hand. It stopped me. Surprised me.

That's your chance.

As much as I wanted to continue exiting the observatory, I forced myself to backtrack down the hall.

"A handshake to seal our deal," he stated flatly.

I met the man's solid grip with mine. Immediately, I saw the second shadow. But it was deeper than that. The presence coursed throdgh me. Stronger than anything I'd ever felt. And different. It was foreboding, uninvited, and magnificent. I recoiled at his touch.

"My name is Marquis," he said coolly.

The man looked at me in puzzlement. I struggled to

maintain eye contact. I wasn't sure what I had just felt. It was pure power. He was definitely something else. A Royal.

"I don't like to be crossed, Dante. Five minutes ago, you and I had never spoken to each other. We had no agreements. Maybe we didn't see eye to eye. Maybe we were positioned to be at odds. I can't blame you for your previous thoughts or actions, however ignorant. But now, you and I have come to an understanding. We've shaken hands. We know each other by name. Now I will place all blame on you if you fail to follow through."

I backed away. "Got it." Spinning around, I made for the door. The hallway felt too long, but I resisted the urge to run and marched without looking back.

Halfway there, the door opened. Eladio rushed in from outside. "Boss," he called out. "Christian is gone."

The big man was ahead of me, and as I approached him to pass, he spread his wide arms to cover the hallway. Behind me, the others hurried to catch up.

"Yeah," I said, turning to Emilio and Marquis. "That's how I got in. I saw some guy wander away so I just came inside." I said it nonchalantly, wondering if I could make a run for the door.

"No," stressed the big man, rubbing his head where the laptop had hit him. "I mean, he's standing out there, but he's *gone*. He doesn't remember anything."

Understanding registered on the Royal's face. Large hands clamped down on my shoulders from behind. They knew I was aware of their secret.

"Hold on—" I said hastily. Eladio shoved me towards his

brother. I braced myself against the wall and put my other hand up, showing that I didn't want to fight. Two of them were too many. Three would not have ended well. I cowered under the strongmen as Marquis pressed close.

"How do you know about us?" he asked. "*What* is it that you know?"

I squeezed my back into the wall. "I know that you're not you. I know that Red Hat is a network of shades."

The black man looked from one of his guards to the other and chuckled. "What? Don't be so dramatic." He motioned for the men to give me some space. They backed away only a few feet, standing on each of my flanks. "So, you are the type of person who *knows*. You're one of us. I suspected as much."

"I'm nothing like you."

"Save it. I don't need to hear your reasons. We all have them. Is it our place to justify our knowledge? If we're not meant to inhabit others, then why can we do it?"

Marquis didn't get it. He thought I was a shade. It made sense, I suppose. How else would I know about them unless I was one? How else would I truly believe?

But he didn't know *my* secret. No one else could sense the second shadow as I could. Probably not even the Royals. It was just something I could always do. It made the hunt natural for me. As Marquis had said, if I wasn't meant to root out shades, then why was I so good at it?

"Whatever," I said. "I didn't lie about Soren. I was making sure he wasn't in your particular kind of trouble."

"There's truth to that, I suppose, but deception as well.

Why go through so much for a man whose last name you don't know? No," he said, pacing away from me. "There's something else."

"You're wrong," I said through gritted teeth. "I'm just concerned for Soren."

Marquis flashed his expressive eyes at me in disappointment. There was something he didn't tell me. Something he'd wanted me to say. Did he really want Soren so much that he would let me go this easily?

"It's lucky for you that I didn't like Christian very much. He was idle. And simple. But he did serve a purpose. Red Hat is less without him than with."

"Just think of it as a practical lesson."

"There is a lesson here for both of us, Dante. We are not even. Accounts need to be settled. Now, I don't care if it is Soren or not, but you owe me a soldier. And reneging on agreements is distasteful."

I looked at him in disbelief. "So you don't care that I know about Red Hat? The shades?"

"You're forgetting about the two types of people, Dante. The only ones who would listen are the ones who already know. That information has no power over me."

"And how can I trust you?"

The Royal softened his stare. "We are men, not savages. We must do right by each other. If I make a deal with you, I will honor it. Find Soren. Full disclosure. It's his choice."

I didn't try to hide the scowl on my face. "If he knew what he was getting into, why would he choose Red Hat?"

For the first time, Marquis looked stumped. It was a brief

moment, but he didn't understand why I didn't understand. Before I could puzzle it out, his face relaxed. "Full disclosure," he repeated. He turned and told the others to take me outside.

"Let's go," said Emilio, placing his hand on my shoulder and pushing me through the door.

"Wait. I got it," said Eladio. He waved his brother off and escorted me towards the crowd. The cut on his head started bleeding again, and his eyes burned with mischief.

Chapter 39

Getting kicked out of parties is always embarrassing. You can try to act tough and hope you impress a girl or two on the way out. Usually that just adds more fuel to the fire. Best to go for nonchalant and hope nobody notices. Usually, there's no good option. One way or another, attention is called to you.

"You really don't need to walk me out," I said in protest. As I was shamefully escorted past the crowd, I scanned for Soren. One last check. Again, I couldn't find him anywhere. But I did see John the drug dealer smirking at me. "Eff you," I mouthed.

"Keep moving, little man," said Eladio.

We passed the security line in the parking lot and I turned around. "Well, it's been fun—"

The bloodied man shoved me. "Move."

I put my hands up, aware that we were in public now and

other people could be watching or recording. I stepped back for a moment, then spun around, disquieted by the fact that the strongman was still on my tail. Maybe he just wanted to make sure I left. Or maybe he had more sinister intentions.

"You know, Eladio, the chandelier thing... It was all very heat of the moment."

"You better stop talking about the chandelier, bro."

"In my defense, you did pull a machete."

"You mean this one?"

That's when I noticed the knife was already in the Mexican's hand. As we descended the sloping street, I considered making a run to my car. It was still a good five minutes down. Maybe I could lose him and get out of here.

"Dante," we heard from behind. The click-clack of heels echoed on the street as Eva ran to catch up to us. She had never looked so good. "Where have you been?"

"Oh, just trading mustache tips with my luchador friend here."

Eladio protested as she slipped by and hugged me. "Luchadors wear masks, asshole."

"Might be a better look for you." Eladio grumbled and tightened his grip on his blade.

"Get out of here, Eladio," said Eva, slapping the man's gut softly.

"I got him," he said.

"No. He's taking me home." She batted her fake eyelashes at him. "Don't worry, I'll keep an eye on him."

I was going to interject but I thought that would only complicate matters. Besides, it actually looked like the big man was listening to her. They exchanged glances and Eladio stopped following us and we resumed our way downhill. I turned around a couple of times to make sure. Machetes will do that. The strongman stood at the perimeter with a scowl. When we were out of earshot, Eva must have sensed I was unsure how to break the silence.

"What did you do?" she asked. "You don't want to piss him off. Trust me."

I frowned. "Do you think he's the type of guy that gets pissed off when you kick his ass?"

Her eyes widened. "You didn't."

My short friend wrapped her arm around my waist. I tried to ignore the second shadow inside her.

"How do you know those guys?" I asked. I wasn't sure I wanted the answer.

She shrugged. "They work at Red Hat. Why?"

"And what about Marquis?"

She stopped. "You saw him?"

"Sure. He was inside. You know him too?"

She laughed. "You went inside the observatory? No wonder you got kicked out."

We arrived at my car and I pulled my keys out. "This is me."

I unlocked the dark gray Z and checked up the street. We weren't followed. Then I suddenly wondered if Eva was the kind of girl that cared how expensive my car was. I liked sporty cars but this one didn't exactly break the bank. Next thing I knew, she opened the passenger seat and sat down, without a mention of it.

"What are you doing?" I asked.

"You're my ride," she said matter-of-factly.

"You weren't lying? Where's Liz?"

"She's with some friends. I came with her. Now I'm going with you."

I couldn't say I was bothered by the news. As I sat in the low bucket seat, the back of my skull hit the headrest hard. I rubbed the sore spot tenderly.

I eyed the petite girl in the tight yellow dress and marveled at my luck. Ten minutes ago I was mostly concerned with staying alive. Now I had more ambitious dreams.

"Where do you live?" I asked.

I held the flame above the pipe and pulled deeply, letting the skunky smoke filled my lungs. I usually don't like pot. Especially the overly strong medicinal variety. It makes me paranoid. Believe me, when you know ghosts are everywhere, the last thing you need is more paranoia. But the ecstasy I'd gotten from John was wearing off, Soren's coke was long gone, and Eva still wanted to party.

We sat on the carpet of her studio apartment. The cheap IKEA coffee table was Eva's workspace. An open green pill bottle of weed rested next to a crumpled paper that once held K. She had music on, some hip hop or whatever that I wasn't really listening to. The only other noise was our occasional laughter.

The room was dark because she had duct-taped a sheet over the window to act as a blackout curtain. Despite her best efforts, I could see the sliver of light along the edge that meant the sun was coming up. The drugs had helped me forget about the pain from the brawl. Now I was just plain exhausted. I gave the pipe back to her and leaned my head against the seat cushion of the couch. I needed to tap out.

"I win," she said, taunting me. I studied her. She was so cute, even without any make-up on. She had dressed down to get comfortable, wearing only panties and a long white T-shirt.

"I should've gotten more X. Weed isn't my thing." Next time I came to this house, I thought, I needed to bring a six-pack. Alcohol had a way of keeping me level at times like this. I slid to my side and rested my head in her lap. She leaned down and gave me a kiss. Heaven. Until she blew some smoke into my mouth.

I pushed her away and emptied my lungs. "Really," I said, "I'm done." It was a little unnerving. The joke was a bit too similar to the times I'd exsufflated shades. Shit, *she* was a shade. What was I doing here?

Her thighs were too comfortable for me to abandon, though.

Eva winked at me. No longer did her face sparkle with glitter. No longer were her eyelashes double-length. But she was still beautiful. It was hard to think of anything else when she smiled.

"What are you thinking about?" she asked.

Her. That I was fucking high. About Red Hat, and Soren, and how stupid I was for being here. I was thinking about her tits right above my head. And what I knew Violet would say if I had bothered to take the watch out of my pocket.

"I don't know," I answered. "Just wondering how much people really know each other. Why people do the things they do."

Her smile softened. "Why do *you*?"

I tensed up for a moment. She knew. Wait, did she? That was the pot talking. There was no way she saw what happened inside the observatory. No way she had time to talk to Marquis after I had gotten the boot.

"What do you mean?" I asked.

"Program. Make video games. Why do you do that?"

I relaxed again. "Eh, it's nothing. It's fun. Coding's like solving puzzles and finding the best ways to organize things. It's—" I laughed, and she followed suit. "It's hard to talk about when I'm high. But it's very ordered and logical. It makes sense."

Eva picked up the pipe again and gave it a short drag. It was barely lit, but she didn't need that much more. "You like order," she said.

I never really thought of myself in those terms. It was true, I guessed. Shades should stay with shades, the living with the living. I think Violet had said something like that.

"Bullshit," she said, countering her own point. "You

drink. You do drugs. You sneak around. You get in fights."

"Blame that on the Mexicans," I said.

"I saw you at Avalon too. What were you doing in the bathroom?"

"Oh." I'd forgotten where we first saw each other. At Avalon, I didn't know if she noticed Soren, but she saw me going into the closed bathroom. It was only afterwards that we spoke outside. It was probably obvious I had been fighting. "I guess you have a point. What about you, then? Do you like guys who get in fights and stay up all night and sleep in late? 'Cause I am not waking up tomorrow morning."

"I never said you could sleep here." She tilted her head close to mine. "And those guys are all right if they can hold a good job."

"I knew it. You want me for my programming skills." I laughed. "It's a common problem. It's difficult keeping all the chicks at bay."

Eva put her hand on top of my face to shut me up. "It must be so hard," she said, getting serious again, "to be so black or so white all the time, never realizing that most of the world is gray. Everything doesn't always fit into a neat little box. Sometimes you just need to go with it."

I sat up and put her hands in mine. "The only place I'm going is there." I pointed to her small bed in the corner of the room. The sheets were disheveled. We had messed around a little bit already but things had stayed pretty tame. This time my plan was just to pass out.

Lifting myself up was difficult. Remaining on my feet

through the sudden rush of dizziness was even more so. I shuffled to the sink and filled a glass with tap water.

"Do you have any aspirin?"

"Second drawer," she said.

Good. She didn't object to my sleeping here.

I opened the drawer and saw a few small boxes of medicine. They were colorful and had bold Korean lettering on them. One of them had a picture of what I thought was ginseng. I sighed and closed the drawer. I'd stick with the water.

I laid my clothes on the floor beside the bed, not bothering to empty my pockets. I made sure they were mostly folded so I didn't look like a slob. Eva turned the music off and disappeared into the bathroom. She must have been in there a while. I nodded off.

Next thing I knew, she was waking me up. I was so exhausted and my head hurt. But she smiled. She was naked, and I didn't feel like sleeping anymore. I kissed her. Her mouth was fresh with mint flavor. It helped cover the feeling that there was another girl possessing her. I pulled her small frame against my chest and then pushed her down on the bed. I wondered what to do as I looked at her pale breasts. What could I do?

I put the blacks and the whites of the world out of my mind and rolled on top of her.

I jolted awake with subtle urgency. Something was wrong. But I was relaxed. Eva was asleep next to me. Everything was peaceful. Then I felt it.

The bed was swaying gently. No. The whole room. An earthquake. It was as though we were on an ocean with minuscule waves, rocking back and forth. There was a low rumbling sound. I think I felt it more than heard it.

I just lay on my back, staring at the ceiling, reveling in my awareness of it all.

I'd never really noticed Los Angeles earthquakes before. One time I was in a restaurant with big glass windows and everybody stood up and started looking outside. I'd thought there was a fight or a car accident or some other city drama. Afterward, somebody told me it was an earthquake. I just shrugged and finished my burger.

Before I could fully grasp the sensation, completely appreciate the scope of it, the bed lulled itself to sleep. The hint of movement was gone. I tried to close my eyes, but my comfort was empty now.

My phone said it was noon. I usually checked the watch but I didn't want to talk to Violet right now. I put my pants back on. It was still dark in here, but I knew the sun would be blinding outside.

I admired Eva's unconscious body on the bed. My hand brushed the box of cloves in my pocket. It would be so easy to do it right now, I thought. Instead, I pulled a strand of platinum hair away from her face. I wanted to kiss her on the forehead, but I was afraid that would wake her up.

I scrolled through my contacts. My head was still fuzzy. I thought I remembered everything about the night, but I wanted to be sure. Yes. I had Eva's number. That made me happy.

I scratched my head and tried to wake myself up. I had to go. I had to figure out what was going on with Soren. With Marquis. I had to get some real sleep tonight. At my own place.

Chapter 40 - Saturday

Even though it was starting to darken outside, it was still the morning for me. I'd slept as long as I could, but that didn't save me from feeling like a dried up sponge after a bout of sewer cleaning. The Advil helped, as did the half-finished bottle of Gatorade that sat beside me on the kitchen counter. My feet hung over the floor in dirty socks. I wore old jeans and a ten-year-old T-shirt from Miami. It said "Duffy's Tavern" on it and was issued to all employees. It was only supposed to be a month long gig, but I ended up wearing that shirt every day for twelve. Despite the grease stains and moth holes, it was in better shape than my head.

I forced the last bite of my PB & J sandwich down. Sad, I know. I just hadn't had a chance to go shopping this week. Right now I needed was sustenance. The last thing I wanted was to leave the apartment. Some more Gatorade, some TV, a shower, maybe another snack, and then it would be bedtime. Just like Saturday never happened.

I'm the last person that should be saying this...

I rolled my eyes. Violet knew not to talk when I was hung over. I didn't even know why I'd taken the watch with me.

You and Eva goes against everything we've worked for.

"Jealous that I found another troubled spirit?"

Please. I'm twelve.

"You're a hundred and twelve."

Whatever. Not only is she distracting you from very pressing matters—she's taken. And on top of that, she works for Red Hat.

I kneaded my temples. "I admit she has some baggage."

She's using you. She's watching you. She's gonna—

"What? What's her motive?" I put my hands on the edge of the counter and slipped down to the linoleum floor. "Keep in mind that I hit on her at Avalon. I approached her at the observatory. And I have no idea what that Mexican freak show intended to do with me. Eva saved me from a beatdown at the very least."

Violet didn't say anything. She didn't have to. What I was doing might not have been wrong but it certainly wasn't right. I just needed time to figure it out. I put the empty plate in the sink and took a gulp of lemon-lime-glacier-ice (or whatever edgy name Bob from Marketing had come up with). Then I grabbed the watch and left the kitchen.

"I can't do everything at once," I said to her. "There's only so much time in the day and, I might add, this one's almost over already." I didn't want to worry about pocket watches or estranged fathers or Royals or even smoking hot

Asian chicks. I just needed some Netflix and maybe some Cheetos. Some downtime, is what I'm saying.

I tossed the watch on the cushion of the sofa and collapsed next to it, then realized the TV remote was out of reach. I didn't move to recover it. It felt good to be motionless. Free of worry. Responsibility.

Dante, you might be right. Maybe Eva has nothing to do with any of the plots we're looking in to. But she's a shade—

"You're a shade, Violet." I couldn't contain it anymore. My voice rose with my anger. "Are you gonna give me some more advice about how you're the only shade I can trust, then lie to me about the things you've done? Do you wanna go visit Catriona again to see your work?"

I made a mistake!

"*A* mistake? You've made plenty of mistakes, Violet. I don't know that you could ever have saved Aster, but you could've chosen not to be a part of it."

He was my father! I did what he told me to. He—

"He's a twisted fuck, Violet. If I could kill him I would!" I launched myself off the couch, no longer comfortable sitting. I didn't think Violet disagreed with my words, but I said them to hurt her anyway. She needed to feel pain. As the others had. "This one man has probably done more harm in his life than all the shades I've expelled put together. And you helped him. You realize that? He needs to go down, one way or another. For Catriona. For Aster. For..." I trailed off when I realized I was going to say something nice. I was going to say that I needed to stop Ambrose for his daughter. For Violet. But I was too mad at her. I didn't know how to soften my hard edges now.

He does. And we can stop him. But we need to stop Red Hat too. And—

"You don't think I know that, Violet? *All* shades are my enemies. Every single one. They're all gonna be taken care of. But I need to work with some to get others. That's why I'm laying off Marquis."

So, what? You're just going to sleep with Eva and buddy up with Marquis and join the Red Hat corporate team?

"I joined up with you, didn't I?" My voice had reached a pitch that the neighbors could hear. I stopped myself and massaged my eyes. The headache had almost been gone. Riling myself up had forced it back.

Violet didn't say anything. I had just told her that her dad was Hitler and she had enabled him. I had just said that this world needed to be rid of all shades. We both knew that working with Marquis was like making a deal with the devil, and I had equated that to working with her. I was pissed, and those things sounded true enough at the time, but a part of me still felt I had crossed the line.

I heard crying again. Crying that reminded me of the little girl in my dream, trembling under the scorn of her father. Terrified of him. Disappointed in him. Hating him. I stood silent, trembling myself, thinking I had said enough.

The front door of my apartment shook as something heavy pounded against it. The sudden commotion startled me because I was still on a short fuse.

"What now?" I screamed. I stormed over to the door when there was no answer. A quick peek through the peephole did not settle my nerves.

"What do you want?" I demanded through the closed door.

"Open up," said the man. It was one of the strongmen from last night.

"Are you the chandelier one?"

"I'm Emilio," he answered, as if that helped.

"Do you know how much I drank last night? Are you the chandelier one or not?"

"No, that's my brother, Eladio."

I leaned my elbow against the door and buried my head against it. Was a little TV too much to ask?

"Any large jungle knives on you?"

"Open up."

I answered with a heavy sigh. Looking to Soren's iron ring hanging above me on a nail, I decided it best to open the door before Emilio had a chance to break it down.

"How did you find me?" I asked him face to face, not hiding my annoyance.

"We scanned your ID, remember?"

I didn't remember that. But they did take a look at it. Was I going to need to move now?

"What does Marquis want?"

The man blinked plainly. "He wants to know if you've found Soren yet."

"What? That was like, a few hours ago."

"Seventeen."

I ignored his passive-aggressive correction. "Marquis asked me to bring him by the Hollywood office. I'm gonna need until tomorrow, at least."

The rotund man nodded. "I just wanted to make sure you didn't disappear."

"Don't worry. I'm here. When I find him, I'll call the office to make sure Marquis can meet us. If Soren wants to come, I'll bring him in." I started to close the door but Emilio jammed his foot in the way. As I pulled back, I checked the horseshoe ring skeptically.

"If he doesn't want to come, bring him anyway. My boss doesn't like when people don't keep their commitments to him."

I frowned at the ring, thinking I was an idiot for even trying it. "Yeah. It's his thing. I got it. Anything else?"

Emilio furrowed his brow, ducked his head down, and peeked up. "What do you keep looking at up there?"

"Uh, it's nothing."

"What is that?"

"This. Um. It's a horseshoe."

Emilio pulled back. "Humph." He stood there, watching me with a quizzical expression. His bushy eyebrows and mustache made him look like a cartoon. And then I noticed the band of metal around his neck. It was a single bar without a clasp that had been bent around in a circle, almost like a nearly closed horseshoe.

"What do you know of cold iron?" I asked.

The strongman reached to his neck but didn't complete the action. He backed out of the doorway and turned to go. "Tomorrow then."

"Yup," I said. "Or Monday."

"Wha—"

I slammed the door shut. Then waited until I saw the shadow disappear from the peephole. Once I considered him gone, I locked the door and retreated to the couch.

"Great, now I have two goons showing up at my door." I buried my face in my hands. This was awful. Especially when I realized I'd forgotten to grab the remote again.

What happened to us? We used to be so careful.

I shook my head slowly and spoke softly. "We used to be a lot of things..."

Again silence. And it was welcome. I listened to my breaths. I let the oxygen revive me. I wondered what it felt like to be a shade, taking in the sage. Realizing that their bond to the living was slipping away. It was cleansing. Almost beautiful.

Five minutes must have passed without a single word. It was peaceful, for a time. Then I imagined Eva's face. Her naked body close to mine. I recalled her second shadow. Another girl about her age. I didn't know anything about her or who she was. Or actually, she was the only one I *did* know. Everything Eva said and did was a result of her shade. It was the little Korean girl with bleached hair I didn't know.

It was an unsettling thing to imagine. I tried to think of anything else to keep my mind off it. Of all the things, I came up with Emilio's goofy face in my hallway. He had a funny look. Puzzled by something I'd said about the cold iron. He reached for the bar on his neck, then stopped himself short, as if he didn't want to expose a secret. What was it?

I pulled my laptop close and did some image searches for the jewelry. They were called torcs. They were an actual thing. From the Iron Age, primarily, but still. Stiff rings of metal worn around the neck. Usually permanent fixtures.

I didn't get it. What did Eladio and Emilio need the theatrics for? I had joked about them being circus performers but they were really just bodyguards. Like Bedros.

I thought of Soren's horseshoe ring. Cold iron. A metal ring that repelled spirits. And then it hit me. Soren had been difficult to expel. He was wearing the iron during the fight. He'd resisted the sage. Until the end, when I was choking him out. That's when the large ring fell off his finger. Maybe it wasn't that the cigarettes were weak. Or that he was strong. If spirits couldn't cross a loop of iron, then wouldn't it be a two-way street? Maybe the horseshoe wasn't meant to keep shades *away*, but to keep them *in*. It was a form of armor.

It suddenly made sense and I knew I was right. Ten more minutes of silence allowed me to do some research, sparking ideas for how this information could help me. But the momentary satisfaction didn't last. I had figured out the puzzle of the ring, but there were much larger forces to unravel. Only now, I was on a roll, and couldn't think of ignoring the problem. Marquis. Alexander Ambrose. Soren. They were all involved in an intricate dance. Only I didn't know the moves.

"None of this makes sense," I complained. I'd gone

through the thought in my head already but I wanted Violet to chime in. I wanted to invite her into the conversation without saying I was sorry. "Marquis is a man of resources. He doesn't need me to find Soren. What do they want from me?" I shoved my laptop aside with my feet as I placed them on the coffee table and slid down the leather sofa into a more relaxed position.

You did say you were his friend.

"Sure, but Red Hat can pick up the phone just as easily."

So Soren must be hiding from Marquis.

"Avoiding his calls. Not going home. Sure, that's a possibility. Or..."

Have you considered that Soren may no longer be Red Hat's priority?

"I..."

He wants you, Dante. He can make the same calls you can make, but he wants you working for him. He wants you comfortable with him.

"He'll get to know me better than that."

That's what I'm afraid of.

I frowned. Violet was a little girl who'd fallen victim to the temptation of immortality before. She knew the pull it had. Perhaps she was afraid I'd be drawn to it. But I wasn't a helpless kid, dependent on somebody else's twisted morals. I was good. They were evil. It was that simple, even if others wanted to muddy the distinction.

"Listen," I said, taking a neutral tone. "Right now we need to think about Soren. We can't deliver him to Red Hat. I'm not gonna do that just to save my skin. But if we want to protect him, we need to find him. There's another possibility besides him simply avoiding Red Hat. And that's that he's in trouble. I still think he would've made that party if he could have."

It's possible he changed his mind. Found something better. Maybe his fiancée wanted him to stop being a DJ.

I tilted my head in concession. "Girls *are* hard to get away from." I looked down as the obvious came to me. I chuckled and picked up my cell phone. "Maybe I was selling myself short. It seems I do have a contact that Marquis doesn't." I scrolled through my contacts and made a call.

Who are you calling?

"The girl," I answered. "They're hard to get away from."

She picked up, surprisingly, on the second ring.

"Hi Pam."

"Good to hear from you, Dante! I can guess why you're calling."

"Really?"

"Sure. It's Saturday night. Almost six. Time to start doing the rounds and finding the right crowd to go drinking with."

The thought of alcohol almost caused me to throw up in my mouth. Pam was wrong. Besides, I never put out feelers until ten. That didn't stop me from playing along though. "You got me. What are you two up to tonight?"

"Funny you should ask! Look, I'm not really supposed to talk about it. Soren hasn't been speaking with anybody. He hasn't been home in two days. But he's working on a big deal right now."

"I know. He told me about Red Hat at the party."

"Oh good! Then I don't need to keep it a secret from you."

"Keep what a secret?"

"The deal," she said. "Red Hat Events. Initially they only wanted him as a DJ, but their music manager said they liked his ideas. They said he had a good feel for youth trends or something like that. Can you imagine?"

I didn't know what to say. I didn't expect to hear that he was in touch with Red Hat.

"Anyway," she continued, "we can't hang out because we're headed to dinner at eight. The music manager wants to celebrate the signing of the contract. His lawyer made reservations for all of us at Perch. Can you believe it?"

I couldn't. Soren sounded like a hot commodity, no matter who I talked to. "You're eating dinner with a lawyer?"

"I guess. You know how it is. Their executives have a whole entourage. They're even picking us up in a limo. Anyway, I have to go. I've never been to Perch before and I still need to finish my hair. But we'll definitely check in with you next weekend."

I didn't try to extend the conversation. My head was still fuzzy and I hadn't been able to digest most of it yet. I congratulated them and told her to have fun and hung up. Violet couldn't make sense of it. I called Eva to see if she knew any details but her phone went to voicemail. I didn't bother leaving a message. Chances are she knew less about Soren than I did.

"What are we missing?" I asked Violet after several minutes of silence. "Why is Red Hat looking for Soren when he is going to dinner with them tonight?"

Maybe they just found him. Emilio wasn't notified yet.

It didn't feel right. "I don't know. Pam made it seem like Soren had been in contact with them for the last couple of days. If she's telling the truth—"

Then Marquis was lying.

I nodded. "If that's the case, then the strongman wasn't here about Soren. He was just checking up on me."

I told you they want you now.

I cursed and sank down further in the sofa cushions. "It just seemed like Marquis was telling the truth. I thought I got a good read on him."

He's a powerful shade.

"He's a bastard. I know. But something about him struck me as honorable. I thought he would keep his word." Violet didn't say anything. I knew she disagreed but she didn't want to press the point. Talking about it to death wouldn't help matters. "No. All our troubles started with Soren. It's him they want. Could it be that even Marquis doesn't know what's going on?"

As we thought about the question, my eyes fell to a glossy black envelope on the coffee table. The side had been ripped open when I removed the invitation. "Ambrose. He has to be involved."

My father? I wouldn't put anything past him. We know he hates Red Hat.

"It makes sense, given his history. There's some link

we're not seeing." I put my feet on the floor and sat up. "Let's go over it, from the beginning."

Avalon.

I nodded. "Soren was just another burnout. A loner without a family. He probably had too many dependencies, but who am I to judge? We know that, somehow, Soren is an accommodating host. Pam said he had been acting differently for three months. That's longer than most."

Compared to my father, a few months is nothing.

"Granted. There are some people—Ambrose, the Royals, maybe even Bedros and the strongmen—who are much more powerful. Until now, we'd made it our business to clean up the street level scum. You've told me that shades come in all shapes and sizes. Ambrose said many powers and abilities are unique. We're not working with hard rules here. There's too much variability to make assumptions. But we do know the vast majority of shades out there have weak holds on their hosts. But not the fiend inside Soren."

On the Dead Side, he was a mess. I broke apart his form easily enough.

"That's the thing. Neros wasn't especially powerful. But we know about the iron ring now. He was able to stay in this world longer than most. Maybe that attracted attention. Maybe he was being watched."

My father doesn't know about the properties of iron, but we have to assume Marquis does. His bodyguards wear torcs.

I bit my lip. "So we're left with Soren. As a host. The difference is that he's susceptible. For whatever reason, shades have a strong bond with him. Easy entry. Usually, after someone smokes my cigarettes, their tie is cut for a long time, if not for good. The people I help can usually avoid repossession. Yet Soren is as popular as ever."

That's assuming they know you banished him.

"Maybe they do. Maybe they don't. Isn't it curious that, as soon as I do, Sal is escorting him out of the club? Your father passed right by us, and you wanted to follow."

I didn't know for sure it was him. I just sensed something familiar.

"But you suspected. And maybe, after four years on the lonely streets, we were bound to cross paths. That would be especially likely if Ambrose was looking for the same people we were."

Dispossessed souls.

"Recruiting for Red Hat is what he said. But he made me following him. He ducked into the bathroom at Mel's. Distracted me with an owl somehow. Neat trick. Obviously, we know he has friends and that he can body hop. He shook me. You were so mad about it that you met me on the Dead Side for the first time. I could see you were shaken up. I pushed and you let Livia's name slip. Then I was on Alexander McAllister's trail. I knew it!"

I stood up quickly, gripping the pocket watch in my hand again and pacing in the living room. "I don't believe in coincidences. I was investigating Sal and I was looking into your past and Red Hat came up both times. What were the odds? But both of those seemingly independent inquiries were started by the same question: why was Sal talking to Soren?"

But we answered that already. My dad was either working for Red Hat or pretending to. What we know for sure is that he introduced Soren to Marquis. They planned on accepting him into their fold.

I nodded excitedly. "Yes, but that didn't happen. Unless I'm wrong, the Royals are still looking for Soren. Which means—"

He's not having dinner with the real Red Hat.

"Exactly." I yelped the phone number and called Perch. When the hostess picked up the phone, I asked if she could confirm a reservation for me.

"What name?" she asked.

"McAllister."

She mumbled under her breath as she went down the list. "I don't see it, sir. Are you sure it's for tonight?"

"Yes." It was only a hunch, but it had to be right. This wasn't just about Marquis looking for Soren. Something more was going on. "Actually," I cut in, changing my mind, "I had my lawyer set the reservation. I think it's under his name. Try Glickman."

Another moment. "Yes. Glickman, party of four. You have a private balcony reserved for eight-thirty."

I thanked her and hung up. I didn't bother telling her it would be a party of five.

Chapter 41

Pershing Square was my Red Line exit. The metro station was named for the block-long park nearby. The square used to be a Downtown hub, famous for hosting war rallies and political functions, but it never really found its stride and had to be reinvented several times. Originally, it was known as Central Park and would have appeared as a miniature version of the Manhattan icon we know today: a patch of trees in a valley of skyscrapers. It was then renamed for a famous general after the war, fitting its ensuing role as an area for social activism. Eventually, the entire park was demolished and an underground parking structure was built in its place; now most of the green is asphalt and many of the sculptures are modern geometric eyesores. What was once an oasis amid concrete was swallowed up by it.

Today, the biggest reasons to visit are probably the concert stage and the seasonal ice rink, although both had failed to ever draw me. I'd never had more than a passing association with the park. Instead I was downtown for one of the lumbering stone giants across the way.

As I ascended the escalator from the underground station to the street, I zipped up my gray leather jacket to fend off the breeze and took in the city. In my dreams, I often walked between these old behemoths. Every single time, I felt tiny and disconnected in the darkness of the world. Somehow, this evening was different. I had the confidence of purpose. Of justice.

In the night sky, amidst the lights of the traffic and buildings, stood a stately fossil. The Pershing Square Building is a masthead of the old Los Angeles style. The exterior stonework features ornate details and reliefs of griffins and cherubs. Bold framing and cornerstones command a presence that isn't imitated today. The impressiveness continues inside. Sculptured brass and Italian marble is a mainstay. As I walked within the high halls with curved ceilings and crisscrossed stone tiling, I thought it an apt place to catch Alexander Ambrose. He was a man of tradition, and he was a Downtown lifer all the way.

I stepped into the elevator and faced the bronze plate that framed the call buttons. The top button had a metalwork bird welded next to it. It was the thirteenth floor. Like many buildings in Downtown Los Angeles that were built before the nineteen-fifties, this was a limit-height building—only zoned to stretch one hundred and fifty feet into the air. Where I was headed was near the roof, but thirteen, unlucky as it was, wasn't the destination.

I was dropped off into a hallway. A quick walk brought me to an unassuming room with old frames on the wall. A man in a suit stood at attention and opened another elevator door. So much for height limiting.

"I'm going to the dining room," I told him. He nodded as I entered, pushed a button for me, and resumed his post outside.

Perch is an upscale French restaurant, a slice of Parisian wonder precariously resting on a Los Angeles rooftop. The door slid open to reveal a bustling crowd of drinkers. I was deposited immediately beside the hostess stand. I slipped past into the large room of antique-styled chairs, tables, and sofas. The expensive tiles created an intricate pattern the color of cream and sky. Large, arched windows framed patio doors and allowed a night view of the Downtown skyline. A building with the words "ONE WILSHIRE" emblazoned across the top stood in the distance, lit the same color as the moon that floated quietly above it. I stepped into the chill air on the balcony. Below me, a trail of lighting caught my eye and I saw the ice rink of Pershing Square.

It was 9:30 p.m. I was late because I'd stopped at an army-navy store on the way. It was no matter. There were only a couple of places Soren could be and they'd just be finishing dinner. I strolled along the balcony edge, sliding my fingers on the clear glass railing, until I reached a private corner area. Offset from the other tables, it had its own fireplace and a lovely view of the city. Not a long view, as you might see from a mountainside or on a postcard, but the real thing: a sight of the city from within its bustling confines, above the activity but somehow still a part of it, still drawn to it.

Soren, Pam, Mr. Glickman, and Alexander McAllister sat sharing a wine bottle. They did not notice my approach.

"Don't I count as a family friend?" I asked, interjecting myself in the middle of whatever they were talking about. Pam was startled. Mr. Glickman and Soren looked confused. Alexander, however, flushed red with anger. He was still in a wheelchair but seemed to be in much better health. He chose not to make an outburst. While they remained seated, I leaned against the glass balcony railing next to the heating lamp. "I notice Bedros isn't here either. Maybe you thought he'd scare off your marks."

I put my hand in my pocket and fingered Soren's ring. I figured I would return it to him. Tell him I had found it in the bathroom or something. Maybe it could stop Ambrose from taking him.

"Dante," said Pam, the first to break the stupor. "What are you doing here?"

"Sorry Pam, Soren. I hope you at least enjoyed your dinner. I don't think Alexander McAllister has been fully honest with you."

"Dante, dude," protested Soren, "this isn't cool."

"He's not who you think he is, Soren."

Alexander's complexion returned to normal. He finally spoke up. "And you, sir, have you come clean on your end?" His voice was strong and confident. A far cry from the feeble man in the loft.

"What are you talking about?" I asked.

"Only that the night my promoter ran into this gentleman, he had just been assaulted in a nightclub."

Uh-oh.

"Dante knows about that," said Soren. "I've told him. Besides, I'm not so sure I didn't just fall."

Alexander scoffed. "Ridiculous. You were attacked. Have you considered that your stalker here may have played a part in that?"

Pam turned to me with cold eyes. "What?"

"That's not true," I said. "Soren, that doesn't even make sense, man. We were hanging out. I didn't even see when you left or where you went to."

Soren started to shake his head, then stopped. He was trying to recall what had happened. I knew he would remember hanging out with me, but the minutes surrounding the brawl and the banishment were gone forever. "No—I was in the bathroom alone," he concluded. "Dante didn't come in with me."

I nodded reassuringly, but I had the feeling Soren wasn't the one I needed to convince. "Pam, he went ahead of us. I was sitting with you. Don't you remember?"

Her face softened. She didn't say anything but I saw a slight nod. Alexander would need to overplay his hand to give them any certainty. It would look too suspicious on his end to know too much about the situation. But I realized with a sigh that I couldn't just hand over Soren's ring now. I had just told him that I didn't know he went to the bathroom.

I decided to blow the shade's cover before he dug deeper

into mine. "Let's talk about you, Alexander. We both know you don't work for Red Hat. You were in a coma until a couple days ago."

Soren stood up. "That's what this is about?" He looked to Pam and understanding swept over his face. "Dude, I already know that. He has friends at the company and found me through them. He initially told me he worked with them so I wouldn't think some creepy guy in a wheelchair was stalking me. But he came clean. He told me he was friends with my father and wanted to see how I was doing." I must have shown my disbelief. "I know. It sounds like bullshit. That's why I didn't say anything to Pam until I found out more. She thought he was Red Hat management until an hour ago."

Alexander was a step ahead of me. He had inside information about Red Hat, but it was a flimsy cover that he couldn't link to McAllister's persona. So he used that to get close to Soren. To get him away from the party. It was clever. However, this story about knowing his father couldn't be true. Or maybe it could. Did it matter? I instinctively pulled the pocket watch into my hand.

"Ah," said Alexander, "so this is all just a misunderstanding. It is good of you, Mr. Butcher, to watch over your friends so."

Pam pulled her fiancé back into his seat and everybody relaxed. Mr. Glickman was the only one who remained on edge. How was he involved in all of this? Either he was just doing his job or he had more sinister motivations. It was impossible to tell.

Before the silence grew too uncomfortable, Pam spoke up. "So, the both of you know each other?"

Alexander smiled and looked to me for an explanation. "Yes," I said. "I knew... his daughter. When she was alive."

The mood at the table became more solemn. Soren nodded. "He told me about her. It's very sad."

"Yes," agreed Alexander. "I am thankful for your friendship." I couldn't tell if his words were true or if he was just playing along. I looked at the four of them. A disparate group that didn't belong together. And I wasn't an exception. I understood what Alexander wanted. A young body. A strong host to start over with. But what was Soren's stake in all this?

The inheritance.

Violet's words ran through my mind like a cleansing stream. Of course. A sick man. Friends with an orphan's father. If anything could make friends out of strangers, it was money.

"He's giving you his money, isn't he?"

Soren was clearly surprised but answered quickly. "Yeah. Alexander cares about family—legacy. He wants to pass his things to somebody before he dies. He said he owes it to my father."

And it made sense. From the very beginning, from the moment Ambrose had approached Soren in Avalon, he was after the body. Mr. Glickman had said that McAllister woke up several times at Keck and the doctors were expecting an imminent recovery. That was the perfect time for Ambrose to lay the groundwork for a different future.

And I didn't have any way to warn Soren without sounding like a madman.

"Why don't we get you a chair so you can sit down," offered Pam. She looked back for a waitress but Alexander put his hand up.

"That is not necessary. I do confess that I have some business with Mr. Butcher. I must have been so wrapped up in our affairs that I woefully neglected him. Perhaps we should cut the night short. I do apologize. My solicitor can see you home."

The excitement had been enough for Mr. Glickman. He approved of the plan and expeditiously convinced the other two to go with him. When Soren stood up, I noticed he held a walking stick with a white rose. It was Ambrose's, from the dream.

Alexander saw my eyes catch it. "I certainly don't need that heirloom anymore," he explained. Then he rapped the armrest of the wheelchair. When everyone was standing except him, I wondered if that was a ruse as well. Could Alexander really walk?

I thought to stop Soren and Pam from leaving, but wondered if they wouldn't be safer away from McAllister. I decided to play along. For now. When I shook Soren's hand and gave Pam a kiss on the cheek, I noted they were both clean. It was as I thought. A few moments later, the audience was gone.

I sat across from Alexander McAllister.

Chapter 42

"Have some wine, young friend." He poured a small amount in a new glass that was dropped off at the table and finished the bottle into his own. Given the situation, I normally would have declined the offer—but it was a Zinfandel from Paso Robles.

Don't drink with him.

"Don't worry," I said under my breath. I held the wine glass in my right hand. Alexander looked at the pocket watch in my other. Of all the people in the restaurant, only the two of us were aware that we sat at a table for three. Four, if McAllister and Ambrose counted double.

"How was last night's party?" he asked.

"A clever diversion on your part."

Alexander scratched his tan hair and feigned sympathy. "I am sorry it turned out to be a waste of time."

"I didn't say it was."

His eyes searched for the meaning of my words. For some reason, he then felt the need to defend himself. "You were on to Red Hat's trail without me."

"I was on to Red Hat's trail *because* of you."

Alexander's face remained firm. "Regardless, I gave you the in that you wanted with the company. Our reasons are vastly different, but they are an enemy to us both. I was not lying about that."

The wine had a deep oaky flavor that went down briskly. "I won't let you take Soren," I stated plainly. McAllister smiled. "All that talk about repentance and becoming an honest man. That was bullshit. You served your time on the Dead Side when McAllister was in a coma. Just like you did when Finlay was in prison. But your ambitions never wavered. You still intended to steal the lives of others."

Alexander McAllister carried the formality that Ambrose had in the dream world. No longer was he the tired and confused man I had met in that dusky loft. He spoke with more drive and had a boldness that wouldn't bend. "You know so much yet so little, Mr. Butcher. Don't you see that Soren, and all the others, are yearning to house our kind? He is weak and looking for escape. He seeks inner strength, a strength greater than his own."

I raised my voice. "You can rationalize that bullshit all you want, but it's still crap."

"Sir, you will address me as a gentleman."

"Oh come on. That facade of propriety isn't fooling anyone. You can convince the world you're doing it a favor, but I'm never going to buy that."

"You don't need to, Mr. Butcher. You can live without ever living, if you choose. You can waste away in death like so many other souls. That is your right; just don't impose your narrow will on me."

My frustration must have been evident. The man was intractable. As I fumed, I realized there was only one eventual conclusion to our conversation. I lowered my voice to a whisper. "I don't know how but I'm going to stop you."

Alexander smiled confidently. He knew he had set off my temper. He reveled in it. "You have much to learn. You have this power yet do not understand it. It tugs at you. You grow weary."

I took a breath. It was true. I was losing my cool. But this man, speaking of power in a way that insinuated he knew more about me than myself, made it difficult to be levelheaded. It wasn't easy to admit that a nemesis had the advantage in knowledge and experience. Maybe even strength. That's why I had to do things the way I was planning. It couldn't be done alone.

"You often speak of power," I said. "And yours is a great one. You're different. I can understand how it makes you feel invincible." Alexander looked at me intently as I spoke. "Most shades fight hard for their bonds with the flesh. Simply staying in this world is enough of a struggle."

Alexander was losing patience. "Many of us are above that trifle."

"And I have you to thank for bringing that to my attention. Violet never did. But I'm talking about your unique gift. You know how to jump into other bodies."

"At least for a short while," he admitted. "Finlay had some gangster friends that I worked. They set up my return to wealth."

"And Sal. And who knows how many others. You laid the groundwork through them for this."

"I did. But those were all short-term visits. You are an expert now, no? With my daughter's help, you had better be. Like all others, I can only truly bond with one man at a time. The others are temporary distractions."

"Did you take the lawyer too?"

Alexander raised his eyebrows. "Mr. Glickman? No, no. He is a meek man, but surprisingly strong-willed. You know that this business only works with acceptable hosts. I am afraid our dear lawyer is in the dark about all of this. He respects Alexander greatly. Even more after recovering from a long hospital stay." Ambrose shook his head. "It is going to shake the poor man."

There was something about what he said that threw me. I couldn't conceptualize his whole strategy yet. But there was another plan. The one he didn't know about. The one I was working. The waitress returned with his check and Alexander signed it. After she left, I casually lit a cigarette.

Alexander McAllister raised an eyebrow. "I believe Los Angeles has laws prohibiting smoking in restaurants now. Even outdoors."

"Yeah, I'm that asshole." I callously blew smoke across the table into his face.

"You do realize that sage won't expel me, Mr. Butcher. I've been at this too long. I know this business too well."

"I don't know that until I try it."

He sat a moment to give me the proof I needed. We both finished the wine. "Well then," he continued, "you certainly are aware that it would be useless to do so, even if it worked. I could just hop into another. Perhaps even Soren."

"Hmm," I said, flicking ash onto the floor. "That's why you sent him away."

"Indeed. And you let him leave."

I smiled sardonically. It wasn't ideal, but it would do in a pinch. "No doubt the limo driver is none other than your bodyguard, Bedros."

"Ah, then we are both abreast of the situation."

Smoke billowed from my nose and mouth slowly. "And what are you planning on doing with Pam?"

The man grinned. "The same that any red-blooded American man would, given half the chance." He must have seen my face darken. "Oh, don't worry. She will be a willing participant. I am not a monster."

I snorted at the appeal. Alexander Ambrose was an old man. He had a century on me. To be doing what he had been doing for so long must have completely broken his sense of morality. A man who could kill his own daughter could justify anything else with ease.

Violet had been quiet until now. Maybe it was her way of avoiding her father. Blocking out the association. But she had been listening. And she was thinking the same thing I was.

My father will convince you he's a good man before you ever change his mind about anything.

Once again, I burned inside.

"How could you do this?" I demanded. "How could you be such a son of a bitch? If not for what is just, can't you think about your daughter?"

Dante... don't.

Alexander didn't even register emotion. His face was stone, and his heart must have been harder.

"You disgust me," I said.

That got a reaction out of him. The man cared more about the respect afforded to him than the lives of others. With a disgruntled look on his face, he wheeled his chair away from and around the table. "If there is nothing else, Mr. Butcher—"

"Where do you think you're going?"

The wheelchair stopped right next to me. Alexander's eyes locked with mine in defiance. "A man is measured by his actions. A lifetime of accumulated behavior bears reputation."

"So?"

"So, sir, I believe you know full well where I am going and what I will do. I also know what you will do."

I swallowed. "What's that?"

Alexander Ambrose settled back in an unnatural comfort inside Alexander McAllister's body. "You will do nothing, Mr. Butcher. We've crossed paths four times before. Four times have we conversed. And four times you have done nothing." He stared dismissively at me. It was as though he didn't even have enough respect for me to harbor contempt.

"You are a talker, Mr. Butcher. You play amongst children to feel large, but when you confront a man, you withdraw. You have no piece to play. No viable action to take. This is a game you are not up for."

Alexander rolled away. He was right about many things but wrong about the reasons. Shades of his caliber were new to me. I hadn't been able to confront him yet because I hadn't known how. His deceptions had thrown me and Red Hat was a significant worry. To have rushed into this match without knowing the rules would have invited defeat. Now, I was far from an expert. But I thought I was getting a hang of the game.

I stood up and dug into my pocket. Crap. Soren's ring. I should have slipped it into Pam's purse or something. It didn't matter. It was a long shot. And it wasn't what I was reaching for.

Alexander wheeled himself into the open elevator with the assistance of the young hostess. I weaved my way through the tables and ignored everything else but the bead I had on him. I had tunnel vision. A single purpose. Nothing would let Alexander Ambrose get away from me tonight.

I shoved my hand between the closing elevator doors and they jerked to a halt and reversed. Alexander was only mildly surprised when I stepped inside next to him. He waited until we were in motion and had the elevator to ourselves to speak.

"More following. More watching," he said.

I grabbed the man by the hand. A strong surge of feeling flowed through me. His second shadow was a force worthy of awe that stood out from the dregs I was accustomed to. Its fingerprints were undeniable. "I'm afraid to disappoint you, Ambrose." I wasn't sure if he was going to remain calm or violently strike me, but he never got the chance. A puzzled look crossed his face as he heard the click of handcuffs locking his wrist to the chair.

"What's this?" he asked suddenly.

"Just something I picked up on the way here."

"Handcuffs?"

"You know, I've been wondering about why you forced Sal off the top of that building. You saw me after you. If you'd wanted to retreat to the Dead Side, you could have."

Alexander kept his gaze on the cuffs. He raised his hand and pulled against the armrest of the wheelchair to which he was bound.

I continued. "Most of the shades I banish, they're easy to explain. They have a single link to the world of the living that they've fought hard for. Leaving their hosts to run from me would likely mean abandoning this world. Never coming back again. They fight like criminals determined never to go back to prison. It's easier for them to, even, since they can't die. But you and Sal, those circumstances were different."

Ambrose ignored my point. "Congratulations, Mr. Butcher. You have succeeded in chaining a wheelchair-bound man to his chair. I do not believe that I have ever witnessed a more useless gesture."

"That's not what I did," I said. It was true that I questioned whether he could walk or not—the man was a liar—but the cuffs had another purpose. He turned to me with curiosity as the elevator door opened.

I smiled naturally at the man standing in the small room. Alexander began to wheel himself out. The armrest he was chained to was close enough to the top of the wheel for him to reach it. He could move himself. But he was slow. And the metal rattled. I impatiently took over his fumbling and pushed him. It would call less attention to the handcuffs.

At the main building elevator, a couple loitered in the hall. They jumped in with us, so it was a long, quiet ride down. Alexander had a strange expression on his face as he examined the metal around his wrist. The other two must have felt the hostility because they stared. Ambrose noticed, and lifted his left hand, casually revealing the cuffs. The girl was shocked.

I put my hands up emphatically. "Grandpa. He'd lose his wheelchair if he wasn't tied to it."

They broke away from us the first chance they got.

Once we were outside, I rolled Alexander through the crosswalk. He broke his silence. "There was very little time to leave Sal," he said, "with you on my trail. A banishment is an abrupt and painful transition, as I'm sure you're aware. A proper retreat would have been too time-consuming. Besides, I wanted to see you up close, with my own eyes. I wanted to see who was following me. That is how I recognized you on the Dead Side."

"And now?" I asked with a cocky grin. "What's keeping you from leaving now?"

The man was silent for a few moments before speaking. "Curiosity, Mr. Butcher."

I sneered at his weak reply. "The answer you're looking for is cold iron, Ambrose. Those handcuffs aren't normal steel. They're vintage. From an old military store."

"Iron?" he asked, placing all attention on his bound wrist.

"You really don't know, do you? That explains why Violet didn't know. Why I had to figure it out for myself."

"Figure out what?"

"The properties of iron. A horseshoe. It can be a deterrent, of course. But it's more than that. A shade can't pass through a coil of iron. It can be on a doorway. Or it can be around a body. I was thinking about how people focus so much on keeping shades out that they never thought about keeping them in. Now, I could be wrong about this, but it's a solid bet that the cold iron around your wrist will prevent you from slipping out of Alexander McAllister."

The man yanked against the chain once more. He didn't say a word.

"Hate to say it, Ambrose, but I think you're stuck with me."

We entered our final elevator, this one heading underground into the subway station.

Chapter 43

Most of the Metro stations in Los Angeles each have their own theme. Pershing Square Station is no different. As I wheeled Alexander McAllister along the island platform between the tracks on either side, I shuddered under the colorful neon lights. Bands of purple and pink supposedly celebrated the very first neon sign in the country, never mind that the car lot that displayed it was six blocks away. It was a tenuous connection and a strange tribute, and right now it annoyed me.

Alexander had been quiet for several minutes. I wasn't sure how he would react to his capture. He could've screamed for help at the first pedestrian that walked by. He could've claimed that he'd been kidnapped. My plan, if that happened, was to take him to the bathroom and put him in a choke hold until he was docile. But I had a feeling that Alexander was above such theatrics. A century of life will teach a man patience, if nothing else.

As it was, I found a quiet end of the terminal and waited for the next northbound train.

"I suppose I was hasty in my judgment of you, sir," the man finally said. I glanced at the chair momentarily and then continued my vigil of the tracks. I sat on a bench next to him but was uninterested in any more conversation. I just wanted to get this over with as fast as I could. When I didn't respond, he kept baiting me. "Do you do all of this for Mr. McAllister? Do you think to save him from his grief? Well, let me tell you that it is too late for him."

I scowled.

"In my experience," he said, "when a man has been other than himself for years, a part of his true being withers. You visited my host when I was not inside. You saw that the loft resembles a crypt more than a home. Didn't you notice his body was failing him? One foot in the grave. Now, my spirit is like a warm glow, giving his flesh an energy it lacked. A drive. Fingal went mad when I left. Finlay was already ill but quickly deteriorated upon my exit. How do you suppose poor Alexander will fare?"

"He has a chance," I countered. "Finlay was abandoned by you when he went to prison. How long had he been taken by that point? A decade? By all accounts, he was becoming a better person inside. Reforming. You were only in Alexander for four years before being struck down. And the coma may have even helped him. It could have re-acclimated his spirit to his body. Maybe he can live a normal life, after all."

Ambrose kept his face relaxed but I caught something he tried to hide. Was he impressed? I was just guessing. Spitballing. But I had to believe that shades didn't permanently destroy those they inhabited. I had to believe there was hope.

"The man has awoken to a world where his loving wife beat him with an iron and murdered his only daughter. He is broken, Mr. Butcher. Hope is meaningless if it is unrealistic."

My face darkened again. "Do you not feel the slightest remorse for the McAllisters? Four generations of a family were destroyed by you. They lived their lives as automatons, struggled with the reality of living with strangers, or were simply murdered. Only two pieces remain. Catriona will likely live out the rest of her life in Willow Gardens, and Alexander will find himself alone in a similar way. But at least he has money. Maybe he can do some good with it. Maybe he can add something to this world."

Alexander Ambrose was not sympathetic. As I spoke about the hardships of the family, not a trace of sadness or remorse crossed his features.

"McAllister," said Ambrose, letting each syllable play in its own beat. "It means 'son of Alexander.' I have often thought it fitting, if not a bit dry." The man rocked in his wheelchair and turned it to directly face me. "The money is mine, sir. I have earned every penny of it, not that... puppet."

"Think of it as restitution."

"I will not. But our difference of opinion on the matter is

academic. As of this evening, the inheritance of Mr. McAllister is no longer his."

I watched the smug expression on his face. He had done it already. He had beaten me to the punch. "Mr. Glickman. Soren."

"Correct, Mr. Butcher. Soren is in control of my estate now. He will forever believe his benefactor was an old friend of his father's, but it matters not. Whatever you tell him, he will cling to the money. It is human nature. But you and I both know that a fortune will not sate him. He will fall into his destructive cycle again. That is *his* nature. He will always be waiting for another shade, if not me."

"How long have you been watching Soren? How long have you wanted him?"

Alexander raised his eyebrows softly. "Soren was only one possibility. There were others. I kept a close watch on all of them. I looked for any opportunities."

"But why didn't you just do what I did? Why didn't you blow him full of sage and take over?"

Ambrose released a rare laugh. Not too loud. Not too long. But it was mirth all the same. "Mr. Butcher, for as much of an expert in these matters as I am, I must concede that banishment was never my priority. Like the iron loop. Simply said, I didn't know how to do it. Until you showed me."

"But Violet was the one who taught me—"

"She's a smart girl, my Viola. Extremely talented. She visited the living in that watch before I ever did. I needed her as a crutch in the beginning. Don't believe for a second that she isn't talented enough to do what I do. She is simply afflicted by morality." He paused in a moment of respect or contempt. It was hard to tell with him. "She must have learned about the sage after we parted ways. Or perhaps she had always known and kept it from me. I cannot say. For my part, I have discovered how to bind with a man while firmly rooted in another. It is not an easy process. It requires some time close to the prospect. But it can be done. As can anything. This world of ours, Mr. Butcher, is a fickle one. There is wonder and disappointment, but most of all, there is the unknown. It is a frontier wrought with mystery. For all I can do, there are others who can do more. Yet they marvel at my knowledge. My ability. Even you," he said, again with a hint of admiration, "you have gifts that confound me. You can see us in this world where no other can. It is a delicate web that we tread upon, never knowing where the next strand will take us."

I had always known I was different. That I was special in some way. That was undeniable, especially after Violet enlightened me. But I had never contemplated it. I didn't care why. Just as Ambrose had stated, the workings of life are a big mystery. In my book, the what was more important than the why.

As the lull in our conversation lengthened, I began to wonder what strange abilities were out there that I didn't know about yet. Could Violet do anything? I remembered seeing her on the Dead Side rendering Soren's shade to light. Ambrose had seen it too. Was that a power? Was that special? Then my thoughts took a foreboding slant. I thought about Bedros and Eladio and Emilio. Even Marquis. Here was a man that was undoubtedly dangerous, maybe even more of a monster than Ambrose. What could he do that the others couldn't? What made him special?

As if reading my face and sensing I was on another topic, Alexander picked my brain. "What are your intentions here? I don't want to hear about your lofty ideals. I don't want your world view. I mean here. Now. What are we doing?"

I looked up at the station monitor and checked the time on my cell phone. I was purposefully keeping the pocket watch put away, keeping Violet from the company of her father. We still had a few minutes and I exhaled a heavy breath. The bench didn't have a backrest so I leaned against both my hands behind me. "My primary concern is protecting Alexander McAllister and Soren."

"Only one of which is currently under your watch."

"I'll find Soren next."

"If you think he'll be easy to find, you're wrong. And even if you knew where he was, he's not alone."

"Don't place too much faith in Bedros. I've tangled with his sort before."

Alexander nodded. "And how do you plan on tangling with a true ghost? With a man that can jump bodies?" He lifted his arm and the cuffs rattled against the wheelchair. "This is only temporary, Mr. Butcher. Your actions have longer ramifications. By now you must be aware that I have bound myself to Soren. The seed is planted. He is mine." Alexander looked around Pershing Square Station. "It is much like this rail. Or better yet, like the Southern Pacific that had a hold on me in another lifetime. The train is barreling ahead. It is an iron horse with the momentum of a giant. Fingal, Finlay, Alexander—they were all stops, not destinations. You can raise trouble. You can slow the titan. My acquaintance with Soren may meet a delay at your hands but it will surely happen. It is a guarantee. You are merely changing the timeline."

I nodded in resignation. "You're right. I don't know how to stop you. But it's not me that's going to."

Suspicion immediately clouded Alexander's face. "What? Where are we going?"

"You were sly when you threw me off your trail. You just needed a little more time to bind with Soren and you got it. But you made a mistake." Alexander listened to my words intently. My smile was difficult to contain. "Did you think introducing me to your enemy was a smart move, Ambrose?" The man still did not register recognition. It looked as though I had finally outmaneuvered him. "We're taking this train into Hollywood. Visiting the headquarters of Red Hat Events. Your good friend Marquis is waiting for you there."

A look of absolute horror consumed the face of Alexander McAllister and the face of Alexander Ambrose behind it. I had him. And he knew it.

"He thinks I'm bringing him Soren," I explained. "I was never going to do that. The innocent deserve a chance. But you?"

"You would cooperate with a demon to bring justice to a sinner? You can't do this!"

"I can," I said coldly. "You completed your service to him. You paid him off and hoped he'd forget about you. And he did. But then you embezzled the riches back through your gangster buddies over the course of Fingal's fifteen-year prison sentence."

"Bah! The man promised me eternal life. What he wanted was eternal servitude. I gave him that life. I sacrificed my future by handing over all of my assets. He still would have taken more."

I scoffed. "Do you hear yourself? You've stolen everything from the McAllisters yet you object to what Marquis did? Even a robber doesn't like getting robbed."

"I improve the lives of these men. They are weak without me. I collect their riches. I build their legacies. Not Marquis. He is a leech. I was supposed to live for him, but I couldn't do that." My expression was stone against his words. He became frustrated. "I am a self-made man. I have provided for myself and lost it all three times over. You talk about morality. Then see me for what I am. A man who was dragged down by the dirty politics of the Southern Pacific Railroad. A man who looked for a way out for his daughter. A man who was tricked into servitude in the afterlife. No, Mr. Butcher. I won't submit to your outlook. I won't be trodden on. I will *not* be a slave any longer."

I laughed as a wash of underground air blew over me. It had a chill to it that made this place feel hollow. When the train approached, you could feel it before you heard it.

Ambrose continued pleading. "You assume moral superiority yet turn to a shade worse than I. How does helping him aid the greater good? You are just giving him another soldier to march for him in the coming years."

"Don't you see the irony?" I asked with scorn. "You talk of servitude—don't you see that you were always free?" The man gaped at me hesitantly. In the distance, the grating of the train against the metal tracks grew louder. I could see a faint light building in the tunnel. "You had a life, Ambrose. You lived it. You found success with the railroad. You had a wonderful daughter. For whatever reason, you decided to end it all."

"Begin it," he corrected, but the confidence in his voice was gone.

"You're dead, Alexander. You no longer belong here. You're supposed to move on to whatever's next. But you cling to this life. To this servitude. Can't you see that Marquis can only enforce his will on you if you remain in his world? If you opened your eyes, if you made peace with your circumstances, you could leave all this behind. The McAllisters, Soren, Red Hat—they would all be of no more consequence to you. You're enslaving yourself."

The man stared with indignation for several moments. He couldn't accept the elegance of my solution. Alexander Ambrose was not like most people. He was callous to the point of indifference. He cared for himself. Others, even his own daughter, were either tools or burdens. It was clear he was a psychopath, with no thought for the pain his actions had wrought.

It didn't matter. Fear could make a man appear repentant. That was why we were here. That was why

Marquis would be left to deal with him.

"You're not saving anyone," spoke Ambrose, finally. "Even Marquis is powerless here. Alexander McAllister is a dying man. Soren will inherit his riches no matter your actions."

I shook my head slowly. I was done with his lies. "You forget that I spoke to the hospital staff, Ambrose. Your lawyer. You're not terminal."

The man's eyes glazed over and he set his jaw. "Oh yes, Mr. Butcher, I am."

Alexander McAllister thrashed his hands hastily against the wheels of his chair. He jolted backwards. I lunged ahead to stop him, but it was too late. The chair flew off the platform and into the path of the oncoming train. In a flash, the cavernous space was filled with a rocket of metal blazing by, trying desperately to stop.

Chapter 44

I dipped out of there with a quick sprint up the stairs. I glided along 5th Street. Blended in with the crowd. Took a right down Spring and a left on 6th. Anything to make sure I wasn't seen or followed. I wondered about the cameras in the station. Were there any? Was I complicit in what had happened? Would running make me look guilty? I decided any possible video evidence could only exonerate me. I didn't push the man.

The handcuffs were a problem. It wouldn't look like a straightforward suicide to the police. Perhaps I should call 911. I could explain that I was worried he was suicidal. That the handcuffs were a protective measure.

Instead, I crossed Main Street near the old center of Downtown. A small crowd congregated around a split in the sidewalk. Steps led down just below street level and exposed a couple of hidden storefronts. I found myself heading to one of these, into a bar called the Association. Now was as good a time to drink as any. Better, even.

Opening the large door with the lion's head knocker, I was greeted with music and a darkness that added to the underground feeling. But the bar inside was inviting. Warm. The red carpet and leather chairs, the chic crowd, dressed nicely but not overly so—it was a good scene. A good place to blend in.

I ordered a Flor de Caña and coke, no fruit. The distinctive spiced rum paired well with cola and was one of the many reasons I liked this bar. I took my drink and stepped up to the seating level, weaving around the ottomans and patrons until I found an open corner under a tilted mirror along the wall. It wasn't empty here—I had to squeeze in between two guys—but I fit in. I tried to relax as I listened to the blend of indie music and dance beats.

When the waitress came by, I ordered another. I was finished with my first by the time she brought it. By then, I still hadn't managed to settle down. I kept wondering if Alexander McAllister was dead because of me. I had believed what I said about him having a chance for a normal life. If I hadn't trapped Ambrose in his body, if I hadn't made that play, then maybe he would have recovered.

I pulled out my phone and pocket watch. With the chain dangling from my hands and the phone in my palm, I pretended I was having a conversation. Nobody could hear me anyway; the music clouded most of my words. But, to the people next to me, I looked normal.

"What the fuck? He killed McAllister."

With the handcuffs in place, it was the only way he could free himself. At least we know that iron works.

"That doesn't make me feel better."

It's okay. We didn't see that coming.

"I should have, though. He did the same thing with Sal, didn't he? People are just pawns to him. When I outplay him, he gleefully wipes the piece off the board and moves to another. How am I supposed to save Soren like that?" I sucked at my highball in my left hand. "Shit. He must really be terrified of Marquis."

I'm afraid to imagine what that means.

"It means I'm fucked from both ends."

That's not true. We know to look for Soren.

"Ambrose told me that Soren would be hard to find. Bedros is probably keeping him prisoner at a hidden location somewhere."

Bedros doesn't need to hold Soren. My father has already taken him. If the bond was already established, and with McAllister dead, my father should have full control now. Permanent.

I swigged some more rum. "So not only do I need to find him, I need to expel him. Except that isn't so easy. I felt him. His second shadow. Like Marquis, he's different."

Different, how? A shade is a shade.

"That's not true. You told me yourself that the Dead Side has disparate effects on spirits. There are no rules. Some people can do things. Some fall into separate categories. It's like the shades that infect their hosts and make them sick. The ones in the hospitals. I've tried exsufflating them before. It doesn't work. There are all kinds of haunts out there, and we've only been dealing with a small subset of them."

So what are you saying?

"There's no way the sage will work on Ambrose. Even if he's unconscious. He can hop around too freely. His bond is too strong. I need another way to stop him."

We stopped talking as a popular song came on and people started singing the chorus. Some girls farther down the booth seat were laughing and one of them almost fell. It was funny. Such a small thing, a meaningless fumble, but it was great. I needed the distraction.

That's why you think you need Marquis. You don't think you can confront my father on your own.

I grumbled when she vocalized it. It was an admission of weakness. But what did I care anymore? "Something like that. And it was working. Marquis remained cordial as long as I could be useful to him. But I failed to deliver."

You need to smooth things over with him. He knows where you live.

I knew that already. I knew I needed to tell him something. I knew I was screwed. Everything used to be so much simpler when I was anonymous. I sighed and lowered my phone so I could see the screen. "Soren's no longer interested in Red Hat," I texted.

It took a minute for him to get back to me. It felt like twenty. "Our arrangement does not allow for such developments."

I shook my head and drank some more and waved at the

waitress for another. There was no point texting back. I didn't bother. Marquis wasn't the type of man who accepted dismissal. I slammed my empty glass on the cocktail table hard enough to skip some ice out of it and waited for my next.

A pair of guys sitting on my right cleared out, leaving a gaggle of girls at my side. They slid along the seat to fill out the empty space. The leftmost one bumped into me and must have seen my depressed face. "Oh my God. I'm sorry. Are you okay?"

"No worries," I quickly responded. I tried to lighten my thoughts and look as if I wasn't hiding from an attempted murder arrest. The girl next to me was short. Mexican. Cute, with long hair. A bit on the thick side, but she had a well-shaped body which she accentuated by wearing a tight blouse that pushed her cleavage up. It was practically in my face. I must have stared too long. "I'm okay now," I said, trying to play it off.

She looked at me with a single eyebrow raised. "Get a good look?"

"Not really," I answered. "Your clothes are in the way."

She smirked almost indecipherably. She didn't know what to make of me yet.

I decided to press my luck. "You shove me again, though. See what happens."

"Is that right? Maybe you don't know who I am." She puffed her chest out like she wanted to start a scrap. She was being playful but it was damn sexy. "I grew up in the hood."

"Oh yeah? What hood is that—the OC?"

She blinked at me in total shock. "Irvine," she said. "How'd you know?"

I laughed audibly despite my best efforts and put a hand to my forehead. "What the hell are you doing all the way in Downtown LA?" I shook my head. "It's almost not even worth it."

She immediately frowned. "What's not worth it?"

I hadn't meant to make the comment out loud. Or not so loud, anyway.

Guys and girls from all the surrounding neighborhoods, even counties, push into the heart of Los Angeles on the weekends to party with everybody else. It has its good points. There are lots of bars and lounges with steady business and a diverse clientele.

But it made for a crappy surprise, sometimes. What use was it flirting with a girl who lived over an hour away? I didn't even have my car with me. Nothing was going to happen tonight.

"Nothing," I said, trying not to be a complete dick. "It's just, I live in the Valley and you live in Irvine. Are you going all the way back there tonight?"

"Of course. We do it all the time."

I winced. "Listen, you're cute but..."

"It's not worth talking to me?"

She stared at me a moment, probably expecting a witty reply on my part. I had nothing. She slapped an open hand against my shoulder just hard enough to show that she wasn't playing around anymore. "Asshole!"

I hadn't gotten my next drink yet but I had worn out my

welcome. The girl whispered to her friends and I was getting some angry glares. On my way out, I gave some cash to the waitress and grabbed my last cocktail from her tray. I downed half of it before I realized it was a Jack and coke. It wasn't my drink. And I hated whiskey. I returned the unfinished highball and apologized, then retreated from the lounge.

Hiding wasn't as fun as I'd thought it would be.

Walking back on the streets of LA, I thought about the girl's cleavage once more and shook my head. If only she lived close-by. I could have used a safe place to crash for the night. But Irvine? She was crazy. The girl was wrong when she'd said that I meant it wasn't worth talking to her. Talking was fine. It was even fun when I was up to the game. No. I had learned my lesson about girls from the OC. It wasn't even worth fucking them.

Chapter 45

For a long time the Metro in LA closed at midnight. I've never understood why that was. Los Angeles was built on the entertainment industry. It caters to a lot of single people with disposable income. That's a great recipe for drinking. Also DUIs. You would think it's in a city's best interests to get its drinkers home safely.

Back in Miami, the bars stay open all night, 4 a.m., 5 a.m.—alcohol is still served. I've always thought it strange that a mega-city like Los Angeles turns off the taps at two. With that in mind, closing the subway early was even more ridiculous. Surely it could've matched last call?

Well, sometime over a year ago, someone had finally gotten some sense and extended the operating hours on Friday and Saturday night. Whoever that political figure was, I thanked them silently, because I would have missed my train if it wasn't for them.

I walked out of my way to the 7th Street Station to avoid returning to Pershing Square. The train would have to roll through it, though. Because of the delays, the car was packed. I settled for standing near the doors and thought about what Ambrose had said. He was right. You can't stop the train, only delay it. Before the Pershing Square station, train traffic was redirected to a single track, slowing our entrance. I realized it would've been faster if I had walked to the Metro station that was *after* the suicide.

Through the soiled windows, all the passengers stared at the platform filled with emergency officials. Transportation workers, police, security guards, and paramedics all hustled around the scene like ants. All with a focused job to perform. All contributing to the greater whole. That's society for you, and whether insects or people, this shared vision of order is what makes it work. I looked away with disgust and wondered how many people would have faith in humanity if they knew about the dead that refused to let us be.

Once we were through the terminal, we picked up the pace. Over time, the train emptied. The backup began to unclog and outward appearances returned to normal. Except for the gangbanger lurking around trying to cause trouble. He was a kid with a ragged skateboard who kept punching walls and seats for no reason. Like he wanted to unsettle the passengers. To pick a fight. He was pretty close to me and I was almost in the right mood to accommodate him.

Instead, a black dude who had been sitting peacefully stood up and punched the kid. Just like that. Out of nowhere. I was surprised the boy didn't go down. Then they both started waving their arms and yelling and getting in each other's faces. Neither would back down. Some of the passengers pushed to the ends of the car and watched with fear. I wasn't as careful.

The kid started to take a pounding. He was in over his head and he knew it. He used the skateboard to compensate, swinging it around in an arc. Before I grasped the danger, it clipped me on the side of the head. I stumbled back against the train doors, at first attempting to get out of the way, and then realizing I was too late.

My head was full of stars. I applied pressure to dull the bleary pain. Then I looked at the asshole who started this. I wasn't concerned with leaving it a fair fight anymore.

After another wild swing, I lunged at the kid and socked the back of his head. Again. The black guy took the skateboard and backed away. To the other set of doors. I kept punching. Not noticing as the train stopped. The doors opened. Passengers left the car. Shuffling by me in a dizzying scurry. I looked to my feet and saw the kid lying on the floor. Unconscious. He hadn't even seen what hit him.

The doors didn't close as they were supposed to. The train wasn't going anywhere. I glanced outside and saw a fat security guard approaching me in a stilted walk. The slightly hurried pace was only for appearances, but the older man couldn't muster much. All he saw was this kid on the floor and my hand in a fist.

I faltered back a step.

"What happened?" demanded the transit security guard.

Somehow, he still sounded bored, like I was interrupting his coffee.

I looked around for the black guy with the skateboard, but he was gone.

"This banger was causing trouble." I waved my arm to some of the onlookers. "Ask them."

Before he got the chance, a strange nausea overtook me. I was still a little dizzy but my head wasn't the problem. I didn't feel right. Without warning, a stream of vomit erupted from my mouth. It was messy. It wasn't that much but it managed to get on my shoes, the kid, the train, and the station brick as I ran outside the car.

I steadied myself against a wide pillar. The world continued to move.

"Step aside," I heard from behind the crowd. I noticed a cell phone recording me. As the audience shifted, a police officer cut through.

"Motherfucker."

I'd never gone to jail before. Mind you, I probably should have a handful of times for offenses much worse. But no. I was always clear. And then this stupid kid got on my train that happened to have a cop walking by, and here I was.

The police dragged me into the Hollywood station in

handcuffs. Steel, not that it mattered. I didn't know what happened to the kid. Never found out. I told them he was the one who started it. I tried to explain what happened. They didn't want to hear it.

"Hey man, I got smacked in the head with a skateboard. I probably have a concussion or something."

"Yeah?" asked the younger cop, strutting me down the hallway as if he was walking to theme music that only he could hear. "If you're hurt, I'll take you to County. Get you looked at. But trust me. You don't want to go to County. They won't treat you as nice as us." I clenched my jaw. It sounded more like *he* didn't want to go there.

They chained me to a long wooden bench with a metal railing that sat in an even longer hallway. And they just left me there. All alone. Why was the bench so long?

The cuffs were tight. I was surprised at how fast thirty minutes passed and how quickly my arms became sore. Still, I sat quietly, deciding not to say anything else. I wasn't getting any help here. Maybe I could get Mr. Glickman to get me out of whatever jam I was in.

As I mulled over my future options, an officer opened the door at the far end of the hallway and announced, "It's time!" The boys in blue all laughed and crowded around the side rooms, leaving the hallway clear. Then the officer nodded and a girl walked in. Two steps inside and she stopped, raised her hands, and spun in a circle. Everyone laughed some more. Jeers and whistles were added to the mix.

Then another girl came in after her. And another. It was

a line of prostitutes, but most of them were treating this like a modeling show. As the girls neared, I realized the rub. They weren't girls at all. Every single one of them was a guy in drag. There must have been at least ten of them and they all filed in and were handcuffed to the bench next to me.

"Oh, hello handsome," said the nearest guy in a thick Latina accent with a lisp. He slid flush to me and leaned his head onto my shoulder.

"Come on," I appealed to one of the cops walking by.

"I think she likes you," was all he said in return. A few of them had a chuckle at that and I wished I had finished that Jack and coke.

The rest of the night was kind of like that. Ridiculous, bureaucratic, and pointless. My possessions and shoelaces were stripped from me. When they took the pocket watch, I thought about Finlay losing it for fifteen years in a similar manner. They put me in a holding cell where I was allowed to use the phone. I tried to call Trent but he didn't pick up. I briefly thought about Eva, but I didn't want her to know. There was no one else so I just waited. Eventually, they threw me in a small cell with other guys. The cops weren't really telling me much, but I assumed this was the drunk tank. I was hoping I'd spend the night in jail and be released in the morning. No harm, no foul.

I collapsed on a thin mattress and closed my eyes.

Chapter 46 - Dream

The dizziness followed me into the dream.

It was difficult to see. The night was pitch black, the street lamps ineffective. I drifted aimlessly along the only path I could make out. The street here wasn't too wide. I didn't recognize it but it was somewhere downtown. The unmistakable buildings surrounded me, threatened to close in.

I had proven before that I could master the haze. Solidify the mist. Where once I was a passenger I had become the captain, guiding the environs at my pleasure. But not this time. The storm clouded my senses. My thoughts. Was that panic over my shoulder?

I spun around. "Violet?"

There was no answer. No movement. I trudged along the lonely streets and it seemed I was the only thing not frozen in time or fog. I walked backwards for a short while, making sure no one was following me. I didn't see or hear anyone else. I turned again.

Were the buildings closer now? This wasn't a main thoroughfare. An alley, maybe. Why was I here? What was I looking for?

What was looking for me?

I forged ahead. Not so much out of a sense of purpose, but of dread. Keep moving, I told myself. Focus. Put my shoe to the street. Feel it. Touch it. Press it. Press on.

The glamour of the haze made me weak. I tried to fight against it. I tried to push it away. But I wasn't a man. Not here. This wasn't my world. I didn't belong.

What was that?

A shadow where the world was dark. A lapse where the rumbling in my head was silent. Was that my mind? The pain. It came back. Perhaps it had not yet arrived. But now my skull felt like it was about to burst.

I tried to scream but I was one with the nothingness. All about me, the shapes were out of focus. Transitional. Shifting, yet still. No one was around to hear me so I made no noise.

I failed. I released the tension in my mind. I unclenched my jaw. I let go of the fight because my fingers were too weak to make a fist. If this world would have its way then I would not protest.

Nothing else worked. I had nowhere to go. Sometimes clarity can only be gained by looking inward. Relaxing. Sometimes, to hear what isn't there, you just have to forget

about everything else and stop.
But it was there. And it spoke.
You are not alone.

Chapter 47 - Sunday

This Sunday morning started out very differently from the last. A week ago, I woke up after a successful hunt. I had banished Nero. Hung with Trent. I'd even had a one night stand with... What was her name again?

I rubbed my head. It throbbed with a dull pain that lingered in the background. Well, that part was about the same as last Sunday. Except I didn't have any aspirin or glasses of water, and the only toilet was a pitifully dirty bowl without a cover (or privacy) in the corner of the room. It was currently being used by a large Samoan man.

So I was in jail. Besides the headache, I had none of the comforts of a lazy morning in my apartment. Or the desire to sleep in. But even worse than wearing shoes loosened by their lack of laces was the fact that I didn't have the pocket watch with me.

"You okay, bro?" The voice came from a young Hispanic

guy, about the same age as the kid who had clocked me with the skateboard. I nodded. "You looked pretty shaky last night. What'd you do?"

I sat up on the bed and examined the small cell. It wasn't like the movies. There were no metal bars, just a glass wall set against painted brick. Six beds were stuffed in the cramped quarters and every one of them was taken. The other five guys were awake and staring at me, waiting for my answer.

"I got in a fight on the subway," I said dispassionately. "And then I puked on the guy."

Everybody laughed. I admit, it made me smile too. It was pretty funny.

"What did he do?" asked the kid.

"Hit me in the head with a skateboard." They laughed again but saw that I wasn't joking. I wondered what I looked like. There was no blood on my hands. I didn't feel it caked to my skin either.

Another kid, this one younger, nodded. "We thought you grabbed a bike or something. Tried to fight the police."

"Grabbed?"

The older kid spoke up. "It's bullshit. I was walking down Hollywood and I see a bike lying in the middle of the sidewalk, you know? So I picked it up to, like, put it against the building, out of the way. Next thing I know, cops be jumping out from everywhere, telling me to put my hands up on my head."

The younger kid agreed. "Me too. I wasn't gonna creep it. I was just moving it a little bit. That's all."

I chuckled, more to share their pain than poke fun. "You guys got caught in an organized bicycle sting?"

"Yeah man," answered the original one. "Like I said. Bullshit. If you were walking down the street and you saw a penny on the floor, you would take it, right?"

Hell no, I thought, but I didn't want to interrupt his story.

"It's the same thing. I saw a bike. No one else had it. It was just... there."

I shook my head in feigned agreement. "Bullshit."

"I know, right?"

I thought of all the prison movies I'd watched. The scene came to mind where the prisoners traded stories about what they were in for: "I killed a man for looking at me funny." That type of thing. Granted, I was only in jail, but I had never imagined how ridiculous the stories could get.

There was a white guy in a grungy Eagles jersey lying on his side, paying attention with tired eyes. "You guys are lucky," he said with an accent that suggested he was raised in a trailer. "Tomorrow morning you'll go to court and be cut loose." He heaved himself to a sitting position and shook his head with resignation. "Not me."

I wasn't sure if anyone else had heard his story yet. I asked anyway. "What happened?"

"My girlfriend's got a restraining order on me. But, see, I was living with her for the last seven months. You know how that is." He said it as if we'd all been there. I just nodded. "Well, we had an argument a few nights ago because I forgot to record her show and she called the cops.

They said there was nothing they could do. She had the restraining order so I got arrested."

"Even if she had welcomed you back in?"

"Doesn't matter," he said. "The bitch of it is that this was the second time they caught me on it. I can pay a fine or I can serve ninety days. But I don't got no three thousand dollars." The man leaned back against the brick wall, as if he had exerted enough energy for the day. "Nope. Better to just wait it out in here."

There was some other small talk but I paid less attention to conversation from that point on. I had thought I was in the drunk tank or something. That I would be kicked loose this morning. But everyone else here was talking about bail and court and staying long-term. What had I gotten myself into last night?

I began planning a course of action. I decided I needed to make a phone call and get out of here today, not tomorrow. That meant calling Trent again, probably. I had some money in my account. I could pay a fine. But I didn't feel I needed to. I didn't do anything wrong last night.

Before I could get past that stage of thought, a police officer walked up to the clear plastic wall. "Who's Dante?"

"That's me."

"Let's go."

The others in the cell looked at me with a combination of envy and pride. I was just with them for a short time but they were happy that *somebody* was getting out. I was too. It's weird, the type of camaraderie that can be built up in special circumstances. It's always better to be a victim in a group. I shook their hands and followed the officer.

"What happened?" I asked.

"Bailed out. Walk through that door, sign up front, and pick up your belongings."

"What was I charged with?"

"I don't know. But I'm sure they told you. If you weren't drunk, you'd remember."

"I wasn't drunk. I got hit on the head with a skateboard."

The officer furrowed his brow. "That some new slang with the kids these days?"

I let out an audible snort. If there was a definition of doing the bare minimum, this guy was doing less than it.

"Who bailed me out?"

The man just looked ahead and shrugged. I doubted he still remembered my name. Shit, of all people, I guess I couldn't hold that against him. I stopped asking questions.

I gave my signature at the desk and turned to see Emilio leaning against the wall. His hardened expression seemed at home in the Hollywood police station. I sighed. This was turning into a hell of a morning. I gathered my scattered articles into a heap and held them in my hand.

There you are.

"I don't want to talk about it, Violet."

The strongman held the front door open and motioned outside with his head. Yeah, no shit, dumbass. He led me down the sidewalk to a nearby red limo. The engine was running and Emilio invited me in. I decided to get this over with as soon as possible. I was hungry and needed a shower.

Chapter 48

The seats in the car were a deep burgundy and did a decent job of matching the paint color of the exterior. The rest of the trim—carpet, felt ceiling, tints—was black. I'd never seen a limo quite like it. Marquis sat across from me, wearing a soft yellow shirt and gray vest. Once again, his collar was raised like some sort of one man fashion statement.

"I assume you need a ride?" he asked.

I nodded and dropped my belongings on the seat beside me. The car pulled out and headed north. Emilio was also inside, but seated at the other end. With us but separate, as I'm sure Marquis preferred. I couldn't see the driver. Nobody said anything as we headed up Cahuenga and got on the 101. By then I was almost finished lacing my shoes.

"I don't think there's much to the assault charge," said Marquis, watching me. "I've spoken with my lawyer. He'll call you tomorrow. I'm sure you can plan on the DA dropping the charges altogether."

I wanted to tell him that I didn't need his help. That I could handle it. But it sounded like a good deal. "I don't want to owe you anything."

"But you already do," he said firmly. "I'm just protecting my investment. Don't worry about the lawyer. It will only be an hour of his time and he's on retainer. The only matter I want you to concern yourself with is my soldier. Tell me about Soren."

"He's off the table."

"Unacceptable."

"I'm telling you, Marquis. He's come into money. He doesn't need a job with Red Hat."

The man rubbed the wiry gray scruff on his neck. I couldn't tell if he was disappointed or pleased. "That is your choice, then?"

"It's his choice."

"I'm afraid you're confusing Soren's deal with the one you and I made. In our arrangement, you have a choice. To make up for banishing Christian, you are to deliver Soren to me. Or you may deliver yourself." Marquis nodded to Emilio. The strongman leaned forward and locked his hands together menacingly. "If you refuse one, you are implicitly agreeing to the other."

"There's another option." I finished with the laces and rummaged through my belongings. No money appeared to be missing. I still had Soren's ring. Everything was in order. I returned the items to my pockets, one by one, but I kept the watch in my hand. I waved it to catch the attention of Marquis.

"The Hamilton pocket watch," he said, "I've seen one like it before. It is your crutch, is it not?" I peered at him with questioning eyes. He immediately explained himself. "Your conduit to this world. Is it the watch?"

"What are you talking about?"

He studied me plainly. "You do have a conduit between both worlds, do you not? The Dead Side draws us all. The watch is what strengthens your bond here."

I sighed, already fed up with the man. "I told you. I'm not like you."

He brought his lips together in a frown. "I understand your hesitation, Dante, but you are too wary. Trust is the foundation of relationships."

"Listen," I said, holding the timepiece up, "you're telling me you don't recognize this exact watch?"

"I recall one similar to it, ages ago. I forget who it belonged to. I've lived a great many years, Dante. Small details elude me."

"Dude, this was Alexander Ambrose's railroad watch. His daughter held it as he killed her. Seeing as how you had a hand in that, you should have the decency to remember."

He thought in silence for a minute. I figured he was surprised, even if he refused to show it. "I see," was all he said.

"That's it? That's all you got? I say that name and you pretend not to be interested?"

A loud squealing sound interrupted us. Emilio was

sliding closer to me and his leather pants rubbed against the seat. Marquis waved him off. I shook my head, impatiently, thinking I was being jerked around. Marquis saw my reaction and explained. "Alexander was an associate of mine at the turn of the last century. He was a headache to maintain but he paid his dues. At the end of his life, we parted ways amicably. He may not have been my best investment, but he completed his contract. Unlike you." The man suddenly leaned forward and glued his eyes to me. "Tell me, you're not Alexander, are you?"

"Me? No, man."

He rested against the seat again. "No, of course not. You don't act very much like him, barring the headache. Besides, that would be impossible. But yes, I do remember the watch now."

I snorted. I wasn't sure what he meant, but it didn't seem like anything was impossible these days. Marquis had been oblivious to Ambrose all these years. There was a lot he didn't know. But the man still knew more than I did.

"Maybe you could fill me in then," I said. "Tell me about him."

"I'd prefer not to discuss my business."

"Why don't you look at it as the foundation of our relationship?"

Marquis smiled and nodded his head in acquiescence. His tenor made it clear he was humoring me, but he talked. "Alexander was an ambitious man. He came from poor stock, like myself. Unlike me, however, his skin color did not hold him back." I wondered exactly how old Marquis was but I didn't interrupt him. "Given a shave and a bath, a fresh coat, and proper parlance, Alexander came across as a gentleman. But I was never fooled by the veneer. Alexander was a hustler. An opportunist. He climbed the ranks of the Southern Pacific Railroad, a company more corrupt than any other at the time. And that's saying a lot. Pay-offs, dirty deals, blackmail—the monopoly influenced many State interests. The railroad controlled growth. They decided which cities were prosperous—wealth was literally carted along the tracks. Los Angeles was not above the extortion. But eventually the public backlash and rise of regulation called for a number of scapegoats, and Alexander was among them. He spun the plates for as long as he could but they were bound to shatter. He was a proud man who desperately needed a way out, and I was happy to oblige."

"What's special about the watch?"

"Perhaps I should tell you a little bit about myself," he said. "Many in this world have gifts. And many have curses. Some men die and look to ascend into the ether. Others yearn to return to their old lives. Neither is possible, as we both know. The majority die and leave their fate to chance, arbitrarily drifting where the Winds take them. But I was never a strong proponent of chance."

"You can control it."

"I have a special gift. A Touch. It is with this that I can snatch a spirit from the aimlessness of freedom. My grip bolsters a singular focus. A single desire."

"To remain on the Dead Side. You can ensure the dying turn into shades."

He nodded in confirmation of my statement.

"And you can return them to the world of the living?"

"I can hold them back from the Endless Winds. For them to return here is another trick entirely. It must be worked into them like a soldier sent to boot camp. This can take decades. Alexander did it in twelve years."

"He used the watch."

"His daughter did. She was the first of Alexander's deceptions. The girl was never supposed to be killed. Alexander had volunteered himself into my service, not her. He was to commit suicide with a personal item, something valuable to increase the chances of it not being destroyed. The watch was that item."

I never knew it was important. I had always liked holding it. He let me hold it.

The picture began to solidify in my mind. "So Ambrose decided to take his daughter with him and gave her the watch. But how did he know that he would ever see her in the world of the dead? You didn't use your Touch on her, did you?"

Marquis shook his head. "There must be an indignance in death," he answered. "But it is never certain. Not without me."

"So he took a chance. He gambled and won?"

"I would say so."

I thought about it some more. "Unless he knew what he was doing."

"Impossible. How does a man truly know about death before his own? There would have been no way for him to predict what would ultimately happen to his daughter back then. But Alexander is long since beyond us. Why are we speaking of him?"

I looked intently at the Royal, eager to ruin his smugness. "He's still here," I said dramatically. Marquis barely raised an eyebrow.

"Among the living? Well, if that's true then perhaps he was stronger than I'd given him credit for. I'm still failing to see—" The man stopped himself and rubbed the ebony bald spot on the back of his head. "Ah. You mean to supplant Soren with Alexander."

"And myself. If I give you Ambrose, you cut ties with both of us." Emilio chuckled and Marquis shot him a deathly glare.

"You forget that he was practically more trouble than he was worth. Why would I want him?"

"You just admitted that you underestimated him. Look at him now. He's here, and he's not even relying on the watch."

Marquis shrugged dismissively. "A conduit is not necessary. It only helps. It can strengthen the bond with the host. Keep them from being..." He trailed off, as if he didn't want to tell me anymore.

"Expelled," I said. I knew some spirits were stronger than others, but maybe Ambrose shrugged off the sage because of a conduit. Initially, in his early years, he'd always kept the watch around. Whether he shared it with Violet or her bond had helped him, I wasn't sure, but I did know that he began to carry the watch less and less. He left it behind.

He did his own thing. It would fit if he had his own conduit. "What if Ambrose figured out how to make his own conduit?"

"Impossible," said Marquis again. He was a little heated. First, upset that he had accidentally educated me on a banishment technique. Second, perhaps, because of his ego. He didn't want any others to rival his power. "He is only a man."

I contemplated his eyes as he said that last part. What did Marquis mean? How old was he? What did he consider himself, if not a man?

The Royal regained his cool. "No," he said again. "You interest me. I believe we can help each other. Failing that, I will have Soren follow me."

The car exited the highway and headed northwest on Lankershim. We were in North Hollywood, almost at my apartment.

"The thing is, Ambrose is after Soren now too." The expressive eyes of Marquis lit up as he finally began to understand.

"He means to possess him?"

"If he hasn't already."

"And he is skilled enough to do this?"

I gripped the pocket watch securely. "I have reason to believe he is."

"Well then, that makes the choice easy for you. If Soren has already fallen victim to another, you should have no qualms delivering him to me."

"You don't understand," I stated decisively. "It makes

everything more difficult."

The Royal glanced at Emilio and then back at me. He was operating on an entirely different set of morals, but he came to understand my dilemma. "You intend to free Soren. Except you are torn because, in banishing Alexander, you no longer have him to give me." He saw the confirmation in my troubled face. "I will make this easy for you. I want Soren, not Alexander. And he's no good to me without free will."

The words of the Royal tripped me up for a moment. Maybe I'd been an idiot, but I finally realized what Marquis wanted to do with Soren. Just then. "You don't want him for a host, do you? When you told me it would be his decision to follow you or not, you weren't lying."

Marquis didn't say anything. To him, it was obvious. Considering him a liar was insulting.

"Except you never get your hands dirty. You're looking for someone to kill themselves and serve you in another life. Another soldier. Another Ambrose." Marquis was a man of questionable morals, no doubt, but he placed importance on keeping his word. Even though I felt like I was in the presence of evil, I took some comfort in that.

I decided to use his honor against him. "I don't think you realize how much you want Alexander Ambrose. He has deceived you quite a bit. And you've told me that reneging on agreements is distasteful."

Marquis leaned toward me, ever so slightly. I had his attention, if only for the sake of curiosity. "He paid me my dues."

"He robbed you blind. He learned how to hop into other bodies, starting with Finlay, Fingal's son. He handed over his inheritance to Blush Bonnet Clothiers, then set up an elaborate scheme to siphon the funds back his way using gangsters in your employ. Of late, he's been working for you, without your knowledge. He was the one who possessed Sal. Except Ambrose really only works for himself. He set you up with Soren, but even that, Ambrose decided, would be his. He's become a rich man and has lived freely in this world. Not only in spite of you, but by stealing from you. And he's been right under your nose the whole time."

Each word filled Marquis with more rage. My knowledge of the details of his business garnered authenticity. He could see I wasn't lying. He could see, at least, that he wanted Alexander Ambrose.

"Where is he?" he demanded.

"I'll find him. But you need to give me time. You need to lay off me. And that means no thugs on my doorstep." We passed the North Hollywood Metro parking lot as I said this. My apartment building was in sight.

The Royal's voice was no longer overconfident and calm. There was a dire edge to his words, though, that still commanded respect. "No games, Dante. I will have one of you. And I am getting impatient." The car stopped and Emilio swung the door open. Our talk was over.

"Actually," I chanced, "I'm pretty hungry after the night in jail. Would you mind taking me up the street for a burger?"

Chapter 49

I sat in my car eating cold In-N-Out. Marquis hadn't accommodated my request and I hadn't eaten in half a day, so I didn't even bother going inside my apartment. I'd walked straight into the parking garage and drove to the fast food joint. It wasn't until I had been sitting there in the drive-thru, with a moment to myself, that I realized how I could find Soren. Whether he was hidden or not, whether he planned on turning tail or stepping boldly into the limelight—it didn't matter. Alexander McAllister was dead and he had a will that needed attending.

The more I thought about it, the more I realized Ambrose was always planning on killing off Alexander McAllister. It was part of his cycle. His rebirth.

I desperately needed a shower to wipe the stench of jail off me. Hell, I probably needed a bucket of bleach. But I didn't have time. I'd headed straight to Mr. Glickman's office. Once I was sure the lawyer was inside—and Soren wasn't—I had decided to wait in my car and watch. So I ate my single, no cheese, ketchup, mustard, whole-grilled onion, with a cheese fries, well-done, and settled into my stakeout across the street.

I hate to be the one always warning you—

"No you don't," I interrupted. Violet pretended she didn't hear me.

But I don't like Marquis at all. He's everything we're against and you're buddying up with him.

The bad taste in her mouth was moving into mine, ruining my food. "I don't trust him any farther than I can see him. He's just a means to an end."

A dangerous one. I'm not going to pretend my father was a victim in all this, but it was Marquis who introduced him to this life in the first place.

"I've got it under control."

Do you? You're making a deal with the devil to catch one of his flock. Aren't you afraid you're helping the scarier monster?

I hadn't considered it, truthfully. "I'm pretty confident Ambrose will never help Marquis again. I think you know that too." Confidence wasn't a hard truth, but I could only handle one crisis at a time.

I threw the wrapper and napkins into the paper bag, balled the whole thing up, and tossed it to the floor. Then I leaned back into my bucket seat. It felt good to be driving again. Really, anything felt good after spending the night in jail.

Freedom is easy to take for granted. It's invisible, but

comes crashing to the forefront of your mind when you realize you can't take a crap without gawkers. Next time they'll need to pry the internet from my cold, dead hands.

Now, I enjoyed all the little things. Driving especially. Lots of people hate the car culture of Los Angeles. People like being able to walk everywhere. Not me. This is my element. Back in Miami, the neighborhoods and hot spots have a similar sprawl. Being able to check out every corner of the large city, becoming intimately familiar with the quirks of every street, is a great coming of age ritual. It says the city is your home. Your place.

A stretch limousine pulled up to the curb and parked. It was black and longer than the ride I was in earlier. I couldn't see the driver through the dark tint but the door opened and Soren stepped out.

"Damn, does everyone have a limo these days?"

I wasn't afraid of him seeing me. I had dark tints on my windows. It wasn't legal but neither was speeding. I considered the tickets a tax and kept doing my thing.

Soren was dressed more formally now, with a suit and a bow tie. Alexander's influence on him was quick. There was little doubt that Soren was now taken. As he walked inside the office building, I waited, thinking he might only be a few minutes.

So what's the plan?

I didn't really know. "Well, I don't have my handcuffs anymore so I can't hold him." The words hung in the air on a sinister thread, like a silkworm waving in the night wind. The thought twisted into a darker meaning.

You don't mean to kill him?

"Of course not," I exclaimed. "That's how shades think. I may make mistakes once in a while, but I don't lose sight of what's important. Your father, Marquis—they're only concerned with personal gain. They shove everything from their path that doesn't help them. Life has no value to them. Once you go down that road, you're irredeemable."

Violet didn't say anything. I thought I heard a sniffle. Then I realized: in condemning Marquis and her father, I did the same to her.

"What's wrong now?" I asked, a little too harshly.

Not all shades are the same.

The hurt in her voice was palpable. She didn't only want redemption, but friendship. She wanted to be past this. To be normal. I felt like scum all of a sudden. It hurt me that she had lied about who she was. It hurt that I had to find out from her father, of all people. But did she deserve to be hated? Dismissed?

"I'm sorry, Violet," I finally said. "I didn't mean that. I know you're trying to make up for your past. I get that. But Marquis and your father, they're not twelve-year-old children listening to their parents. Don't equate your situations." Her crying slowed. She must have known how difficult it was for me to say as little as I did. It wasn't my thing. I tried some more anyway. "You know, your past, it's not as important as your present. The here and now is what matters."

Thank you, Dante.

Her crying halted with a whimper.

I'm sorry I wasn't letting you be happy with Eva. I just want you to be careful. Don't fall into the same trap I did: caring for someone you can't depend on.

"I know," I said softly. "It's just that girls are hard to get away from."

So is family...

Now it was my turn to be silent. She was right. Again.

After a decent childhood, I had spent my teen years having problems with my burgeoning abilities. Having problems with my parents. They were always fighting, blaming me for their discord and using me as ammunition in their arguments. I was just a burden to them. Like Violet, my circumstances shaped me. Unlike her, I'd managed to escape. I moved out when I was seventeen. Slept on some couches. Crashed with some friends who built computers. Had a few places of my own for a couple of years. I learned how to program. I played games and made some mods. When I was twenty, I was all too glad to leave Miami. I missed my friends, sure, but the city was too old-fashioned. Lawyers and bankers and bars. Los Angeles was where I could get a good job with my skills. Reinvent myself. Maybe Viola Ambrose needed Violet to do the same.

Thinking of how the little girl had kept her past from me, I realized I'd been no different. It wasn't sinister, but I was a closed box. Hard to read. My past was just as much a secret.

"I needed to get away from my parents too," I told her. "It's easier than you think, once you make the leap. Once you understand you have the final word." It wasn't a lot. Yet it was freeing. It was a step.

She sniffed again.

Do you ever remember the good times?

"I never forget them."

The minutes ticked by and the car heated up. I ran the engine again to kick up the AC. I played the last Silversun Pickups album and we listened, not bothering with small talk. To me, good friends can be comfortable with each other without saying anything. It felt good.

When the album was half over, Soren reemerged and got back in his elongated car. As it pulled away, I followed, maintaining two car lengths between us. We couldn't hurt Soren, I kept thinking, but Ambrose needed to be stopped. What could make that happen?

"Let's pretend that some of these shades—Ambrose, Marquis—are too strong to be affected by the sage. Even if rendered unconscious. How else can I dislodge them from their hosts?"

It was a question spurred by Ambrose's taunt. He was too experienced for me to take him on. Which pointed out the obvious problem. I had a very limited skill set: sage and salt. The latter only worked on animals. It was weak. The hold of the dead on creatures was tenuous and easy to slip. I also thought about iron and checked my pockets. I still had Soren's ring. It could be helpful. Then I tried to imagine what Marquis would do if he managed to get his hands on Soren. Did he know another tactic? Or did he rely solely on his Touch?

I don't know. I'm new at this too. I only heard about the sage a long time ago. I never even saw it in action until I had you try it.

"What? You never told me that before. You're saying that I put my ass out there on unfounded speculation?"

...You had it under control.

I scoffed and I smiled. "Your father was right. You really can't trust shades." She laughed deviously.

The moment of levity helped, but only a little. It also served to emphasize the mismatch between us and our opponent. We were out of tricks. Out of tools. But the job wasn't done yet. There had to be a way to coax Ambrose back to the Dead Side.

The limo drove down Eagle Rock Boulevard until the entrance to the 2. After a short stint, they merged onto the 5 South. It was Sunday so it only took ten minutes to get to the 110 heading into Downtown. The limo exited on 6th Street, drove to Hill, and made a right. Past 8th. 10th. To an area of the city beyond the central hub. This was a sad, desolate stretch of road with buildings that looked set for demolition. It wasn't that the neighborhood was overly trashy; it just looked like a downtown that belonged in a smaller city. Outdated. A far cry from the revitalized urban epicenter a few blocks behind us. There was no need to drive this far down Hill Street unless you were headed somewhere old.

As if on cue, the stretch limo slowed and pulled to the sidewalk, parking next to an identical limousine. At first I was confused. There was nothing here. But then I saw it. You'd be forgiven for passing it completely: the facade of the Belasco Theater was nice enough in its own right, but grand it was not.

"There's something going on here," I said to Violet. "Some kind of party." One limo was a lark. Two was an event. There were no lines or crowds gathered on the pink sidewalk, however. Whatever was happening, it was small.

Soren climbed out and rapped on one of the parking meters with his walking stick. Ambrose's walking stick. The bow tie and suit weren't enough. The man needed to press his sense of fashion no matter how anachronistic it was. I didn't know if it was ego or for appearances but, somehow, that would be his undoing. In step behind him was Bedros. No one else exited the vehicle.

As the two approached the entrance, a guy walked out and patted Soren on the back with a tattooed arm. It was his best friend, Greg. Poor guy had no idea he was greeting a complete stranger. After a quick discussion, they disappeared indoors.

I let a few minutes pass. I needed to get in the building but was hoping the limo would leave. The driver was still inside. He could be a problem. If he was just going to wait out the show while parked, then I would need to sneak in without him noticing me. I figured if I gave him some time to relax, there was a good chance he'd have his eyes closed.

When the time came, I turned off my car and got out. No one else was on the street except for another car coming by. Instead of passing, it stopped in the middle of the road. It was an old-timey Cadillac, peach-colored and fancy.

Another limo. All I could think about was the Rule of

Three. Maybe it didn't apply here, but something was going on. I ducked behind my car.

The far door opened and two girls in yellow dresses hopped out. Was one of them familiar? They reached their hands into the Cadillac and helped another girl out of the backseat. It was Pam. And she was wearing a white wedding dress.

Chapter 50

Los Angeles is full of old places from another time. Thin streets, stone foundations, meticulous detail work—it all represents society's shifting tastes. Old theaters are perhaps the epitome of such antiquated glamour. They're lush with textured carpets and wood carpentry and wall reliefs. They bring a warmth to open spaces that's rare in modern architecture.

The Belasco Theater encapsulated all of that. Entering was a sudden transition into a vivid world, beset by hosts of colors and manicured touches of splendor. A pleasing assault on the senses.

A hundred years had brought vast changes. I tried to imagine being a man who lived before cars were invented. Seeing electricity become commonplace. I envisioned a ghost of the past learning about refrigeration. Rockets. Computers. As old relics were left behind, new ones were created. It was hard to envisage.

The lobby was empty and I moved quickly. My hand slid along the carved wooden railing as I raced up the carpeted stairs. If I was right, everybody would be in the main theater. I could get a nice view of the proceedings from the balcony.

The raised floor ran along the entire back wall of the theater. Starting at the top, the mezzanine was divided into three levels split by railings. Tufted leather chairs lined the back wall of each section and looked over a vast complex styled after the Spanish Renaissance. The ceiling was a dramatically lit dome that set the stage for the events below. I inched towards the railing and watched a small crowd seated in a single row right in front of a rounded wooden deck. It looked like a dance floor that was flush with the carpet. Like Avalon, this theater had been converted into a nightclub. But it was more elegant. More entrenched in the trappings of yesteryear.

The couple stood in the center of the hardwood floor, atop a crest depicting a crowned shield with wings. Two bridesmaids on one side, two groomsmen on the other, and the officiant at their head.

"And me without my suit," I mumbled.

I didn't see Bedros. After assuring myself that he wasn't on the balcony and that I hadn't been seen, I stepped down to the next level and settled into a seat. I stayed in the middle section because I thought it might be best to keep away from the main edge of the balcony—I wasn't invited after all. So I sat inconspicuously and studied the crowd.

Soren didn't have parents but I saw a man and a woman who could pass for Pam's. Her maid of honor could have been her sister. She smiled and giggled as the ceremony started. The other bridesmaid was someone I'd met in the Echoplex, I thought, but it was hard to tell with all the hair and makeup.

It was a strange affair. They rented this huge, elaborate theater but only catered to fifteen people. The negative physical space was creepy. Even more distracting was the complete lack of music. The Belasco had a state-of-the-art modern sound system, but they were without a DJ. Except for Soren, of course. It was obvious this ceremony was planned quickly and at the last second. As with Finlay upon being released from prison, Ambrose moved to get married and begin his legacy immediately. I winced as the couple proclaimed their vows and kissed each other. Luckily, it was over pretty quickly.

A couple of waiters walked in with trays and served cocktails. The audience chairs remained but most of the guests moved to high tables to the side. People mingled and laughed. Pam cried. The entire time, Soren strutted around confidently, holding the walking stick with the alabaster rose head. And that's when it hit me.

I didn't have much of an opening, and it was a long shot, but I explained to Violet what I needed as I slipped downstairs. It felt wrong, especially after our little breakthrough in the car. That didn't stop me from flagging down one of the waiters as he passed through the lobby, giving him a twenty, and then placing the Hamilton pocket watch into his hand. He dipped into a restaurant in the adjacent hall and returned with a tray of appetizers. I nodded at him and he returned the gesture, then he entered the main theater and I went back upstairs to watch.

This was reckless, I told myself. If ever I felt like a dick, it was now.

From above, I scanned the crowd with worry. I was forgetting something. The bodyguard. Why wasn't Bedros around? Maybe he was in the restaurant. It might have been weird for him to intrude on this personal affair. Maybe Ambrose didn't want to scare Pam. My eyes caught the waiter I had bribed passing by the crowd. His tray was emptied and he returned to the lobby. I had missed the handoff.

"It's a good plan," I said, then realized I was talking to myself. Violet wasn't by my side anymore. It wavered my resolve.

That's when I finally saw Bedros. He came from a side room. A bar. No tracksuit today, he'd squeezed into a suit like every other sucker down there. He moved to his boss and whispered in his ear. Soren inspected the surroundings. I thought he may have glanced my way. If Soren noticed me, he didn't show it. After a momentary exchange, Bedros walked off again. Ambrose was working on something. He let the cocktails and appetizers settle for another ten minutes. Then he put his arm around Pam and whispered to her. She shrugged and nodded, and he kissed her on the cheek. Moving back to the stage floor, the man addressed his small audience.

"Excuse me, everyone. I'm sorry." Soren rapped the metal tip of his walking stick on the wooden floor. "I'm sorry. Excuse me. Yes. It has come to my attention that there has been a mix-up with the restaurant reservations. They have them for an hour earlier than they're supposed to. No, no. It's not a problem." He waved his hands and plastered a grin across his face. "If it's okay with you, I'd like to cut this short so we can head to the reception. The limousines are outside waiting for you. Please file in. Take your drinks, if you please."

Ambrose was getting rid of the guests. That meant I *had* been seen. I moved to the end of the balcony, in the middle level along the wall, to blend in to a dark corner. The waiters were scurrying but the guests were milling about, taking their time.

I leaned back, waiting for the inevitable. Wondering if my plan was ruined. Trying to come up with an alternative. I should have been looking over my shoulder.

"I didn't know you were here." I snapped my head around at the voice. It was Greg, holding a cigarette. "Why aren't you down with the others?" he asked.

I swallowed nervously. "Weddings aren't really my thing."

He nodded and took a long drag, then blew the smoke carelessly to the side. "I was going outside for a smoke but decided to look around. This place is impressive. Have you been here before?"

"For a party once." I watched as he admired the fleur-de-lis accents lining the floor.

"Not me," he said. "I'll need to come back some time when we can really let loose." He tugged at his tie as if it constricted his air.

I nodded vacantly and glanced at the main floor. Half the guests had filed out. Pam and Soren were arm in arm, talking to her parents. They looked around, trying to keep tabs on everybody.

"You're not joining them?" I asked.

He shrugged and took another long drag. "I don't know. These things are always so fake. What do I want to talk to Pam's parents for, you know? I'm actually happy that Soren decided to do this so hurriedly. Saves me the pain of a long dance."

"I suppose so." Greg didn't know the real reason this wedding was rushed. I kept my eyes on Soren down below, to see what his next move would be.

"But I don't need to tell you about it. You didn't even put on a suit or go downstairs. You know what I mean." Greg fumbled in his pockets for another cigarette and dropped his old one in a garbage can. "Shit, you got a light? I must have lost my matches."

I pulled mine from my pocket. It was a cheap plastic number from 7-11. I tossed it his way and he snatched it out of the air. Then I returned my attention to the crowd below just in time to catch Soren and Pam walking under the balcony towards the lobby. Everyone else followed.

"There they go," said Greg. "Man, I might not even go to the reception." He lit his cigarette and inhaled satisfactorily.

"You're the best man."

"I did my duty. I had to help set up around here, you know. Soren wasn't around for that. And I stood there for that dog and pony show. That doesn't mean I need to do the dinner thing too. Knowing my luck, I'd have to sit next to Pam's sister. Have you ever talked to her for more than five minutes? I'll give you twenty bucks if she doesn't text someone in that time."

I chuckled. But I was troubled. The main theater had cleared out. Most of the guests would be outside by now, getting into the limos. If nothing happened now then it would need to wait until after the reception. A restaurant wouldn't be private enough. It felt bad to just sit waiting, but I couldn't do anything else.

Greg walked to the railing and blew smoke into the grand emptiness of the room. "Can I ask you something?" He turned and placed my lighter on the small square cocktail table next to me, then sat down in the adjoining chair. He put his elbows on his knees and leaned forward. "How do you know Soren? I mean, he mentioned Perch to me. And now you're sneaking around upstairs at a wedding you weren't even invited to." He saw me shuffle nervously in my seat and he waved his tattooed arm. "No, no. Don't worry, man. I don't give a shit. I just wonder: why the strange behavior?"

Greg waited for my answer intently. He was friends with Soren and probably had genuine concern, but I got the feeling he was more curious than anything else. Neither of us really fit in with the crowd downstairs. There was a mutual sympathy in that.

"I'm just making sure he doesn't fuck up," I said. It was as truthful as I could get without tearing the veil open on a whole other world.

He leaned back, disappointed. "I don't know. That doesn't really sound like an answer. There's something inside you that drives you. This isn't about Soren."

I just shrugged and stood up. There wasn't anything else to say. I swiped my lighter from the table and moved toward the steps. That's when I noticed, for the first time, that Bedros was standing there. He was upright, at attention, his callous face revealing his intentions.

"Again with you," said the Armenian.

He didn't make a move and I didn't either. We just studied each other. He didn't have any conduits or iron armor. I decided the only way to expel him would be to knock him out. That made this a one-on-one fight. Fair if you looked at the numbers, maybe, but Bedros was in a different weight class.

Behind me, Greg spoke up. "I just don't want you ruining this night for Pam and Soren." I turned to him. He still leaned casually in his seat, puffing away. "It is an important step for them. The beginning of long lives at each other's sides." Greg's eyes flashed wickedly.

I was a fool. Bedros, I knew, was a wild card. But I'd assumed everything else would be straightforward. I'd been so busy watching Soren I didn't even think that Ambrose could've jumped into someone else.

Heavy feet pounded the floor behind me. I lifted the side

table with both arms and swung it around. Like a matador trained in the art of avoidance, I sidestepped the lumbering brute as he crashed through the boxy table. He tumbled down the steps to the lower level with a groan. I backed up the stairs, keeping an eye on both of them.

There were two things that made my enemy dangerous. One was that he made strong connections to his hosts, who changed from generation to generation. The other was that he could temporarily possess others, like Sal. And I had totally not accounted for it.

"What's this, Ambrose?" I demanded. "Keeping me busy while Soren slips away again?"

Greg didn't bat an eye. "That is one way of looking at the situation. But really, Mr. Butcher, how did you expect all of this to play out in front of that crowd? You really must think these confrontations through."

The big Armenian dusted himself off and regained his feet. This time he climbed the steps more intentionally. He'd be more careful not to trip himself up again. I moved to the top level. The floor was brick, more of a walkway than a seating section, with more space to maneuver. High bar tables, small round pieces of wood attached to metal poles, lined the railing. I hefted one in my hands and slammed it into the floor. On the second blow, the wooden surface jarred loose, and I kicked it away with my feet.

"Come on, big guy," I taunted, holding the metal pole like a Louisville slugger. It was an awkward weapon that was weighted wrong and had table legs extending from the tip, but I was in a pinch.

Bedros came at me with a couple of feints, trying to get me to swing and miss. I kept myself in check, backing up when he got too close. When I saw an opening, I swung as hard as I could. Bedros put his arm up. The metal slammed into his shoulder and shoved him aside. He let out a bellow but the heavy blow didn't have a lot of momentum behind it. The big man easily tore the club from my hands and it clattered to the floor.

I lunged at him and planted my knee in his stomach. He grabbed my legs and held me to his body. My fists rained into his face and the top of his head wildly. It shook him. But not enough.

The Armenian charged the back wall and crushed me up against it. My side spasmed in pain. I tried to kick Bedros off, but he released me at the same time. I dropped to my ass hard. Now it was his turn to kick.

I blocked a couple of quick blows. Before he could really connect, I sprung off the wall and thrust my shoulder into the same spot my knee had softened. He was much larger than me, but my leverage had gotten him off balance. He fell backwards, trying to catch himself with several panicked steps. I kept pushing and the small of his back snapped against the metal balcony railing, sending him over the edge to the middle section, on top of another table.

I had just about fallen forward over the railing as well. I leaned upside down, precariously hanging on to the metal with both hands. It was only a five foot drop, but I fought against it. In my struggle I caught a momentary glimpse of Greg, sitting on the same level against the wall, watching with patient interest. Then my hand slipped.

I tumbled into Bedros as he was trying to get up. He snatched at me with his large fists but I stood up and kicked them away. I climbed atop a leather booth and grabbed the metal railing above me again. Bedros clutched at my leg. I sent my foot into his face. Then I pulled myself up and over. I was on the top once more.

Bedros and I sat on our separate floors, leaning against something for support, catching our breaths. As I slid away from the railing, I noticed Pam standing at the top of the stairs coming from the lobby. She stared at me with a tear in her eye and a pained expression on her face.

Greg followed my gaze and abandoned his nonchalance. He rose to his feet. "Pam! Go back downstairs. Don't worry about this."

I brushed my hair from my eyes, stood up, and confidently approached her. Ambrose remained a level below.

"How'd it go?" I asked her, and held out my hand. Pam placed the Hamilton watch in my palm.

"Fuck you," she said. Her head twitched, and another tear streamed down her cheek. "I hate this."

Bedros took advantage of the breather and remained still. Greg, however, inspected us in confusion. "What's this?" he asked.

I held up the pocket watch and let it swing by the chain. "A spy," I answered, turning to Ambrose. "Violet, where's Soren?"

It wasn't the pocket watch that answered.

"I made sure he went outside," said Pam, "with the others." Greg dropped his jaw as he realized what had happened. He'd been fooled by his same trick. But it wasn't over. "I got it," said Violet. Then she handed me Alexander Ambrose's walking stick.

"You hypocrite!" cried Greg, his jaw shaking with rage. But he wasn't glowering at me. I watched Pam tremble under the weight of his words. It wasn't as if she needed them, though. She already hated herself enough.

Pam spasmed more obviously this time. Violet had always had trouble remaining inside hosts. She didn't like it, and she wasn't good at it. I wondered which one caused the other.

"Get out of here," I said. "Join up with Soren. And free her from this."

Pam nodded and raced down the stairs, unable to hold back her sobs.

I stood triumphantly on the top balcony level, tapping the metal tip of the walking stick against the railing. The two men below me both stood now, glaring at me with angry eyes.

"What are you planning on doing with that?" asked Ambrose.

"I wonder..." I said. I slowly walked along the railing, letting the metal scrape as it slid. "How powerful is the famed Alexander Ambrose without his conduit?"

Greg scoffed. "Ridiculous," he said. "It is just a tool, Mr. Butcher. My true talents are what ensure my stay among the living." He plucked the nearly finished cigarette from his mouth and flicked it at me. I ducked to the side and it bounced harmlessly on the brick.

"Maybe," I said. I banged the stick against the railing harder and harder. The metal rang loudly in my ears, and Greg's eyes seared into me.

"Get him," he snapped.

Bedros hopped up to my level again and marched my way. He reached his fists towards me and I rapped them tightly with the walking stick. The Armenian rubbed his knuckles in annoyance. Then he jumped at me.

Once again, the bull was enraged and the contest was mine. I forced the stick between his clawing hands and stuck Bedros square in the Adam's apple. Not too hard. I didn't want any permanent damage to the man whose body I beat. Then I spun under his retreating arms and wrapped myself around his back. I locked my legs around his waist, making the big man support my full weight. Each end of the stick securely nestled in my elbows. My hands pushed the back of his head; the stick: his neck. Bedros could no longer breathe.

The giant thrashed. He clawed at my eyes. His neck. He tried to knock me over the railing. He slammed me against the wall. All his efforts failed to throw me. His actions slowed as his face grew more distressed. Then the two of us collapsed to the floor.

I reached into my pockets and withdrew a white sage clove, then searched for the lighter. I tapped at my left side, then right, and then my back pockets. Shit. I had dropped it at some point. Where was it?

"You don't happen to have a light, do you?" I asked

Ambrose.

Greg anxiously watched. "I'm afraid I'm fresh out."

I eyed Bedros lying unconscious on the floor. I needed to make sure he woke up a different man. This was my chance and I didn't even have a match. And then I saw it.

I paced a few yards away and picked up the cigarette that Greg had flicked at me. It was still lit. I held it against my clove and pulled the smoke inside me. Then I threw the used stub back at Greg.

"I won't let you banish him," he asserted. "He is too important to me."

"What, are you going to get your hands dirty?"

"You don't think I can, Mr. Butcher? You don't think I can beat you until you have nothing left to break?"

I narrowed my eyes as he joined me at the top of the mezzanine. Greg was a scrawny guy. Like me, but he didn't work out. He looked like a stoner all the way. But I knew he'd have some inner strength that came from Ambrose. From another world.

Heavier footsteps concerned me, however. A pair of them. Behind Ambrose, stomping up the carpeted stairs, was Emilio. I spun around and saw Eladio at the other end of the balcony, rising in unison with his twin. They must have followed me. Neither said anything, but Ambrose knew he was in trouble.

"You fools," said Greg, facing one strongman, then the other. "What do you intend to do here? I can release myself from this body and rejoin Soren."

Marquis casually strolled up behind Emilio. "Please do.

Soren is with my people outside."

Greg's face filled with horror as he laid eyes on his old nemesis. "You can't hold on to Soren forever," he proclaimed, but I'm not sure he believed it.

"You were supposed to give me time," I scolded. "I had things under control."

Marquis shrugged. "No worries, Dante. It appears that you did. But after your struggles last night, you can hardly blame me." The man tugged at his vest and stood as tall as his short frame allowed as he examined Greg. "Is that really you, Alexander?"

Greg stepped back and inched along the top railing. "You are a hypocrite, Mr. Butcher. You condemn me for my actions yet use possession for your own benefit. My own daughter, against me. Then you consort with the enemy for your own gain. How much of your noble mission is built upon guilty compromises?" He was trying to keep away from Marquis and Emilio but that brought him closer to me. Eladio lumbered behind me but kept his distance as well. That was good. He made me nervous.

"What of you, Ambrose?" I asked coldly. "You claim to be the ultimate victim of circumstance. You say that morality has never given you justice, but you were never a just man. You were cornered by your own corrupt dealings in the Southern Pacific. You ran from the blame. From justice. You killed yourself and your daughter. Still running. You tried to cheat death, but you only cheated yourself and your daughter out of proper lives."

I'm back.

Good, I thought. I clutched the watch in my left hand and the alabaster rose in my right. Things were getting a little messy, but I had the two items I wanted.

Greg laughed maniacally. "We did what needed to be done. For the city. For our families." He raised his voice in rage, as if to convince himself of its merit. "I am a great man!" he boomed.

I shook my head slowly. "Men are remembered by their worst actions, not their best." I turned away from him and walked back to the sleeping Armenian.

"Don't do that," said Marquis. "I could use a soldier like him."

"That wasn't the deal. One for one. I'm giving you Ambrose."

"Like hell," said Greg. As soon as he had reached a middle set of stairs, he bolted down to the lower balconies. I planted my foot on the metal railing and leapt over. Suspended in the air, I snapped the walking stick on the top of Greg's head. It was an immediate knockout. Ambrose melted into the carpet. I landed on my feet.

I tilted my head to each side to crack my neck and strode back up the steps. Eladio stood over Bedros now. I stared hard at him and shoved by. Then I kneeled beside the sleeping bodyguard and blew the smoke into his lungs. Marquis put his hand up to hold off the strongmen and watched me with interest. After a few moments, I rested my hand on the big man's chest and saw that his soul was clean.

"It's done."

Marquis nodded and Emilio stepped down to the front of

the balcony and approached Greg.

He's here.

I smiled. "No," I directed. "Not him."

"Dante," said Marquis, "one for one. You said so yourself."

"I'm giving you Ambrose, not Greg. Not an innocent." I plucked the horseshoe ring from my pocket and let the watch dangle from the same hand. I tried to slip the ring over the end of the walking stick, but the metal tip was too wide.

Hurry. Before he realizes.

I started to panic. My whole plan was about to crumble because the ring was too small. I'd assumed it was large enough. It was, but the metal tip prevented the fit. Then I realized. I gripped the alabaster rose in one hand and the tip in the other and brought Alexander's walking stick down hard. It splintered in half on my knee. Then I slid the cold iron over the wood. It caught several inches up as the base widened. I made sure it was tight.

"Are we good?" I asked.

Yes. He's still down here. He's going crazy.

Marquis didn't realize I wasn't talking to him and answered. "I suppose we are, Dante. You've certainly gone to a lot of trouble to minimize the collateral damage." He held out his hand and I gave him the broken stick. He examined it with interest. "A man who has the power to jump into a multitude of men is now stuck, attached to a single piece of wood. I have seen something like this before. Clever. But how do I know that he's really tied to this?"

I shook my head. "If you can't see it like I can, I'm sure you have ways of confirming it. You have agents on the Dead Side, don't you?"

"More than I have here, Dante. It will upset me if this was all an elaborate deception."

"We are men, not savages," I said calmly. "We must do right by each other." He smiled as he recognized his words.

Emilio glanced around, trying to appear useful, then shrugged and returned to our level, leaving Greg in peace.

"There's one more thing," I said, "before you go. Ambrose also buys Soren. If your people are holding him outside, they need to let him go. Soren will never agree to join your crew now, anyway. He'll never kill himself. He's a newly rich man. Just married. His future is bright without you. Let him go."

Marquis signaled for the strongmen to head down the stairs and they wordlessly led the way. After they passed, the Royal nodded. "Reneging on agreements is distasteful."

He was a wicked man, and undoubtedly my next enemy, but I knew he was telling the truth. He turned halfway and hefted the walking stick in his hand, then paused and looked back at me. "You have proven reliable and resourceful, Dante. My offer to you is still extended. Come with me. Join my employ."

I looked at the man without blinking. "Not a chance."

He started down the steps. "Well, I'll keep my eye on you anyhow. Consider it, at the very least. You have my number."

It was some time after he was gone before I recovered

myself. I focused on the Hamilton 940. "One down," I said.

Many more to go.

I nodded with determination, made sure Bedros and Greg were okay, then turned to go. On the way out, at the last second, I retrieved the bottom half of the broken walking stick.

Chapter 51 - Dream

Violet sat on a large husk of concrete, its purpose and usefulness long since past. Her small frame rested easy atop the slab, black combat boots swinging in the air. She sat just at eye level but was out of my reach, not in form but in thought.

We were in a large open span of ground next to the LA River. Train tracks skirted us on either side. Behind us, a block away, was the vague vestige of old Downtown, but that's not what held Violet's attention. A large structure that looked like a Moorish castle served as a terminal for absent train cars. In the forever gloom of the Dead Side, it looked especially uninviting.

"I've never seen this place," I said. I was trying to shake Violet from her reverie, but in a careful way that showed consideration. She was probably mad at me. She should have been, at any rate.

"This depot is La Grande Station," she said. "I don't think it exists in your world anymore, but it was instrumental in mine. A bustling terminal that was the heart of the Southern Pacific in Los Angeles. Before Union Station was built." Violet continued her silent vigil of the building. It had large, empty windows on the bottom floor, and rounded parapets, but its main iconic contribution to the skyline was a large, central dome and spire. It looked small from a distance, yet somehow magnificent.

"Your father worked here." Violet's focused silence gave me the confirmation I didn't need. After everything that had happened, as evil as Alexander Ambrose was, he was still her father.

"My memories," she said, "they're all jumbled now. When you live a hundred and twelve years, if 'lived' is the right word, things get mixed up. I've had different lives. Different names. At least for a time. My real life is so far away that it's hard to identify with anymore."

"The present is what matters. It's who we are now that counts."

She turned to me. "Who are you, Dante?"

I kicked at some gravel with my shoe. "Why is it that everybody asks me that?"

"Do you think you're special? Do you think you have a purpose?" She looked away again, not expecting me to answer. "Do any of us matter?"

I scratched the back of my head, already uncomfortable. I wasn't good at this sort of thing. I didn't know what she wanted. What to say.

"Some of my favorite memories are of riding the Southern Pacific with my father. He was a busy man. Always so concerned with making a living and becoming respectable. I guess, for a while, he succeeded at both." Violet fumbled with her dad's pocket watch. "I never understood it back then. For a little girl, it just came across as harsh. Strict. But when he let me ride the train with him, all of that disappeared. We stood side by side and watched as we passed by the lives of so many other people trying to make it in this town. The wind against my face felt good. Sometimes I want to feel that wind again." She turned to me with watery eyes. "Those were the few moments we could be together without feeling the weight of the world. I loved those precious experiences. He did too. I like to think he found joy in my happiness. I like to believe that... at one time... he really loved me."

I wanted to tell her he did. That he was just a man who made hard sacrifices for his family. That he eventually succumbed to his destructive tendencies, but for a time, at least, he tried to do good by her. But I didn't say any of those things. I didn't know what they would sound like out loud. And at this point, after everything we had been through, I didn't want to lie to her.

"He's in there," she said. "Right now. He's mad as hell."

"Has he tried any—"

"It's not me he's concerned with. You've locked him out of any other connections with your world for as long as that ring circles his walking stick. The man of great power is now nothing more than me, a shade with a window to the living."

"But both of you are down here now, together. Aren't you worried about crossing paths?"

"He'll leave me alone. He's let me take care of myself for decades. It was a blessing that he left me behind, really. The more twisted he became, the more corrupt, the easier it was to shake free. After Finlay, Livia and Aster, and especially after all of this, I don't know if my father will ever seek me out again. In a way, he knows that's the best thing he can do for me."

I nodded. She was right, as usual. Violet had managed to avoid her father for many years down here. Hiding wasn't even necessary. How could a twelve-year-old girl draw the ire of a father? If anyone, it was me that Ambrose resented.

Her face showed relief. Having someone to talk to, to really divulge inner thoughts to, was something the girl hadn't had in a long time. Maybe not since the days of riding the Southern Pacific with her dad. Giving her that much was the least I could do.

But the cuteness of her childlike cheeks couldn't hide the vast atrocities that would forever stain her eyes. The black eyeliner, the purple hair and lipstick, it was all a mask. For better or worse, it was who she was now. Viola Ambrose was a jumbled memory. A fantasy. She was dead.

"I heard what he said," she started. "My dad. About us being hypocrites. Obviously, I know our intentions were noble. We're not the same as him. But can we excuse ourselves for our actions? Should we just pat ourselves on the back and move on?"

"Violet..."

"I can't jump into people anymore. I break them when I do that. It breaks me." She looked down again, holding back the tears that would surely come later, when she was alone.

"You were only inside Pam for five minutes," I said.

"She still didn't handle it well. She's having nightmares tonight. I guarantee you that much."

"Violet, Pam was a little shaken up by your intrusion, but she would have voluntarily done it to save Soren. I believe that. And that's what makes it okay."

"No. Nothing makes it okay. That's why we do what we do. That's our purpose. Now that my father is stopped, I'm done."

I nodded softly. It was her right and I wouldn't tell her otherwise. Violet had a long history of troubled possession. It wasn't in her to control it as well as her father. Maybe that's why she could be saved.

But what did she mean about being done and having a purpose? "What about you?" I asked. "You've taken care of Ambrose. You've made your decision about the living. Isn't it time for you to move on?"

Violet wiped the water from her eyes and looked at me earnestly. Determined. "I'm not finished. I've still caused way more harm than I've helped. I think I'll stick around a little while, see how much further I can tip the scales." There was something about her purple lips. Was it a smile? "You know, Dante, I feel better already. I don't think you're a half-bad friend. A bit of a dick, though."

I laughed. I didn't know what I had said, but if this

troubled girl could see a bright side, then so could I. I paced in the depot for several moments. Smiling. Thinking of the sun even though it was absent here. I realized I would have missed her, if she had left. It felt good knowing she'd still be at my side. In my pocket.

"Red Hat is still out there," I offered. "They're a whole other can of worms we don't fully understand yet."

She hopped down from her perch and landed with a thud. Her boot kicked up dirt and she brushed at the red and black stripes of her dress. "No more little fish, then? No more finding marks at clubs?"

"If you think I'm gonna stop going out, you're crazy. I can do my thing at clubs and still investigate the big boys. They're both worthy causes."

"Well maybe you can cut back on the drinking at least."

"Not a chance."

"Oh well," she said, smiling. "Worth a shot."

We stood there, blinking at each other, satisfied without words. It felt like a new beginning. We all needed those sometimes.

"They're watching us now. Marquis knows your tricks."

I tilted my head in a playful shrug. "Then we'll just need to come up with new ones."

"We can't go in blind."

"I never do," I said.

"You always do."

I scoffed. "I've got it under control."

She chuckled and ran at me with open arms. I kneeled and grabbed her in a big hug. The cockiness was contagious.

After all, we couldn't do what we did without it.

Like all things, the innocence of the moment had to end. By our very nature, we could only experience highs if they were riddled with lows.

"You never gave me an answer," she said, breaking away from the embrace. "Did we compromise our principles? Are we bad in our own way?"

I stood up again and smiled. "I've heard that not everything in the world is black or white."

Her light purple eyes were piercing. "You don't believe that."

Epilogue

It was a bittersweet day.

I was in lighter spirits after the chapter on Ambrose closed out. I didn't allow the tasks ahead to consume me yet. Instead, I'd found time to hang with Trent. Watch Netflix. Do the little things. I especially liked my moments with Eva. It was nice being happy.

We spent the whole day together doing mundane things. Going to the mall. Dinner. We went to Lock & Key for drinks. Then we capped things off at her place in K-town. This time I'd remembered to stock up on beer first.

We smoked out and had sex. Watched some TV and had sex again. By then, even though it was still dark out, Eva passed out. It was a satisfying conclusion to the kind of day we all wish for.

But these moments don't come so easily or intentionally. We all live our lives and try to get our way and hope we cross paths with complementary people. But it's all dumb luck. Something like this can't be manufactured. It just happens. And when it does, it's magical. This was like a one night stand, except both of us had wanted more. That providence in a sea of possibilities was what made it so special.

I didn't nod off so easily. I lay in bed and watched her sleep. Alone with my thoughts, my mind became burdened with the words of Alexander Ambrose. I couldn't find peace. Even though his shade could no longer visit the living, he haunted me. And Violet, who had told me that I only believed in absolutes, by measuring degrees in black and white, seemed determined to deny me a little bit of gray.

I thought about the girl's cursed life and the sacrifices she had made since. Compared to her, I was lucky with family. Girls were another story. It's not that I didn't meet any. The party scene had some perks. Cute girls were the biggest one. Still, I kept them at a distance. I'd always thought that was what I wanted. Now, I wasn't so sure.

"That was amazing," whispered Eva. If her voice wasn't so sweet she would've startled me. She spoke as if she hadn't been asleep at all, as if our bodies had been locked together just seconds before. I smiled at her sadly. It *had* been amazing. At that moment, I felt more guilty than ever.

Her arm brushed against my chest and she turned her head slightly. Half her face was buried in her pillow. A mane of platinum hair obscured much of the rest. I could see a lazy eye blinking slowly, straining to keep me in its gaze. I put my hand on her back. Eva looked so small under it. I rubbed her spine and she flinched as the touch gave her a chill.

"What do you look for?" I asked her. "In life, I mean. What do you really look for?"

She rolled to her side and my hand brushed her breasts. Small. Perky. She was beautiful. "Sex..." she answered. I traced the back of my hand to her neck and across her cheek. "Companionship. Love."

"Me too," I said after some thought. I was miserable.

"How do you know when you've found it?" she asked. As Eva spoke, her tired eyes closed some more. Her fingers ceased their play on my skin and her arm relaxed. I put my cigarette to my lips, grabbed the thin bedsheet, and pulled it up over her naked body.

I watched longingly as Eva drifted further into an induced sleep, then blew more sage into her face.

-Finn

Connect

If you're reading this, it means you demand more from your urban fantasy. Shades are spooky, but they're nothing without a layered cast of characters and realistic plot drivers. *The Dead Side* is my stab at a cut above the rest: unnerving mystery, stubbornly fighting against impossible odds, and themes that hopefully make you put the book down and ponder, if even for only a minute.

My writing process demands quality control at every step of development. I hope you agree *The Dead Side* is the premium product I strive to make it. Unfortunately, doubling down on originality and quality in an on-demand world has drawbacks. It's simply not possible for me to get you a brand-new novel every month or two. The process takes time.

That's where you come in. Together we can build a better book.
All you need to do is connect.

- Join the Outlaw Underground, our private Facebook group. (www.facebook.com/groups/dominofinnfans/)

- Leave an all-too-important review where you bought the book. Each one helps more than you know.

- Recommend this book to your friends. Link it on social media.

- Join my reader group newsletter, get a free story, and hear from me only when I have new releases or important news. You'll never miss another launch sale again. (dominofinn.com/newsletter/)

Simple, right? Five minutes of your time makes a world of difference to me and Dante. Thank you for your heartfelt support. I'll keep writing as long as you keep reading.

- Domino Finn

Also Try:
Black Magic Outlaw

Did you know Dante isn't alone in talking to the dead?

Did you know he's part of a wider shared universe of hard-luck heroes?

Did you know that sometimes the good guys use a little magic too?

If you're into bullets, black magic, and an extra helping of action, check out Cisco Suarez, a too-cocky-for-his-own-good necromancer in a tank top.

Dead Man

Black Magic Outlaw Book One

Waking up dead is the worst. Trust me. I know these things.

The last time I woke up this hungover I was naked, soaking wet, and wrapped in a Cuban flag.

This time, at least, I had clothes on. I couldn't see them in the pitch black, but I could feel them. I could feel other things too. Raw pounding in my head. Enough tightness in my chest to make every breath a chore. I was in ten kinds of pain. Apparently that wasn't enough because my leg was asleep too.

There was more. Cold, wet, grimy more. Flies buzzed around my face, circling the stench of death. My arm was slimy. I shifted my weight and something crunched beneath me. My hands and feet pressed against the tight confines of a box.

Smell of death and decay. Check. Some kind of giant coffin. Check. I'm no mathematician but things were starting to add up.

Despite the evidence of my apparent death, I didn't panic. You see, I'm a necromancer (among other things) so I know a little about the subject. I couldn't tell you where I was or what happened the day before to get me here, but I had an inkling I was still alive. Even if just barely.

I tried to sit up. A stabbing pain pulsed through my body until I relaxed again. Request denied.

Okay, deep breath time. I focused inward to calm myself, then reopened my eyes. A thin sliver of light crept through the seam of my crypt overhead, but it was too weak to illuminate the interior.

Good thing I knew a trick or two.

I stared into the darkness, more deeply than before. Not into the box or any physical place, but into a place within me. The pupils of my eyes leaked and my green irises filled with black, and with a blink I could see.

And you thought the necromancer thing was all about wearing black and growing your hair long. I hate to burst your bubble but I'm not a walking death metal stereotype. I don't wear a trench coat and I have a crew cut. I live in Miami, for fuck's sake. It's hot and humid *in the winter*. No sense getting a heatstroke to appeal to northern sensibilities.

Not only that but Cisco Suarez (that's me) isn't just a necromancer. He's a shadow charmer too. That's the magic I just called on. The darkness all around me, it was still there—I could just see through it now.

The thin razorblade of light now stung my eyes. I avoided looking directly at it and checked the rest of the tomb. Crushed cardboard boxes. Stuffed plastic bags. My accommodations weren't as morbid as I'd feared. This wasn't a coffin but a dumpster.

Maybe I wasn't dead after all. Just down for a nap. A bed made of beer bottles. My pillow? A dead sewer rat.

That would've made most men jump, but remember: necromancer. I scrunched my nose and reached for it.

The simple act of limberness was a battle of pain. My muscles were sore. Dry and withered like the old husks of a toppled tree. My bones creaked and my joints were half-dried cement. I stirred up more dust than the Mummy. But I pushed through the agony until I dangled the dead rat by its tail.

It had been decapitated. A tribute. Sacrificial magic, and not mine. That spelled trouble.

I checked for other signs of ritual or binding. Charms. Runes. Burnt sacraments. Scanning the contents of the dumpster, I spied a couple of dark-red cowboy boots on my feet and literally hopped in place. (I almost knocked my head on the dumpster lid.) You see, the rat I could handle. My wearing a bona fide pair of alligator boots was unacceptable.

Don't get me wrong. There was nothing magic or cursed about them. It's just that the modern Cuban doesn't wear cowboy boots. Cisco Suarez doesn't wear cowboy boots.

That's me again, by the way. Shorter and catchier than Francisco, it always reminded me of a comic book name. What kid didn't want to be a superhero? I liked the sound of it so much I picked up referring to myself in the third person. My fatal flaw.

Enough about my name. Let's talk spellcraft. I'm what you call an animist: an everyday human who happens to tap into spirits for magical energy. Wild, huh?

I know what you're thinking: A cleric deals with gods and a wizard with books, right? Well, put the Player's Handbook away and forget everything you think you know. Gods and books have plenty of overlap. (The most famous book in all history is a notable example.)

Fact is, magic is a universal force in the world, pure energies known as the Intrinsics. They're the building blocks of all creation. People like you or me can only manipulate them through spirits. That makes us animists.

Everything else is just a title. Wizard. Cleric. Learned men like to use mage (it's more sophisticated). You see shaman or witch doctor applied to primitive peoples. Or if you wanna vilify animists, call them witches and warlocks. You get the idea. I'm sure some academic somewhere compiled a list of unofficial "official" definitions—but you'd have a hard time running into that terminology on the street. And the street is where the real stuff happens.

Case in point: the dumpster I was lying in.

Some alarm in my head screamed that I was hurt. Maybe fatally. The thing was, besides stiffness, there wasn't anything wrong with me. I wasn't dying, anyway. I kinda felt like a homeless vampire more than anything else. Which would be a lot funnier if I didn't know vampires actually existed. After all, right now I had a hangover from hell—maybe hell was where I came from.

You're probably bored by now, right? Sorry. I think too

much. It's a problem I'm trying to address.

With a strained kick of an alligator boot, the lid of the dumpster flew open. Blinding light engulfed me and seared my senses. I literally hissed and uselessly threw my hands up in defense. Maybe I was a vampire after all.

But I didn't burst into flames. After I took another second to get my head on straight, I realized I was still drawing upon my shadow sight. I drained the darkness from my eyes, my lids pushing out black tears, until it was safe to look.

A blue sky. Fluffy clouds. Palm trees.

I was in South Beach.

Not the pretty coastline with white sand they show on TV during football games. That was never far in Miami Beach, of course, but the back alleys were far less picturesque. I was just off Washington Avenue somewhere, outside a dive bar. The alley was empty. I heaved myself over the dumpster wall and landed on the concrete with a thud. I wouldn't win any vaulting medals but it got the job done. Standing and walking involved entirely new kinds of pain, but either it was wearing off or I was getting used to it.

Normally I'd assume this predicament was my doing—it wouldn't be me if I didn't go big—but the dead rat was a bit much. It was also a dead giveaway that someone else was involved.

I padded at my jean pockets. I had a cell phone but no wallet. Was I robbed? It seemed unlikely given the evidence of spellcraft. A beatdown, then?

I frowned. I'd annoyed people, sure. I'd had minor run-ins with gang tough guys and stirred up the local talent, but that was life as a small-time hustler. I was too young for real enemies. No reason anyone should wish me dead.

The preternatural fog in my head wasn't going away. I couldn't think clearly. No amount of head-scratching helped.

With my head on a swivel for danger, I staggered to the pink sidewalk. (Miami Beach, remember?) I was ready for anything. What I didn't expect was to be ignored.

Small groups of shoppers strolled up and down Washington Avenue. Horns honked and cars inched forward and came to a stop at the light. I got a few odd looks but nobody confronted me or threw any blood curses my way. It was just your average whatever-day-it-was in South Beach.

A man strolled by and held his hand out to me. While trying (and failing) to make eye contact, I accepted his offering. A nickel and two pennies. He avoided my puzzled expression and continued on his way.

That was random, but I couldn't be accountable for the South Beach crazies. Cisco Suarez needed to stay on task. Since everything appeared normal outside, I considered pumping the bar employees for information.

The car that was stopped on the road in front of me clicked its doors locked. I looked and the woman in the passenger seat averted her eyes. Bitch. Then I got a glimpse of myself in the window reflection.

I would've locked the doors too.

Besides my healthy tan, nothing of my disheveled appearance was recognizable. My usually close-cropped hair hung over my shoulders in a wild mane. My eyes were permanently frantic, sporting the raised-by-wolves look. The full-on homeless beard didn't help. And my clothes. Besides my jeans and red cowboy boots, of all things I wore a yellowed and bloodied tank top.

Tank tops were never really my look but, to my surprise, I actually filled this one out. My chest strained against the thin fabric and my bare arms looked carved from marble. Still in disbelief, I flexed a bicep at my reflection. Maybe the car windows were made from magic fun-house mirrors.

This warrants an explanation. I may be a little cocky and reckless at times, but one thing I'm not is a gym rat. I was always that scrappy skinny kid who was too stupid to stay down. Yes, that means I lost a lot of fights. I wanted to be a superhero but lacked the dedication. What animist would spend time working out anyway? The power of the world at your fingertips, wasted by repeatedly picking up and putting down heavy things.

No, I was never out of shape, but I was supposed to be thin. Now I suddenly felt like Peter Parker after running into that radioactive spider. I was straight buff, is what I'm saying.

My jaw glued to the floor, I stared like a lunatic. The driver floored the gas at his first opportunity. In their place, a matte-black jeep slammed on its brakes. Which was weird since the light was green and the cars behind it honked. I snapped out of my shock as the group of Haitians in the jeep focused on me, anger in their eyes.

They yelled, "Dead man!" and dismounted, brandishing light automatic weapons.

I threw seven cents at them.

Pick up DEAD MAN
where Domino Finn books are sold

Also by Domino Finn

<u>SYCAMORE MOON</u>
The Seventh Sons
The Blood of Brothers
The Green Children

<u>BLACK MAGIC OUTLAW</u>
Dead Man
Shadow Play
Heart Strings
Powder Trade
Fire Water
Death March
Blood Craft
Open Season

<u>SUMMONER FOR HIRE</u>
Tooth and Nail
Hell and High Water

<u>AFTERLIFE ONLINE</u>
Reboot
Black Hat
Trojan
Deadline

About the Author

Domino Finn is an award-winning game industry veteran, a media rebel, and an armchair ghost hunter. As a grizzled author of urban fantasy and litRPG, his stories are equal parts spit, beer, and blood, and are notable for treating weighty issues with a supernatural veneer. If Domino has one rallying cry for the world, it's that fantasy is serious business.

Take a stand at DominoFinn.com